TWO AGAINST ONE

Both bandits had ducked behind the other side of the building and were taking turns firing. Lockhart worked his way around the gray horse and back toward the raised sidewalk. Reaching the sidewalk, he crouched below it, snapped several shots at the hidden gunmen's position and placed one pistol on the planked platform. He yanked loose his black mustang's reins with his free hand and flipped them toward the animal. Without looking, he fired again toward the bandits. A quick wave of his hand further encouraged the mustang to get away from the shooting. Only the gray horse remained and it was rearing and kicking in a frantic desire to be somewhere else. Lockhart decided against trying to let it loose. That would take too much concentration—and time he couldn't spare.

A bullet spit a chunk of wood from the edge of the raised plank sidewalk, thudding inches from his taut face, and he ducked instinctively. But he had seen enough to know what he would do next....

OTHER BOOKS BY COTTON SMITH:

BROTHERS OF THE GUN
BEHOLD A RED HORSE
PRAY FOR TEXAS
DARK TRAIL TO DODGE

Spirit Rider

Spirit Rider

COTTON SMITH

The characters and events portrayed in this book are fictitious. Any similarity to real persons, living or dead, is coincidental and not intended by the author.

Printed in the United States of America.

Published by AmazonEncore
P.O. Box 400818
Las Vegas, NV 89140

ISBN-13: 9781477842300
ISBN-10: 1477842306

To my newest treasures:
Katie, Bobby and Gus.

This title was previously published by Dorchester Publishing; this version has been reproduced from the Dorchester book archive files.

Chapter One

Nothing warned of the disaster to their village ahead. Laughter and victory banter rippled through the returning Oglala Sioux hunting party. It was the Moon of Yellow Leaves, and a small herd of buffalo had been waiting for them as promised by the tribe's holy man, *Hanble Tunkan*, Stone-Dreamer.

Twelve proud warriors were dressed in their finest, befitting their success. Long, flowing hair was highlighted with coup feathers; faces were carefully painted with spirit medicine. Their ponies had been rubbbed down with sweet grass, then feathers tied in their manes and tails. War shields were uncovered and carried on bronzed arms. With them were packhorses laden with sacks of buffalo meat, ready for cooking and drying.

Wide smiles on the warriors' faces were easy to read: The food stores of their village would be full for the coming winter. Generosity, the true indicator of a warrior, would be amply demonstrated to all. More horses carried heavy buffalo hides for clothes and robes. Another carried only buckskin sacks of bones for making tools and medicine. One fine hide was carried by itself on a handsome, brown-and-white pony. This hide would be consecrated to their brother, *Tatanka*, the buffalo, for his generosity in a suitable thanking-ceremony back at the village. They had already laid sacks of tobacco in thanks to the spirits of the Buffalo Nation, their close relatives, at the site of the kill.

Overhead *wambli*, the eagle, screeched a fierce challenge as the Oglala hunting party rode confidently through a thick wall of cottonwoods, dripping with morning dew. The sacred forest, with its roots deep in Mother Earth in four directions and its branches touching the sky, served as a protective circle around a secluded valley where the tribe's lodges would remain during the long winter. It seemed farther than three miles away, for they were eager to show off their bounty to the waiting tribe. Adulation for their success would be fittingly generous, especially from the women, young and old.

Panther-Strikes and Touches-Horses rode side by side as they usually did. Brothers. Or at least they felt like brothers. They were best friends and had been since they were boys. Brother-friends. *Kolas*, tied together in loyal friendship for life. Now they were also brothers-in-law; Panther-Strikes had just married Young Evening, sister of Touches-Horses. Both rode matching brown-and-white horses, trained by Touches-Horses. Panther-Strikes's magnificent mount was a wedding gift from his best friend.

"Once again, your father—the most holy of men—heard the stones singing. They even brought him the spirits of the Buffalo Nation to guide us," Touches-Horses said in the Lakotan tongue of the Oglala Sioux. He spoke quietly to Panther-Strikes, who was the taller and stronger of the two young warriors. His words barely cleared the banter of the other warriors.

Panther-Strikes smiled self-consciously and said, "Yes,

my brother. It is a rare gift from the grandfathers to talk with the most ancient of living things. I cannot honor him enough."

Panther-Strikes was lighter-skinned and brown-haired as well. He was *wasicun*, a white man, adopted as a boy by Stone-Dreamer. A hunting party like this one had found the child alone in a garden next to a sod hut. He was searching for food after his family died of cholera. They named him Angry Dog because of his feistiness when they took him to their camp. His white name was Vin Lockhart, but he barely remembered that now.

"You honor him every day, Panther-Strikes. The *was-icon* Firestick is magic in your hands. You have already led three successful war parties. Only Bear-Heart and Thunder Lance are seen as greater warriors—and they are much older," Touches-Horses responded enthusiastically and added, "You are also *skaiela*, a white speaker, and can talk the words with our *wasicun* visitors. And you were chosen for the Dance of the Sun at the gathering of all Lakota. Any father would be proud of such a son."

"But I do not hear the stones sing. They did not come to my vision. They do not come to me in my lodge or in my dreams. I bring special stones into my lodge, but they do not speak to me as I prepare for war or ready myself for the hunt. I call out to them, but they do not answer. I know it has hurt his soul. I know he has fasted and dreamed to receive understanding from the spirits."

"Few hear the stone songs, my brother. The panther is your spirit helper instead. That is a strong life-guide, and your deeds in war show it."

"But I am…the son of Stone-Dreamer," Panther-Strikes answered sadly.

His father tried to hide the disappointment of his son not receiving a stone-vision or owning a stone-song. But Stone-Dreamer had always assumed Panther-Strikes would become *wakanlica*, connected to the spirits through the stones, from his vision vigil. Others didn't see this frustration, but Panther-Strikes did. Nothing the young warrior did—no honors of war or hunt, no greatness of generosity, not even the terrible sun dance—filled this unspoken gap between the father and son.

To worsen the relationship, Stone-Dreamer had formally become a second father to Sings-With-Stones, a younger tribesman who had received a stone-vision. The extended relationship was logical since he hoped to become a shaman and sought Stone-Dreamer's teaching. But no matter how hard he tried, Panther-Strikes's envy of Sings-With-Stones still blistered his mind.

Touches-Horses started to say something about Panther-Strikes being white and perhaps this was the reason, but he was stopped by the arrival of Thunder Lance, who rode up behind them. More than six feet tall and straight-backed, he held a heavy lance comfortably in his right fist. It was decorated with dangling eagle feathers, strips of otter fur, and beads of sky-blue and black to represent the Thunderbeings. A small pouch of war medicine was bound to the lance just above where his hand gripped the smooth staff.

Thunder Lance's face was bright with the sense of accomplishment as he asked, almost yelled, "Do you think we will beat Black Fire's hunting party?"

Both young warriors laughed and shouted their acclamation. Using the sacred stone-song directions from Stone-Dreamer, scouts had found two small herds in separate places on the nearby prairie. A second hunting party, led by the tribe's headman, Black Fire himself, had headed south to seek the second herd at the same time as the returning warriors had headed west. Competitive curiosity about the likely performance of Black Fire's hunters had been a constant subject of interest as the dozen warriors weaved their way through the maze of silent towers.

"Aiiiee! We will ride into the village to magnificent trilling. Three times around we must go," Panther-Strikes said confidently.

His muscled chest was bare except for a breastplate of elkbone, and marked with a set of scars that told everyone he had been a chosen one to perform the Sun Dance for the People. His wide studded belt held a tomahawk and a war knife in an oversized, studded sheath, another wedding gift from Touches-Horses.

"Yes, the women will shout their affections. Our families will yell our names. Tonight there will be much to celebrate—and new songs of victory to sing," Thunder Lance added, jerking his lance in the air for emphasis.

"And Black Fire's hunters will be forced to enter in shameful silence," Touches-Horses said, almost as a whisper, then looked at Panther-Strikes for his agreement.

As he spoke, Touches-Horses slid his hand along the neck of the sorrel he was riding to calm the animal. The young horse sensed they were getting close to home and wanted to run. Possessed with an unusual ability for training horses, Touches-Horses was gentle, shy, and uncomfortable when presenting his achievements to the tribe. Often, another warrior had to do so, and usually it was Panther-Strikes.

Most of the major accomplishments of their young lives had happened together. They had gone on their first hunts and their first war parties together; they had even counted their first coups on the same enemy, a flustered Cheyenne. Although not together, they had sought their life-visions at the same time. Recently, both young men had also become proud members of the Kit Foxes, an *akicita*, one of the special warrior societies protecting the tribe.

Leaning toward Panther-Strikes, Thunder Lance whispered, "I must talk with your father. I have been having a dream that needs his great understanding. I feel it is the spirits trying to tell me something about my life ahead."

Panther-Strikes nodded and said without feeling, "I am certain my father can help you. The spirit world is happiest when they can talk with him." With that, he broke away from the intimate conversation and sang out an honor song. "*Yata hey!* Bear-Heart is the greatest hunter! *Yata hey!* Bear-Heart is the greatest hunter! Our village will sing his praises! Our people will sit and grow fat in their warm lodges!"

His confident manner was that of all instinctive fighters, free of all self-doubt in battle, seemingly impervious to danger or injury, yet generous in praise of the courage of others afterward. His throaty compliment was met immediately by fierce reinforcement from the other happy riders. Bear-Heart, the short, powerfully framed warrior leader, waved his uncovered war shield and lance above his head as acceptance of the compliment. His name had come from eating raw the heart of *matohota*, a grizzly, he had once killed. It gave him the strength and power of the revered animal. Around his thick neck hung a massive necklace of claws from that same bear.

Bear-Heart smiled broadly and said, "Aho, my warriors, see Panther-Strikes! See his skill with the *wasicun* firestick! Aho, my warriors, see Panther-Strikes! See his skill with the *wasicun* firestick! See how many buffalo he brings to our camp! No kettle will be empty. See how many buffalo he brings to our camp! No kettle will be empty."

Often sullen and hot tempered, Bear-Heart was in a good mood. His eyes sparkling with pride, he knew it was a time to be generous. He was intense and single-focused, and even the slightest deviation from what he expected tended to upset him. But everything had gone as he had planned and their return to the village would be greeted with the accolades of his people. He could see this in his mind and was wearing his finest warshirt and leggings, decorated with porcupine quillwork and beaded strips, as befitted such a return.

Touches-Horses put his arm on the shoulder of his step-brother and said quietly, "From Bear-Heart comes a fine compliment. Your feats will be sung tonight. You are a great warrior, my brother. I am proud. Your father will be proud. Young Evening will be proud."

"My honor is due to the great spotted horse my brother gave to me. He is unequaled in the hunt or in war," Panther-Strikes said, and patted the neck of the mustang under him.

Balling his left hand into a fist, Panther-Strikes drove it high in the air and yelled into the echoing pines, "Bear-Heart does me great honor. But our victory is shared by all the brave warriors who ride with him. Look at the skill with a lance of the mighty Thunder Lance…the eyes of Hawk, who found the herd when others could not, even with the words of Stone-Dreamer…the strong arm of Iron Bow, whose arrows are as deadly as the Firestick's iron rocks…and the medicine of Touches-Horses, who makes horses run like no other!"

Touches-Horses beamed at the compliment, but Panther-Strikes was already lost again in his own day-dream of return. The lighter-skinned warrior touched the choker necklace of whitest elkbone and sky-blue stones around his neck. It was a gift from Young Evening on their wedding day just two moons ago. Thoughts of her danced along the back of his mind from the moment he awoke until he finally went to sleep for the night. Young Evening. *Cinca Htayetu.* His lie-beside wife. She was everything the name suggested. Beautiful. Serene. Happy. He could barely wait to see her again and to be alone with her in their tipi. His mind had undressed and caressed her over and over since they began the return to camp yesterday.

A playful breeze broke away from the sentinel of trees and pushed Panther-Strikes's brown hair off his shoulders.

His face was lean, with high cheekbones and a nose that hinted of having been broken once. The tanned, chiseled face was not Oglala, nor were the light blue eyes, but everything else about him was. Next the breeze found the three split and marked eagle coup feathers tied to his scalp lock, honors won against the Cheyenne and Shoshoni, and tried to make them dance. He turned his face toward the gentle winds to let them paint his forehead with their cooling.

"Panther-Strikes, your medicine is, indeed, strong," Thunder Lance said, breaking into the young warrior's daydreaming. "You killed more buffalo than any two of us together. Stone-Dreamer will be the proudest father in camp. And Young Evening, the proudest wife!"

"I am the one who should be speaking of the feats of the great Thunder Lance, not the other way around. I saw you bring down that bull after it gored the horse of Painted Wolf," Panther-Strikes said, and rested his hand on the tall warrior's shoulder. "That was the biggest of them all."

"If your *wasicun* Firestick had not become silent, you would have done it before I even got there."

Panther-Strikes glanced down at his right fist holding a Henry carbine, one of the tribe's few firearms. Bear-Heart had such a fine weapon; two other warriors had muzzle-loading rifles; another had a Springfield carbine. The rest were armed with bows and lances. His lever-action weapon had been taken from a defeated Cheyenne last year in a remembered fight. Fellow tribesmen thought it was a magnificent gun, delivering fifteen .44 rounds through its awkward loading tube. They attributed his rapid-firing accuracy to the ferociousness of his spirit helper, the mountain lion.

Over his shoulder, on long straps, hung a small parfieche holding precious ammunition; a collection of brass, copper, paper, linen, and skin cartridges; and a pouch of powder and loose caps and balls. Some of the cartridges were still in their original wrapped packages of ten as issued to Union troops in the Civil War. He traded dearly for bullets among passing *wasicun*, and they were the first thing he sought among dead enemies.

After relating the story of the great bull, Panther-Strikes and Touches-Horses watched Thunder Lance ride on ahead to tell his story again to others. Panther-Strikes silently cursed the Henry for jamming as it had done yesterday. It kept him from bringing down the largest buffalo he had ever seen and leaving the honor to Thunder Lance. Maybe that would have made his father forget about his not hearing the stone-songs.

"Panther-Strikes, it will be good to see our fathers again," Touches-Horses said, loosening his friend from his thoughts. "Mine will ask us to point out which *pte* we each specifically killed." He looked around for a distinctive landmark, grinned, and added, "And yours will tell us that he saw us talking as we passed—ah, three bent pines beside a large, ugly rock. He will ask if we heard it sing to us."

Panther-Strikes returned the smile and started to answer. Suddenly he was rigid. Against the red morning sky, black cords of smoke were clawing their way above the forest line. He turned to Bear-Heart and blurted, "The village!"

Without waiting for a response, Panther-Strikes kicked his spotted horse into a run. The magnificent animal was in full gallop in two strides, widening the gap instantly between himself and the other warriors. Long fringe from his buckskin leggings fluttered like windswept grass. Decorative owl feathers and strips of panther skin rolled tightly into strings flew from accent points at his knee and mid-lower leg. He slapped the horse's withers with his rifle to push it even faster through the heavy forest. Behind him, fluttered cries to "wait!" from Touches-Horses and Bear-Heart himself went unheeded. He thundered over the last ridge and caught the first glimpse of the village.

Instead of a happy encampment with sixty painted tipis placed in a sacred circle—*cangleska wakan*—to hold in the power of the universe, a half-moon of blackened conical skeletons told him what he had feared was true. Instead of the sweet song of women preparing quillwork on new warshirts or cooking in darkened kettles, he heard the wail of death. Loud, unreachable cries that could not be softened with any words of caring. Instead of the few remaining warriors, old men, and women of the camp cheering the return of the successful hunting party, he saw downed silhouettes with others kneeling beside them. Dogs barked at an enemy long gone. Many lay to rise no more.

He reined the sweating horse to an unwanted stop as a loose sorrel horse cut in front of him, causing his paint to stutter-step backward. The frightened animal galloped past them toward some unknown freedom. Behind it came three more horses, but they reached an open area of undisturbed grass and stopped to graze. He patted the spotted horse on its neck to calm the fiery animal and the powerful neck lowered. A right front hoof began to paw the ground with impatience almost immediately, and Panther-Strikes understood the anxiousness.

It must have been the hated Shoshonis, taking advantage of the tribe's best warriors away on their hunt! It was a blood attack for revenge, not a pony raid for honors. The Shoshonis had been humiliated by the Oglala during the summer when Panther-Strikes and six other warriors made a war party of twice that many turn and run. Songs and reenactments of the coup-counting around the celebration fire were joyful and boisterous after that successful encounter.

Behind him there was movement, and he swung his

carbine toward the thick underbrush. An elderly warrior stood slowly; his face was half gone from blood. A gash above his right eyebrow was deep. Panther-Strikes didn't see how the man had lived this long.

"Blue Rider, what has happened?" Panther-Strikes asked.

"Panther-Strikes, it is you. I am glad. The Shoshonis came. They rushed through the village at the dawn. We had no time. So few of us to fight so many. They must have been watching our camp and knew all of you were gone."

"Have you seen Young Evening?"

"I am sorry, Panther-Strikes, I have not. I fought…" The warrior collapsed into a squatting position, and his head flopped once against his chest and stayed there.

"And fought well, my faithful friend."

Even with their superior numbers, the Shoshonis had not dared to remain long, he decided. They would have feared the return of the Oglala warriors even as they struck. It looked as if a third of the tipis were completely destroyed and half of the remaining lodges carried some signs of torching. The large, unpainted tipi that served as the council lodge loomed large and silent at the northern tip of the tribal circle. His eyes told him it had been left alone. The Shoshonis were afraid of its power, he reasoned.

To his right he saw a burning *Isna Ti Ca Lowan.* In the Lodge of Isolation, a girl celebrated her first menstrual period and became a woman in a sacred ceremony. He rode past the trembling remains of the sacred tipi and saw Happy Bird, the daughter of Yellow Elk, lying there alongside an old woman who had been guiding her through the special ritual. Red marks on the girl's forehead and chin were ceremonial red paint; red marks on the older woman's face were streaks of her own blood. The young girl had been raped and killed, the older woman bludgeoned to death.

He shook his head to rid the repulsion and nudged his horse forward toward the half-blackened tipi marked with his own spirit-helper symbols and his deeds. He was heartened by the structure remaining in place. His eyes tried to penetrate the walls of his tipi to see inside. His mind rejected the scorched side. Everything would be as it was. Young Evening would emerge from the lodge at any moment and smile at him, and everything would be all right.

"Young Evening, where are you?"

The only answer was the wailing of the encampment. He tried to swallow away his anxiety but couldn't. Bile edged up his throat. He swung down from his horse and felt his legs wobble. His eyes were glazed over with the fear that filled him. He was startled by a small boy who ran toward him from behind the tipi. The child was naked except for the tiny, decorated pouch holding his umbilical cord, worn to protect him. Tears covered his face as he ran without purpose.

Panther-Strikes forgot his own concern and stepped over to rescue the boy from his own fear. He kneeled and wrapped his arms around the distraught child and said gently, "Little warrior, do not flee. You are within the circle of the People. It is well."

"My mother? My mother? Where is my mother?"

Panther-Strikes recognized the boy as the child of Storm Wolf and Deer-Singing but didn't remember his name. "Your father, the great warrior Storm Wolf, is coming soon. I was with him. He will—"

"I want my mother!" the boy wailed into Panther-Strikes's chest. He patted the boy's head as his eyes continued to search his own tipi twenty yards away and saw the legs of someone on the ground. Then he saw the legs of a second person.

Two people! Fear galloped through him, spurring his heart into his throat and making it pound. He tried to murmur words to calm the child, but, choked with emotion, he couldn't hold back. He was torn between staying with the child to comfort him and going forward to face the agony he was certain lay within his lodge. He saw an elderly woman approaching and realized it was the boy's grandmother. She, too, was crying but took the lad by the hand, thanked Panther-Strikes, and led him away, talking with a reassurance only a grandmother can give.

After she left, he stood and advanced toward his own agonizing destination. His worried eyes confirmed the unmoving bodies of Stone-Dreamer and Sun Wolf, the father of Young Evening and Touches-Horses. Sun Wolf was dead; he could tell at a glance. Thin tendrils of breath smoke from Stone-Dreamer told Panther-Strikes that his adopted father was yet alive. Neither man had ever raised a hand in violence toward another, but they had obviously challenged their enemies to protect Young Evening.

Like a sudden cold wind, he recalled that his adopted father had told him the *tunkan*, sacred stones, had whispered that something bad was coming from the North. The whispering had come when he poured water on them, as he did daily. Panther-Strikes was certain the holy man thought it was a warning about an early-winter storm. Not this. Misinterpreting messages from the other side could happen, he knew. Even a messenger, like the meadowlark from *Okaga*, the South Wind, would get things wrong occasionally.

Toe stones were the first people and had sung since they created Mother Earth, the sky, and the mysterious power, *Taku Skan Skan*, that moves through all things. It was, therefore, understood that even the most holy of mere men could not always understand their songs until it was too late. That was the way of the grandfathers and had always been so.

He couldn't help wondering if Sings-With-Stones had heard such a message too, and then wondered where the young man was—he hadn't gone out with either hunting party and obviously wasn't here with Stone-Dreamer. Stunned at the sight of his adopted father lying unconscious, Panther-Strikes forgot about Sings-With-Stones and stood without moving. His gaze transfixed on the dried blood knotted on the side of his father's head and released the love he had for this strangely powerful man. That love was returned, even though it had been strained since the younger man's vision had not included a visit from the stone people.

Stone-Dreamer's lithe frame and unwrinkled face belied his age; the only hints were the gray strands of hair among the shiny black. Even in stillness, he had a commanding presence, a noble countenance marked by deeply set, penetrating eyes. They were now unseeing, his eyelids closed. The young warrior knelt beside his adopted father to examine him more closely. The head wound was not serious, a glancing blow that had captured the shaman's consciousness but not his life. Panther-Strikes touched the blackened red glob on the side of Stone-Dreamer's head. Several of the holy man's sacred stones had tumbled from a white elkskin bag he always carried and lay beside him. Like many sacred men, Stone-Dreamer gathered *sicum*, soul power, from holy men, warriors, and animals who died. Each *sicum* he held in a special stone for healing, for gaining wealth, for success in war, and for long life. His fellow tribesmen knew that, if he so chose, Stone-Dreamer could give a collected *sicum* to a dying person and give him new life, but it would greatly lessen his own spirit.

Panther-Strikes's attention was drawn to the handful of stones, distinctive in color and shape. Brown. Black. Clay-red. Shiny yellow. He saw the smooth, blue-green stone from the southwest and knew it contained the *sicum* of the long-dead great warrior Guard Elk. He saw a piece of clear, solid air his father had brought back from the spirit world and knew it was holy. Then he saw a reddish, spiral-shaped pebble tied to an elk-string lanyard.

He hadn't seen the *tunkan* since returning it to his father, who had asked him to wear the sacred stone during *hanbleceyapi*, his vision quest. This *tunkan* contained the *sicum* of Eyes-of-the-Wind, an ancient medicine man, but it did not help the young man receive a stone-vision as his father hoped. Instead, his spirit guide was revealed to him in the form of a panther and he received a man-name. *Igmu Tanka Awapa.* Panther-Strikes.

He picked up the pebble and a rush of memory went through him. After months of carrying the disappointment of not seeing *tunkan* when he went beyond, Panther-Strikes had come to Stone-Dreamer and presented himself.

"Father, I have seen beyond. I have dreamed of *wak~inyan*, a spirit guide. It is the great panther. I have learned the ways of my People. I have gone through the ceremony of making relatives, *Hunka Lowanpi*, and know I am related to all living things. *Mitakuye oyasin.*

"I have been honored with an eagle's feather. I know it is best to die young in the glory of battle. That no pots are to be empty if I am ever to consider myself worthy. I know the four great virtues of generosity, bravery, patience, and integrity."

Pausing to recall the rest of his rehearsed speech, and to swallow away his fear before bringing up the stones, he added, "You have taught me that I am tied to the Great Mystery through my head. You have taught me *canupa*, the pipe, is the connector between men and the *wakan*—and that no man can lie and breathe its power." He paused again, inhaled courage, and asked, "Will you now teach me the songs of the stone?"

"My son, I cannot teach you this. They are powerful songs."

"I know they are so, Father. I know the *inyan* are the most ancient of people. I know they are very wise. I am ready now. See how strong I have grown in the ways of our People. I know the sacredness of 'four' and the wisdom of doing things in fours. I know *skan*, the force that moves everything, that makes us alive, makes the water flow and the birds sing. I am ready to hear the songs of the stones."

"The stones will decide when you are ready, if ever. The songs of the stones come only to a few. The stones choose. Not the man."

"Like they have chosen you, my father?"

"Yes. But you should always listen for them. Their rhythm is in all men. It comes from deep within Mother Earth herself. The *inyan* moves always to the will of the invisible grandfathers. But most men are deaf to them. If you think they are beginning to speak to you, come and tell me about it right away." The shaman smiled wanly and placed his arm on the shoulder of his taller son. Panther-Strikes remembered there were tears in the corners of his father's eyes.

Panther-Strikes stood and slid the pebble lanyard over his head and let it rest on his sweating chest. Deep inside, he whispered to his soul that its power would protect him from what he feared most. He yelled out her name again, and his cry whistled into the smoke-filled air but again brought no return. Dropping his shield, rifle, and the reins of his horse, he pulled aside the wide flaps of the tipi's entrance. Panther-Strikes took a deep breath and forced a half-step inside. An invisible giant hand pushed him to his knees. Their possessions were strewn about the lodge's floor in a wild array, but he saw only Young Evening in horrible death. He screamed, but no sound emerged.

Chapter Two

In bloodied stillness lay the half-naked body of Young Evening. An ugly gash gurgled dark blood from the side of her head. From his kneeling position, he leaped toward her and cradled her unseeing face in his arms. Hot tears tattooed her bared breasts. Moaning like some wounded animal, he held her tightly in his arms and tried to sing her favorite song. Only grunts of despair came out. Her blood swirled across his leggings and chest. Suddenly the arrival of the hunting party jolted him from his agony.

He laid her body down and tried to cover her exposed breasts with the ripped-apart buckskin dress. The softened hide wouldn't remain in place and he looked frantically for something else. He grabbed a blanket burned at one end and laid it over her remains. His mind shouted out that she had been ravaged and he screamed denial.

"No! No! No! It can't be! Oh, no, not my Young Evening, please...please...please..." This time the yell bolted through the crossed lodgepoles at the top of the tipi and escaped into the grayness of the day.

As he pushed the corner of the blanket under her body, his fingers touched an elk-hide bag. Immediately he knew what it was and lifted her limp frame enough to pull the bundle free. Two Navy Colt .44 revolvers were stored in the heavy sack, along with a sack of cartridges, caps, balls, and a pouch of powder. Many buffalo hides had purchased the weapons from a visiting mountain man who had taken them off the body of a dead white trapper. Practice with the guns had been an obsession with the young warrior, far enough from the village so that no one was disturbed or curious. Young Evening had always accompanied him and the outings had always ended with their lovemaking.

Only one other warrior—the village leader, Black Fire—had a six-shooter, and it was considered a trapping of his authority. Panther-Strikes never carried them, out of respect for Black Fire. Yet skill with the Colts had come easily and far surpassed Black Fire's clumsy attempts to fire his pistol. The Shoshoni raiders had not discovered the handguns because Young Evening's bloody body lay across the tightly wrapped elk-hide bundle. It was as if this were her final act of defiance even as they defiled and killed her.

Methodically, as if nothing was on his mind, he sat beside her wrapped body, cleaned the revolvers, and loaded them with caps, powder, and balls. He would save his few precious cartridges. Each hammer was cocked halfway so the cylinder wouldn't be held in place. Powder and bullet were pushed into each chamber, then the loading lever brought the rammer against them. Carefully caps were pushed into position so they fit tightly and wouldn't be dislodged as he rode. Satisfied with the loading, he tied both ends of long leather loops to the trigger guards, then draped each loop and its gun over his neck, joining the dangling *tunkan*. All of his remaining cartridges were stuffed into his ammunition parfleche. He rose and headed toward the flapped opening.

Ignoring the tilt of the tipi due to a cracked lodgepole, he stopped and turned back. His hands went to the wedding necklace at his neck and untied it. He laid the necklace beside her body and choked back a sob that buckled his knees. Wobbly and wretching, he knelt again beside Young Evening. He dipped two fingers into the syrupy blood enmeshed in her hair and wiped it in a long line across his cheeks and nose. He rushed outside, taking huge breaths of the smoky air to try to stop the vomiting that rushed from his soul.

His fiery horse hadn't moved in spite of the fearful smell of blood. He grabbed the loose reins, lifted the war shield from the trampled grass, then picked up his rifle and checked the loads. He looked again at the two downed men and saw a frightened Touches-Horses running toward him.

Without waiting to discuss the situation or comfort him, Panther-Strikes said, "My brother, your father has left us. I am certain his spirit came to warn us. Will you care for my father? He is alive but hurt. I must ride."

Panther-Strikes could not bring himself to say that Young Evening was dead as well. News of his father's death made Touches-Horses stumble. He half turned away as if to reject the words, then realized what the absence of Young Evening signified and what his brother-in-law meant in leaving.

"No, my brother! Wait for the others!"

Touches-Horses grabbed his arm. Panther-Strikes pushed him away and swung onto the spotted horse. Touches-Horses watched his friend ride away with mixed feelings of sadness and pride. Disoriented, Stone-Dreamer raised his head and mumbled something Touches-Horses could barely make out, something about the stones singing for his son.

Two days later, Panther-Strikes found the Shoshoni war party riding carelessly back toward their camp. They were moving through a wide ravine that in ancient days had held a river. From his hidden position, Panther-Strikes couldn't help but compare their attitude to that of the Oglala hunting party's. Stolen horses were herded easily along with their own extra mounts. A morning fog belted the riders, hiding the legs of their horses and ghosting their twenty-four silhouettes, as they entered a narrow valley. "Spirit rain," Stone-Dreamer would later call it.

Their faces and chests carried patterns of colored paint. They laughed and exchanged stories as they rode. Pendants of red, yellow, and green fluttered from leather thongs around their braided hair. Some were further accented with small silver disks attached to the braids; others wore bone and silver earrings. Eagle feathers were stuck in their scalp locks, except for one warrior who was wearing a broad-brimmed white hat, evidently a trophy from a recent raid somewhere else. Another wore a full feathered headdress, but he didn't appear to be the leader, just an honored warrior showing off his coups.

Eight were clad in long-sleeved buckskin warshirts; another six wore bone breastplates over bare chests; one was decked out in a blue U.S. Cavalry officer jacket and one was in a woman's blue gingham dress. The rest were garbed in clothing and other items taken from the Oglala camp. Eight were carrying rifles, a mixture of Springflelds and Spencers; the rest held bows and arrows and lances shortened for use on horseback. Panther-Strikes could also see a few revolvers shoved into leather waistbands. Fresh scalps dangled from rawhide shields, thong bridles, and proud lances.

Panther-Strikes inhaled to calm the seething rage within him. He welcomed death, for it would come while he was striking down the killers of Young Evening. He would be able to join her in the journey to the spirit world.

He spoke the Oglala warrior's call to battle: "*Hokay hey*! It is a good day to die! I am Oglala. Only the earth and sky live forever. It is a good day to die."

Breathing deeply to soak in the confidence, he added the Kit Fox song: "I am a Fox...I am supposed to die ...If there is anything difficult/If there is anything dangerous/That is mine to do." Then he prayed silently for his spirit helper to give him the cougar's courage and stealth. His mind blotted out the possibility of staying alive but made him focus on doing the most damage first.

Touching the sacred stone dangling at his chest, he fingered the hard edges and added one last prayer: "*Tunkan* of Eyes-of-the-Wind, give me strength. Grandfather, sing for me this one time."

He moved the war shield and rifle to his left hand and drew the tomahawk with his right. Sensing his rider's need for stealth, the paint horse eased over the ridge and moved forward like a shadow. Horse and rider slid silently behind the last Shoshoni warrior riding behind the gathered Oglala ponies. The young Shoshoni's attention was on his companions in front of him, enjoying themselves while he was forced to ride alone.

Panther-Strikes's tomahawk drove into his head and blackness followed for the pony guard. The already dead warrior slid from his horse, startling it into a sideways skitter. A dark blossom of blood spread on the trampled earth after the body came to rest with bare legs curled awkwardly together. Putting tied reins in his mouth, Panther-Strikes urged his horse past the frightened animal and focused on the next rider at the front edge of the pony herd.

He was two strides away when the Shoshoni warrior-sensed something behind him and turned. Panther-Strikes's Henry roared, firing it with his left hand like a giant pistol; the war shield bounced on his arm as he pointed the weapon. Dislodged from his horse by the impact, the second guard pitched forward over the neck of his mount and down in front of its stutter-stepping hooves. The sudden gunfire aroused the war party from its gaiety. As one man, they turned to see what the noise was about.

Panther-Strikes thundered toward them, firing and levering his carbine with both hands. His war shield was held in place by the bend of his left elbow. The unsuspecting Indians were ripped apart as he pounded through them, blasting left and right with deadly accuracy. Horses screamed and jumped with fear. Five warriors were killed instantly; another four were wounded and knocked from their mounts. Only the men in the front had enough time to realize what was happening and return his fire. He reined up thirty yards in front of the stunned group and reloaded his rifle from his ammunition sack, using only his best brass cartridges.

Recovering from the unexpected attack, the remaining Shoshonis charged him confidently, yelling their war cries of human defiance and spiritual guidance. Four aimed rifles, two pulled their bows, and two more positioned their lances. Without moving, he coolly aimed and fired, driving five more Shoshonis from their horses. He reloaded again and poured lead into the rest of the wild-eyed war party. On the eighth shot, his rifle jammed. He yanked on the lever and pulled the trigger three, then four times, without success.

Without another thought about the weapon, he threw it to the ground. In the same motion, he grabbed the two revolvers hanging around his neck and kicked the paint horse to meet the unstopped advance of the war party. As he galloped through them again, his sweating horse seemed to take on the same blind rage as his rider. He cocked and fired the pistols as if they were extensions of his mind and body.

Gunfire was so rapid that it sounded like one continuous roar. Everything was in slow motion to him, like he was watching himself from somewhere outside his body. Fear controlled the eyes of the Shoshonis as he drove through them again. He picked his targets as he ducked their swings of lance and tomahawk and ignored their shots with rifle and bow. His fire cracked through flesh while their lances and tomahawks struck wildly in the fog-laden air, producing only glancing blows against the pistol-wielding white warrior or crashing against his war shield.

Swirling dust within the fog made it harder and harder to see clearly—a disadvantage for the Shoshonis, who had already inflicted cuts on each other in trying to reach their lone adversary. This was no coup-counting performance, no colorful warrior tactics the Plains Indian had developed into a high art of selfless courage and daring. No, this was a terrifying whirlwind of death. Something supernatural. Here in their midst was the most savage beast they had ever faced. A wild beast tearing the Shoshonis apart with life-seeking metal while their own weapons were having no effect.

Yet the white warrior's blood seeped black from bullet wounds. A Shoshoni warrior, whose lower face was painted completely yellow had fired at Panther-Strikes twice and struck him both times—once in the left arm, the second in the shoulder. A crease across Panther-Strikes's left cheek spat a thick red stream. His chest and arms were purple with welts and cuts from the blows that hadn't missed. A heavy lance cut his horse along the neck, but the snorting animal kept running.

He reined the paint to a reluctant stop and slung his war shield to the earth. His wounded arm could no longer carry it and shoot effectively. What cartridges remained were hastily shoved into the two empty revolvers while the Shoshonis regained their courage for a charge against him. His hands were trembling from the loss of blood. Dizziness wouldn't leave his head. The wheezing of his horse was more than exhaustion. It was the beginning of the great animal's death song. The Shoshonis' final advance began with one arrow striking his horse's flank, another driving into his upper right leg.

Bullets whined past them as he rumbled with the last of his ammunition. He kicked the great mount into one last charge. Both pistols belched death into the remaining warriors. His last three bullets ripped into the face of the rifle-shooting Shoshoni and the yellow paint disappeared into an explosion of red. Entangled in a leather stirrup, the dead warrior was dragged by his scared horse toward the ridge where Panther-Strikes had come.

That ridge was no longer empty. Oglala warriors had pulled up their lathered horses to watch him pistol-fight the bewildered Shoshonis. Warriors from both hunting parties were in the assembled band led by Black Fire and Stone-Dreamer. Wearing a full-length white elkskin cape over his customary white buckskin shirt and leggings, the shaman was mounted on a white horse with red painted circles on its face and shoulders. He was speaking in an unknown language to the spirits of the ravine. His normal winter wolf headdress had been replaced by a wide, bloody bandage.

Beside him rode Sings-With-Stones, his eyes bright with the joy of being close to his mentor. As the holy man had advised, he was fasting alone in a place where the spirits were known to dwell when the attack came. He had returned only after completing his ritual and was deeply hurt not to have been there to help defend the village. No one criticized his behavior, for he was not a warrior; he had been called to another path.

The Oglalas had come to bring Panther-Strikes back with them, but they froze in awe at the battle before them, as he charged again and again, firing and killing, as if nothing could harm him. Like the Shoshonis, the Oglalas had never seen a man fire so rapidly, so deadly, so often. None had seen a single man destroy such a numerically superior enemy. This pistol fighting was spiritual. Of another world. So was the frost smoke. The spirit rain. No man could do such fighting alone. It had to be connected to the shadow world in some way.

His eyes widening in surprise, Stone-Dreamer pronounced loudly, "See the shadows? See the spirit rain created by the *tunkan* living within this ancient riverbed? See the grandfathers beside Panther-Strikes? See the dead and dying enemies? Panther-Strikes cannot be stopped. The grandfathers have willed it so. Can't you see? The spirits ride with him! Can't you hear? The stones are singing just for him!" His voice trembled with pride; his eyes were wide with a joy he couldn't contain.

The Oglalas strained to see and hear what the holy man described; some nodded agreement; others whispered prayers to their own spirit helpers. Stone-Dreamer dismounted and picked up a flat, whitish stone. A skeleton of a tiny, long-ago animal was embedded in its surface. Many such stones lay in this dead riverbed of long ago, and they, indeed, were *tunkan*. He held it high in the air with both hands. Sings-With-Stones quickly jumped down and squatted, searching the ground with his eyes and fingers. He saw a similar rock, grabbed it, and stood, holding his stone high with great relish, in an imitation of Stone-Dreamer.

Below, three remaining Shoshonis finally broke and ran, urging their froth-covered ponies into a frantic lope, unaware that their mysterious adversary had no more bullets to tear into their painted bodies. Panther-Strikes swung to chase them, but his great paint horse stumbled and fell. Thick cuts streaked scarlet across its heaving, white-covered flank. Breaking free of the fallen mustang, Panther-Strikes took one step, clicked the hammers of both pistols on spent chambers, and collapsed in bloody exhaustion. His horse blew one last defiant snort and breathed its last.

With the urging of Black Fire and the support of Stone-Dreamer, the Oglala warriors rode down to the dying ground, counted second and third coups on the Shoshonis, and bludgeoned any yet alive. *Hu ikhpeya wicayapo!* Total defeat of the enemy and thorough dismemberment of their dead bodies! They scalped for Panther-Strikes and caught seven horses for him as well. Several warriors tried to touch the spirit rain grown heavier with the battle's intensity. Others lifted their arms in prayer to let its power sink into their chests. Many sought a special rock from the bedground to add to their medicine bundles. A few tied them to elk string and wore them around their necks. They could sense spirits all around them, forcing the air close to their faces. It was an uneasy place to be, and they were glad Stone-Dreamer was with them. Yet they knew the spirits were happy; Stone-Dreamer said so, and they could feel the happiness all around them.

Touches-Horses ignored the fallen Shoshonis and rushed to the prone, and barely breathing, Panther-Strikes. "My brother!" he cried out and gently lifted Panther-Strikes's head from the earth, then wiped the mud and blood from his still face. The badly wounded warrior moaned and his eyes fluttered. Stone-Dreamer came behind him and placed a hand on Touches-Horses's shoulder.

"The grandfathers protected him. They fought at his side. They are watching now. Can't you hear? The stones are singing loudly his song," the holy man said, and presented the flat stone as evidence of his last statement. His pride was unguarded, unusual for him.

Looking up, a distraught Touches-Horses said, "I only see my brother dying. Say it cannot be, holy one. Call to the stones and make them understand. Make him live."

The rest of his words blurred into jibberish as he broke down and wept. Stone-Dreamer saw the Eyes-of-the-Wind spirit-stone lanyard hanging from his white son's neck. As he backed away, Stone-Dreamer's face carried a concern different than that of a father for his wounded son. It was the look of a knowing man who had seen something that made everything make sense.

Only Sings-With-Stones caught the expression and said excitedly, "O great teacher, I see the spirits around us. They are happy to be in battle once more. They are happy to ride with your son. I hear the *tunkan* singing. It is to honor you."

Stone-Dreamer stared at the young man for a moment, his forehead rolled into a deep frown, triggering a faint smile at the corner of his mouth. "Young one, be careful of your words. This is a place made hallow by my son."

"But I do see the spirits. I saw my grandfather and he spoke to me. I know this."

"Good. Look for a glowing stone. It will be important for you," he said, and kneeled beside Touches-Horses. Placing his left arm around the distraught warrior, he ran his right hand lightly over Panther-Strikes's bloody body. Sings-With-Stones stood for a moment and then went to find such a rock.

The others were soon involved in battle honors, rounding up the loose horses, both theirs and the emptied Shoshoni mounts, and building a travois to carry Panther-Strikes back to the village. Bear-Heart assumed the honored responsibility of retrieving all of Panther-Strikes's weapons and ceremoniously distributing them to warriors of note to carry back. All were eager to leave the battle ground of spirit rain and dead enemies. But Touches-Horses insisted on building a fire to consume the remains of the great brown-and-white horse before they left.

"My brother would want it so. The winged ones should not have his great heart. Let him run free again in the other world—and wait for Panther-Strikes," he said with a face filled with sadness.

Soon flames were jumping around the horse's body and eventually took it from their sight. Touches-Horses ordered the travois attached to his horse for the return trip. He rode one of the recaptured Oglala ponies alongside the barely breathing Panther-Strikes.

"Remember, my friends, the spirits live around us. Some are seen. Some are not seen. They are the shade. They are the tiny whirlwinds of dust. They are why dogs bark for no reason," Stone-Dreamer said, ending the chatter of the warriors as they returned to their battered village. Sings-With-Stones kicked his horse to place him to the holy man's right. But Stone-Dreamer didn't acknowledge his presence.

As if preparing them for an important message, the holy man reminded the war party that the dead were not gone but lived in a separate world as ghosts. A world connected to their world by the Ghost Road in the sky. If unscalped, spirits were free to go back and forth from the spirit world to earth. Some came to help their living comrades; others came to do evil. Thin as air, spirits of the dead could return in any form, for any purpose. Some came back again to live as regular humans. Certainly it had been proved that owls were reincarnated ghosts. That is why their talk did not echo, like a man's. The silent warriors nodded in agreement and understanding. A few looked around as they rode, searching for proof to his assertions, but they had been taught the way of ghosts since birth and knew it was the whole reality of their journey on Mother Earth.

"I found no glowing stone," Sings-With-Stones whispered, apologetically.

Stone-Dreamer glanced at him and said, "You did not look hard enough. I saw the stone. It spoke to me, and I have brought it as asked."

He withdrew from his parfleche a jagged-edged, white rock with flecks of silver and brown. Without waiting for comment, Stone-Dreamer returned the rock to his pouch and glanced back at the travois carrying his unconscious son. His voice grew louder, his shoulders thrust backward in an authoritative pose. "Around us, always something moves. Always. It only takes to listen. The most ancient of living things, stone, is always moving—but most men cannot see this moving. It is the will of the grandfathers. The most ancient of living things, stone, is always singing—but most men cannot hear this singing. It is the will of the grandfathers. The most ancient of living things, stone, is always powerful—but most men cannot use this power. It is the will of the grandfathers."

Bear-Heart nudged his pony alongside Black Fire's horse. Neither man spoke, only exchanging eye words. From behind them, Stone-Dreamer continued his pronouncements.

"Today, into battle, Panther-Strikes carried a sacred *tunkan.* The stone of Eyes-of-the-Wind," he proclaimed in a trembling voice. "Eyes-of-the-Wind was pleased to be called into battle by my son. It had been too long. He brought along many of our ancestors to ride with Panther-Strikes."

Two warriors behind him reined their horses in surprise. They knew this stone was one of Stone-Dreamer's special possessions. With this *tunkan* the seer had cured people, found many lost things, and given counsel to scouts. Bear-Heart glanced at Black Fire for reassurance, but the headman was listening intensely to the shaman.

- Waiting until the war party settled down from his announcement, Stone-Dreamer proclaimed, "In the battle of the spirit rain, I heard the stones singing just for Panther-Strikes. He is *wakanlica,* connected to the spirits. I saw the ancient Eyes-of-the-Wind riding beside my son in this remembered fight. I saw grandfathers protecting him from the blows of our enemy. I saw grandfathers guiding his strikes upon the Shoshoni!"

Every warrior appeared visibly frightened by this stunning news. Bear-Heart grabbed the bear-claw necklace around his neck and murmured a request to his own spirit helper. Sings-With-Stones looked down at the small, fossilized rock clinched in his fist and whispered to it. Black Fire touched the medicine pouch hanging from his neck and whispered a prayer. Thunder Lance reached out and touched the shoulder of Stone-Dreamer as the shaman began to chant:

"Someone comes into the fight; he hears the stones singing.
His name, Eyes-of-the-Wind. His name, Eyes-of-the-Wind.
Someone comes into the spirit rain; he hears the stones singing.
His name, Eyes-of-the-Wind. His name, Eyes-of-the-Wind.
Someone waits for this one coming; he hears the stones singing.
Panther-Strikes. Panther-Strikes.
Someone waits for this one coming; he hears the stones singing.
Panther-Strikes. Panther-Strikes.
A stone singing, a spirit coming, a man waiting.
A stone singing, a spirit coming, a man waiting."

Stone-Dreamer spoke no more; his manner became more and more trancelike as they wound their way back to the village. They rode in haunted silence for an hour. At the outskirts of the camp, Touches-Horses rode between Stone-Dreamer and Sings-With-Stones, leading his horse with the travois carryng his wounded brother-in-law. Sings-With-Stones didn't like it, but Touches-Horses didn't notice his frown or didn't care. And if Touches-Horses was concerned about disturbing the holy man, his words and manner didn't indicate it.

"Will Panther-Strikes die?" Touches-Horses asked, placing his hand on the holy man's forearm.

Stone-Dreamer stared into the distraught face of the gentle warrior and winced. "He is in the hands of the grandfathers. It is not mine yet to know." Stone-Dreamer looked down at the red pebble in his hand and squeezed it.

"The grandfathers will not let him die," Touches-Horses responded. His voice was thin but gritty.

Stone-Dreamer did not answer, and they rode in silence for several minutes. Finally, the young warrior broke the awkward quiet: "If he dies, will you build his spirit a *Wan-agi Yuhapi*, a Ghost-Keeping Lodge?"

The holy man shut his eyes and answered in a slow, methodical voice as if it were coming from somewhere outside his body: "Panther-Strikes will live. He will not stay with us."

"How do you know this?"

"*Stolwaye.* I just know."

It was not an answer to Touches-Horses's question, but the grieving warrior let it pass. He rode without speaking for several minutes more and said, "I want to build a Ghost-Keeping Lodge for my father and my sister. Will you guide me through the Shadow Ceremonies?" As was the custom, he did not use their names, nor would any Oglala ever again, to honor their memories.

"That is a path of great difficulty," Stone-Dreamer said. "It is usually a path only a father walks for a young son or a favored warrior."

"I have lost two of my family. It shall be."

Sings-With-Stones attempted to enter the conversation and said authoritatively, "That is a hard path, Touches-Horses. You will live alone in the Ghost-Keeping Lodge most of the time. You must give away your possessions to honor them. You must rely on others for food. You must not disturb the air around you in any way, or touch anyone for a year. There is much more."

Without turning toward Sings-With-Stones, Touches-Horses growled, "I know what is expected. Will you guide me, holy one?"

Trying to gauge the depth of the young warrior's determination, Stone-Dreamer said, "The Shadow Ceremonies are, indeed, very difficult. Are you certain? None will think less of you for honoring your father and sister in the traditional way."

"I must do this."

"So shall it be."

As Panther-Strikes lay dying in the shaman's tipi, the village mourned for their dead and prepared their funerals. Most of the dead were older men and women, but six warriors had also died in the Shoshoni raid. Funeral scaffolds were built within sight of the circle of tipis. They rested on a soft hill to the south where all spirit journeys begin. Each dead person would be close to the sky with nothing between him and his journey to the spirit world.

Bodies were dressed in their finest with their faces painted and all of their honors adorning their hair. Layers of wet buffalo robes were wrapped around each body and tied with rawhide thongs. Prized possessions were laid with them as well. The old warriors' best horses were killed and left beside the scaffold so they would have suitable mounts to ride. An elderly man's dog, also killed during the Shoshoni raid, was placed alongside his body. Mourning began immediately, with family members showing the extent of their grief with slashes on their legs and faces. Some women cut off joints of their fingers. Men cut their hair and went without leggings. Some jabbed pegs into their arms and legs. Stone-Dreamer visited each family to offer his counsel. No one dared to ask him about Panther-Strikes.

Two special Ghost-Keeping Lodges were constructed.

One was made for a small boy who had died during the raid. The other was for Young Evening and Sun Wolf by Touches-Horses, as head of his family. The structures were designed to assist the slow passage of the departed to the other side of life. Their spirits would walk among the living as shade until certain rites had been performed to ensure their journeys would be safe ones. A year of demanding privation through the Shadow Ceremonies would aid their travel to the other world. After the special lodges were completed, locks of hair from the departed were placed into special medicine bundles, consecrated, and hung inside the tipis. When Touches-Horses and the other family were properly instructed on the rituals required, Stone-Dreamer left the camp to seek wisdom from the stones. He advised Sings-With-Stones not to assume that he had the power to assist anyone with their spiritual needs and to keep to himself in his own father's lodge. The gentle warrior was greatly disappointed but obeyed without question.

Stone-Dreamer rode out with a solemn announcement: "I am summoned by the *inyan.* The stones have much to tell me about the spirit rain battle and the invisible ones who fought at Panther-Strikes's side. While I am gone, the families of the dead must continue their rituals as I have described them. No one is to enter my lodge to seek after Panther-Strikes. No one. There is much there that is *wakan.* Much that is a mystery"

Honor songs of Panther-Strikes's stunning revenge and the spirit rain battle were savored by everyone young and old. Most had an opinion about what had happened and why. Most thought his victory was a mystery. When Stone-Dreamer returned four days later, he entered the village chanting in an unknown language and holding fire in his raised bare hands. He wore his finest white leggings and elk-hide shirt. Tassels of white winter wolf accented his special dress, along with magical red porcupine quillwork. As his headdress, a winter wolf's head again adorned his head. Mystical owl feathers hung down one side.

The wound on his head was healed with no sign of scab or scar. He had never seemed so aloof yet so vulnerable. A mature widow, Blue Star, tried to get his attention as he passed. Stone-Dreamer did not acknowledge the woman's presence, in spite of her visiting his lodge many nights during the past year. She turned away, tears in her eyes, and walked alone to the river. Without speaking to anyone, he went immediately into his lodge, taking the fire in his hands with him. Sings-With-Stones ran up to him and excitedly told him that he had received another dream, of flying across the land and visiting the shadow world. Stone-Dreamer told him that now was not the time to discuss it, and the young warrior turned away disappointed and confused.

Night was wrapping its arms around the lodges of the Oglala when Stone-Dreamer emerged from his lodge and went solemnly to the council lodge. With great ceremony, Stone-Dreamer took seven small bundles of tobacco outside to a tree nudging close to the lodge and hung them there as a prayer offering. He ordered bundles of sage and sweetgrass to be burned in sacred ritual, then introduced the sacred medicine pipe, *cannunpa wakan*, wrapped in sage, to assist their prayers getting through to the supernatural.

All men and women of integrity and honor were invited to smoke or touch the pipe. After the ceremonial filling of the pipe, each presentation gesture was completed seven times, and prayers offered each time to the east, west, north, south, the earth, the sky, and *wambli.* More sage was added to the fire to help purify their thoughts and bring them harmony as the holy man told a subdued council of what the life-forces of nature had confided in him about the spirit rain battle.

With a tremor of excitement in his voice, Stone-Dreamer began to share his news. "Listen. *Heyapi.* First, I must tell you that our brother, the wolf, came to me before we left to find Panther-Strikes. The wolf was acting as a messenger—as he often does, you know—between the under-the-earth-beings and we, the People. They had heard spirits of this world and the next had been summoned by the *inyan* to ride with a great warrior. Spirit riders would pass through the campfires of the dead along the Spirit Road in the southern sky. Yes, these were the words of the wolf, our brother."

Expressions of concern and fear encircled the assembly. Waiting for the council to settle down again, Stone-Dreamer smiled faintly, shut his eyes, and softly sang the *Yuwipi* stone-working song:

> "Friend, I will send a voice, so hear me. Friend, I will send a voice, so hear me. Friend, I will send a voice, so hear me.
> In the west I call a black stone friend. *Kola*, I send a voice, so hear me.
> In the north, I call a red stone friend. *Kola*, I send a voice, so hear me.
> In the east I call a yellow stone friend. *Kola*, I send a voice, so hear me.
> In the south I call a white stone friend. *Kola*, I send a voice, so hear me.
> On earth, I call a spider friend. *Kola*, I will send a voice so hear me.
> Above, I call a spotted eagle friend. *Kola*, I send a voice, so hear me."

He paused. This was, indeed, a powerful song because it was directed at the entire universe and requested the spirits of all the directions to respond.

"The first to answer me was *Okaga*, the South Wind.

His messenger, the meadowlark, brought these words to me: 'Look for the spirit riders, they come, answering the song of the stones. Look for the spirit riders, they come, answering the song of the stones.' That is what the meadowlark came saying. 'They come to ride into a great battle.' That is what he came saying. *Wakatanhewi kin heyau welo E ya ye yo.*"

His outstretched hands held seven small stones, enwrapped in boughs of freshly cut cedar. Stone-Dreamer continued chanting in a halting voice, "*Wakatanhewi kin heyau welo Eya ye yo.* Messengers from the other Winds also spoke of the grandfathers coming. From *Eya*, the West Wind, came the swallow. From *Yata*, the North Wind, came the magpie. From *Yanpa*, the East Wind, came the crow. All spoke of grandfathers coming to help my son."

His story was building with the growing importance of his sources, and he continued, "*Inyan* sang a song I had never heard before. A song to my son. They sang a song to bring the spirits. Many of these spirits are watching now. You will hear them. You will see them. It is an important time to pray."

Stone-Dreamer held up his outstretched arms and began to sing in a high, throttled voice:

"*Wakatanhewi kin heyau welo E ya ye yo.*
Tunkan sing to him.
Sacred stones sing to him.
Tunkasila ride with him;
Grandfathers ride with him;
He seeks their help.
Tunkan sing to him.
Sacred stones sing to him.
Tunkasila ride with him;
Grandfathers ride with him;
He seeks their help.

Tunkan sing to him.
Sacred stones sing to him.
Tunkasila ride with him;
Grandfathers ride with him;
He seeks their help.
Tunkan sing to him.
Sacred stones sing to him.
Tunkasila ride with him;
Grandfathers ride with him;
He knows their help.
Wakatanhewi kin heyau welo E ya ye yo"

Completing his chant, Stone-Dreamer dropped his head to his chest and stood silently, his shoulders heaving, his body weary from the emotional outpouring, his face twitching strangely. In the far dark southern corner of the lodge, a disconnected voice bubbled eerily for an instant and then was still. Then another voice in the northern corner whined an unknown phrase. Blue sparks appeared at Stone-Dreamer's feet, swirled around his leggings and into the darkness. Whispers encircled the council fire that the spirits were talking. Later some spoke of also hearing hooves and growling and the sounds of other animals. When he finally looked up, the council fire's glow encircled his face and made it into that of an old man's. Not even the bold Bear-Heart dared to ask him if Panther-Strikes would live. No one noticed the faint smile upon the holy man's lips. With his arms outstretched, he thanked the spirits for coming and said that special food was left for them.

Afterward Sings-With-Stones came up to the exhausted holy man and asked if there was anything he could do to aid the healing of Panther-Strikes. Stone-Dreamer stared at the gentle young man with the fine features for a long time before answering.

"No, you must not even think of such things. It might

endanger my son's return. Go to your own father's lodge. My time must be with my son. Your spiritual journey must wait. But you must look inside to find the way. It cannot come from me. Not now."

Sings-With-Stones walked from the great lodge and let the night air cool the stinging tears on his face.

Chapter Three

The village had little time to ponder the mysteries of Stone-Dreamer's announcement before the North Wind wrapped powerful arms around the land and covered Mother Earth with ice and snow. First came the Moon of Frost on the Tipi, then the Moon of Trees Popping. Honor songs for Panther-Strikes gave way to just trying to keep warm. Grieving for the dead gave way to the necessity of caring for the living. New buffalo robes were put to good use. Stores of dried meat were distributed throughout the village. Horses were cared for with bundles of dried grass gathered earlier. Ice was regularly removed from the nearby stream so animals and the People could get water.

Children discovered the snow and turned it into a new playmate. Warriors gathered to tell stories, smoke, and work on new weapons. Women cooked and sewed new garments. Bear-Heart and a handful of warriors hunted constantly on snowshoes. An occasional elk caught in a snowdrift, or a buffalo trapped in a frozen stream, became their grateful find. The white blanket only added to the loneliness in the two Ghost-Keeping Lodges, where sacrificial vigils continued as directed by the holy man.

When weather permitted, Stone-Dreamer conducted his regular healing and spiritual responsibilities with a cheery disposition. He spoke not of Panther-Strikes, nor was the great warrior seen. Some said Panther-Strikes had died and the holy man had created a funeral only a shaman could prepare or see. Others agreed and said Stone-Dreamer appeared to be in a trance, that he was coming and going to the spirit world to check on Panther-Strikes's progress.

Others spoke of often hearing sounds of whirring winds and prancing deer hooves, even the growling of the grizzly bear within the mysterious lodge. Many spoke of hearing strange voices asking questions and Stone-Dreamer answering. All smelled the powerful burning sage, lying lightly on the winter's cold breath, coming from his lodge.

Finally, the return of the generous South Wind was a miracle to be praised, especially by the tribal council, who watched the depleting food supply with growing concern. Thanks was also given to the North Wind for the snow that purified Mother Earth. The Moon of the Birth of Buffalo Calves finally arrived, bringing the promise of rebirth across the land.

But *Yata*'s breath brought a morning of chill to the early-spring-stretching village, and with it, the announcement that Panther-Strikes had died. A mournful song in an unknown language was heard from Stone-Dreamer, standing outside his medicine lodge in the predawn light.

A mounted crier, painted all in black, rode through the camp on a horse painted with red blotches. He called out, "The great warrior of the spirit rain fight has joined the spirit riders and crossed over to the other world. The great warrior who sought revenge for us all has joined the spirit riders and crossed over to the other world. Grandfathers came to greet him and take him home. Young Evening was waiting. Stone-Dreamer asks that you pray for his soul to find an easy path."

Stone-Dreamer disappeared into his lodge and did not emerge anytime during the day. The village was quiet, adults urging their children into respectful silence. Suddenly, at dusk, a mounted crier, painted all in white, rode through the camp happily proclaiming, "Panther-Strikes returns to us! The spirits have guided him back to us. Panther-Strikes returns to us! He is healed! Panther Strikes returns to us. The spirits have guided him back to us!" Everyone in the village stopped to ponder the words. How could this be?

Later that evening a weakened Panther-Strikes walked unaided and alone to the river and bathed. Naked except for a breechclout, he talked with no member of the village nor met anyone's eyes. He was pale and thin; his body glared with the red marks of freshly healed wounds. He jumped into the cold stream to bathe and purify himself. Many eyes watched but dared not be caught being so curious. Old men and women whispered that Stone-Dreamer had given the young warrior some of his own *sicum*, his own eternal soul power. Some said he was *wanagi.* A spirit. Others weren't certain but acknowledged that the grandfathers had definitely helped him beat the Shoshonis. Many were surprised that he did not partake of the spiritual rejuvenation of a sweat lodge first.

On his return, he paused outside the Ghost-Keeping Lodge of Young Evening and Sun Wolf and heard the hoarse ritual singing of Touches-Horses. Through him rushed the realization that his beautiful wife was named for this time of day. Panther-Strikes hesitated and turned away, stumbled, half caught himself, and went to his knees. In a crawling position, he vomited twice. Stone-Dreamer wanted to run to Panther-Strikes and comfort him but knew he could not. Panther-Strikes must find the right way alone; his soul demanded it. The young warrior had even bluntly refused his suggestion to have his soul cleansed in the sweat lodge, even though Stone-Dreamer had encouraged this step. Finally he stood again, headed back to his father's lodge, and disappeared within. He wasn't seen again for several days, spending most of his time sleeping. While his son slept, Stone-Dreamer sat and smoked, watching him regain stolen strength.

Sweet memories gradually took over the lodge. He saw again the eight-year-old he had first seen, emerging from the mists of his mind. Frightened but ready to fight, young Vin Lockhart was surrounded by the Oglala warriors who had brought him to the village. Stone-Dreamer walked over to the young *wasicun*, put his hand on the boy's head, and gently rubbed his already-tossed brown hair. The youngster jerked back, flashing a small pocketknife, and said, "Watch it, mister! I'm Vin Lockhart and I ain't afeared o' nuthin'."

With limited English, Stone-Dreamer said quietly, "No hurt you, Vin Lockhart. Come. Stay with me."

They had named the boy Angry Dog that day for his feistiness, and the boy and the holy man gradually grew close. Stone-Dreamer guided his adopted son's education carefully and patiently, teaching the white boy many important things. Like how all the sacred things were gathered together—the moon, sky, stones, earth, winds, lightning, thunder—to become *Wakantanka*, and all were sacred in and of themselves. And of those the first four were *Wi*, the Sun, *Skan*, the sky, *Maka*, the earth, and *Inyan*, rock. He had carefully explained that stone, the most ancient of living things, was the enduring life-force connected to the invisible grandfathers. That it was the solid form of the spiritual force that created Mother Earth and all its creatures. That stone, moved with a purpose unseen by most men but linked to the will of the invisible grandfathers.

He explained that a man who owned a stone-song, and thus had experienced a stone-vision, became *wakanlica.* Powerful. Mysterious. Close to the grandfathers. Stone-vision keepers even had the memory of a life before this one. "To remember everything," the knowledge that one had prior to this earth-birth, came from this relationship. He had explained how the spirits of the dead went slowly to the other world and how they must be cared for until that journey begins. Sadly, his son couldn't see that now and was refusing the assistance Young Evening's spirit needed. Stone-Dreamer stood and stretched, but yester-days kept rushing in.

"Look closely, Angry Dog, blue paint is made this way." The holy man pointed to the small pot resting on the gray coals. "You must carefully boil rotted wood, blue mud, and duck droppings. Yes, add more mud. Oh, yes, that is very good." The boy smiled at his father's compliments.

More memories followed, like a herd of elk. He saw himself showing the boy how skunk fat would waterproof moccasins and heal skin sores. How buffalo grease could help a sore throat. How wild mushrooms could heal an aching tooth. How the night was controlled by the hushed-wings, the owls, who were sent to the other world at dawn by the red-dawn-coming bird.

Stone-Dreamer even showed the young boy how he performed certain tricks to enhance his image as a man of mystery, like throwing his voice in a lodge to suggest the presence of spirits. With a wry smile, Stone-Dreamer had showed him how the fluid from scarlet mallow could be rubbed over his hands to protect them from scalding hot water or even fire. And how a certain sliver-thin rock could be ground into tiny particles and appear as blue sparkles when the glow of a fire reached them.

"My son, it is important for men to open their minds to allow for healing of the body or for understanding of the spirit world," he told the wide-eyed boy as they sat within the warm confines of his lodge. "Sometimes, tricks are necessary to do that."

He had taught him the ways of the land—and the ways of the Oglala—but not the ways of the heart. Stone-Dreamer feared what the *inyan* had whispered to him years ago, that his beloved son would one day leave the village and return to the *wasicun.* He had held this tightly in his heart for many years and now he was worried the time was approaching—and he didn't know what to do or say. Had he done wrong in telling the village of seeing spirits ride with his son? Should he have kept this to himself?

Should he not have exaggerated the state of his son's health by announcing his death when it wasn't so? He had done it to remind his fellow tribesmen of how great the spirit rain battle had been. They needed such a story, he rationalized to himself. It was expected that the son of Stone-Dreamer could do no less than cross over and come back. Stone-Dreamer knew his son had done so in his unconscious fight to live again. It was so and should be told, he told himself over and over as sleep finally took his mind and the spirits talked to him. Early the next morning. Stone-Dreamer walked around the village, uncharacteristically smiling and greeting everyone cheerily.

Walking with a bearded mountain man who visited occasionally, Black Fire called out warmly, "Aho, Stone-Dreamer! You are looking well this morning. How is the great warrior Panther-Strikes today? The one who rides-with-spirits?"

Stone-Dreamer strolled over, smiled, and said, "He is doing well. Very well. He is weak but gaining strength every day. Mostly he stays with the grandfathers—sleeping. They favor him; it is crowded in my lodge with many spirits visiting." He chuckled at his remark, and both men smiled.

In Lakotan, the mountain man asked, "Is it true, holy

one, that you brought him back from the dead?" His filthy hands were shaking, and he rubbed them together to ease the anxiety within him.

Stone-Dreamer smiled again and said, "Rarely would I refuse a guest of our leader, but that is a question I cannot answer."

Black Fire realized the foolishness of the question as it came out of his white friend's mouth. No shaman would ever brag about his power. That would be tantamount to ending it; *Tatanka*, the buffalo, would take away the gift because the man was not worthy of this special ability. Black Fire quietly told the mountain man of this and he asked for forgiveness from the shaman. Stone-Dreamer graciously accepted the apology and changed the subject to the weather.

For several minutes the three men talked easily about how long the cold might last before spring finally arrived and when the Buffalo Nation would return. Black Fire asked if the sacred stones had sung about their return. Stone-Dreamer said he had not sought their wisdom on the matter but would soon, that several scouts had asked as well. Both Black Fire and the mountain man wanted to ask more about Panther-Strikes but knew they shouldn't. That would be for Stone-Dreamer to offer, if he wanted to do so. And clearly he did not.

At midday Panther-Strikes walked again to the stream, as if sleepwalking. His stride was uneven, like the lumbering movement of a bear risen from a winter's slumber. Again he washed himself in the cool waters, dried himself on the bank, and headed back. Four young boys of eight and ten saw him, stopped their mock battles around the closest embankment, and ran to his side. Chattering with each other, they tried to match his steps.

Wolf Cub, the son of Black Fire, asked what the others wanted to: "Are you really *wanagi*? Huh? My father says so." The boy's eyes were wide with excitement.

Another asked, "My father says the *wanagi* came to fight beside you. He says you cannot be killed because they protect you. Is that true? Are they with you now? Do you see them?"

A third boy chimed in, "My father also says you are *wanagi*! He says you already died!"

Panther-Strikes inhaled deeply and let the frost smoke spill across his face. His expression showed surprise as the boys jumped back from the sight as if the breath was more than a normal thing. He bit his lower lip and tried to think of something to say that wouldn't offend their fathers.

"Your fathers are wise men—and great warriors. They honor me with this story, but I am an Oglala warrior. Just as they are—and no more."

"But why did the crier ride through camp singing your death?" Wolf Cub asked, trying to match Panther-Strikes's strides.

Panther-Strikes stopped and turned to the boy, who was suddenly frightened. "What did you say?"

"I—I—I said…w-w-why did the crier sing your d-death? I—I—I'm sorry. I—I—I didn't mean to—"

"When was this?" Panther-Strikes interrupted.

Wolf Cub looked around at his friends; none would connect with his eyesight, preferring to stare at their moccasined feet. "I-i-it was at dawn yesterday, I think. W-w-we all heard it, didn't we?"

This time the young boy put his hand out to stop the others and forced them to mumble agreement and shake their heads positively.

"I see," Panther-Strikes said, and began to walk again.

"Will you let us walk beside you, huh?" "Where are you going?" "Can we, huh? We won't get in your way, we promise." "We're going to be warriors too, you know."

"You may walk with me, little brothers. But it won't be a long walk. I am going to my lodge—to rest. I am only a man who has been wounded—and is still weak."

After he entered the empty tipi where he and Young Evening had once lived, the boys stood outside for a few minutes, listening, and then ran away to tell of their great adventure. Panther-Strikes stood inside the lodge trembling. It took his tortured mind several minutes to realize their home had been carefully returned to its proper state by caring men and women in the village. The burned outer hides had been replaced. Clothing, buffalo robes, weapons, and pots were put in their places about the lodge floor. His war shield hung on a tripod in the back, facing east. His pistols, rifle, parfleche and wedding choker lay at its base. His lance, tomahawk, and knives were stationed in the west corner, along with his medicine bundle. The only difference was a wide dark stain where Young Evening's body had lain. Panther-Strikes threw himself upon the bloodied mark and sobbed himself to sleep. Tearing at his mind came an awful nightmare.

Young Evening called out to him, "*Igmmu Tanka Awapa!* Panther Strikes! *Igmmu Tanka Awapa!*" She was drowning in a white roaring river. When he ran to help her, the water changed into a field of brilliantly hued flowers. As far as he could see, there were blossoms and more blossoms of crimson, yellow, white, orange, and violet. But when he pushed his way into the flowers, they turned into violent flames and she disappeared, screaming, within them.

His own cries of agony awoke him. He arose early the next morning, soaking wet with sweat. Dawn was little more than a rosy suggestion in the east. He heard the sound of grazing and went to the tipi's opening. A fine black horse was tethered ten feet from his lodge. The animal's quiet manner indicated it was trained by Touches-Horses. The glistening animal's mane and tail were decorated with eagle feathers, reddened to signify personal injury. On its chest and flanks were painted handprints, one for each dead Shoshoni. A magnificent coup stick, decorated with their scalps and finely beaded fur wrapping, was staked into the ground next to the tipi's opening. Gifts from the tribe, he thought, and smiled. Generosity was the mark of all great Oglala warriors.

Then he noticed that four tall cottonwood staffs had been placed in the ground a few feet from the coup stick. From each stick shyly fluttered a different-colored ribbon. Red, black, yellow, and white strips of cloth called for his attention, each representing one of the winds. Tiny sacks of tobacco surrounded the staffs in a circle. In the center of the four directional staffs were four rocks placed in a circle, with a line drawn between the north and south rocks crossing a line from the east-to-west rocks. A foot away and facing south sat a bowl of freshly cooked elk meat and berries.

A tribute to the spirits? What did this mean? He decided they were praying for his recovery and had left the tributes to the invisibles as a part of that effort. After a few minutes he retrieved the food and ate lightly, finding that his appetite mirrored his depression. Later Panther-Strikes rode through the village. He wore only his breechclout; his long brown hair was unadorned with feathers; his face and body carried no medicine paint.

Holding high the coup stick with his right hand, he shouted, "Panther-Strikes is thankful that his People care for him. I ride the great black horse. I carry the staff of honor. I ride to pray for strength."

He choked on the last words and tried to keep from looking at the Ghost-Keeping Lodge of his late wife and her father. A deep breath fought off the advancing anguish. With a nudge of his heels to the horse's flank, he galloped away toward the south. Warriors throughout the village stopped to watch him. Standing next to Black Fire, Bear-Heart said in a low growl, "All spirit trails lead south." The Shirt-Wearer nodded his agreement.

Panther-Strikes returned at the edge of dusk. He talked

with no one, nor let his eyes greet passersby. After tying the new horse near his tipi, he laid crossed sticks in front of the entrance to signify that he didn't want to be disturbed and went inside. From a distance Stone-Dreamer watched him sadly, realizing that his adopted son refused to enter the Ghost-Keeping Lodge where his former brother-in-law struggled with the discipline of the Shadow Ceremonies.

In his heart, the holy man knew it was probably too much to ask for Panther-Strikes to face the horrible loss of his wife at this point in his recovery. Yet the longer he avoided this responsibility, the more difficult his full return to this life would be. Stone-Dreamer stepped inside his own dark lodge; his nostrils filled with the special smell of sweetgrass. He eased himself into a cross-legged sitting position and reached into his white parfleche.

The two stones, taken from the spirit rain battle, were withdrawn and laid on the ground before him. He began a song about a previous existence, when he first walked on Mother Earth with the ancients. As he always did, he sensed a contact with the wonder of creation through the stones, a kinship with the invisible grandfathers that had been his gift since his own *wot awe*, his vision, years before. It had come directly from the grandfathers in the shape of stone.

The vision had meant a special life that few were allowed to follow or could. It was also a hard way, demanding much of body and mind. But it was the only way he knew. He constantly communicated directly with the spirit realm, learning their ways of healing, their songs, how to interpret the dreams of his fellow tribesmen and how to conduct sacred ceremonies. Yes, he understood the spirit world, and he had taken mind-flight into the land of shadows many times. He knew the real world was actually the spiritual world, that humans were only travelers on Mother Earth.

Now he was pulled between soul ache and bursting pride. His son's refusal of the sweat lodge was hard to take. It was not the way of the son of Stone-Dreamer. But that was overridden by the wonderful fact that the village had recognized his son as one strongly connected to the grandfathers. After Panther-Strikes received his vision, Stone-Dreamer prayed constantly to understand why his son had not been given a stone-vision. It was a bitter disappointment he tried to hide but knew his son had seen. Choosing Sings-With-Stones as a second son was a tribal responsibility he couldn't pass, but he knew it had widened the gulf between them.

All of his prayers—and more than he had dared to wish for—had been answered at the spirit rain battle. He was sure the stones had sung to his son. He had heard them himself when the Oglala war party rode onto the holy ground where the many ancient stone-animals lived and where the spirit rain battle was fought. He had heard them clearly. Oh so clearly.

And then, wonder of all wonders, the grandfathers had come to his son's aid! He had seen the telltale swirls of dust, the spirit rain that surrounded his enemies, the special shadows that darted among the Shoshonis and alongside Panther-Strikes. He had sensed their presence near him. But Panther-Strikes got angry anytime he made such comments, vehemently denying any such happening, angrily denouncing any stone singing to him.

He asked the two *tunkan* to tell him why Panther-Strikes denied the significance of the spirit rain battle. Had the battle itself taken that memory away? Was this the will of the grandfathers? For the first time in their father-son relationship, the holy man didn't know what to do or say. For the first time, the stones did not speak to him.

Each morning for the next seven days, Panther-Strikes found gifts in front of his lodge, left mysteriously during the night. Blankets, sacks of sugar and *pemmican*, strips of ribbon, a bag of rifle bullets, a beaded sack of tobacco, and a large war knife in an all-white beaded sheath were among the presents. Reluctantly he took them inside the lodge and stacked them in a pile. Certainly the gifts were generous, and he was moved by their caring, but he tasted another sensation as well. His friends were treating him as if he were a spirit, not a man. This was the manner to court the favor of a spirit helper. A force to revere and fear, and pray to.

His movement about the camp became ghostlike to many because he was rarely seen, and then only for brief moments before entering his lonely lodge. He avoided contact with everyone, even Stone-Dreamer. He would disappear from the village for days at a time and then reappear at dusk, only to disappear into his tipi.

One morning after he had just returned, he awoke to singing outside the lodge. The song was about him. A solitary drum delivered the honor song's heartbeat as the voices swelled into the morning air.

"Panther-Strikes comes. See him coming. Panther-Strikes comes. See him coming. *Wanagi* come. See them coming. *Wanagi* come. See them coming. The fathers of our fathers ride with him, fight for him, give him life. The fathers of our fathers ride with him, fight for him, give him life. The fathers of our fathers ride with him, fight for him, give him life. Praise Panther-Strikes. For his courage, give him a new name. For his courage, give him a new name. He is now *Wanagi Yanka.* He is now *Wanagi Yanka.* Rides-With-Spirits."

Suddenly the flaps of the tipi were thrown back and Panther-Strikes stuck his head outside. He screamed at the gathered singers, "I am not *Wanagi Yanka*! I am only Panther-Strikes. I have lost my beautiful wife. Can't you leave me alone?"

Frightened by his outburst, the assembled tribesmen

immediately disbanded. Some of them ran, afraid the spirits might also be angry. Several of them immediately sought guidance from Stone-Dreamer. What should they do next? They explained the gift-giving and the reverence they had shown. Fear of bringing on the wrath of the spirits was almost too great to express. How did they anger *Wanagi Yanka*? They had only done what the holy man had suggested. The old shaman assured them that he would talk with Panther-Strikes and that nothing would be wrong.

After they left, Stone-Dreamer walked over to his son's silent lodge and called into it, "Aho, my son, it is Stone-Dreamer. May I enter? My body has been purified by sweetgrass."

A long silence followed before Panther-Strikes finally answered, "Yes, my father. You are alone?"

"As alone as I ever am, my son."

"Please come in."

Panther-Strikes lay upon the bloodstain of the tipi's floor. Stone-Dreamer was saddened by his son's weak appearance and hesitated to bring up the subject he had come to address. Panther-Strikes cocked his head to the side and said, "You have come because I yelled at some of our friends, haven't you?"

"Yes. They do not understand. They revere you. You are favored by the grandfathers. I know it is hard now. But you must remember others love you—and worry about you."

"I am only Panther-Strikes. I am favored by no one—and seek no favor. I only ask to be left alone. Is that too much to ask?"

Stone-Dreamer said, "My son, your eyes are painted with soul pain and it saddens me greatly. I wish my powers were great enough to remove its streaks. But I cannot. Only you can do so. It is time to let your beautiful one walk the spirit path in happiness. Can you not go to the Ghost-Keeping Lodge and do this?"

Panther-Strikes was surprised at the statement and didn't answer for a moment. Finally he spoke, gazing toward the sky and away from the shaman: "My dreams tell me I was walking that trail with her, the trail of ghost fires in the south sky, when you came and brought me back."

"Yes, that is so."

"I wish you had not."

"I see."

"No, you don't. No one does. I ache for her. I cannot breathe. I cannot see without, without—"

Stone-Dreamer interrupted with a stern tone to his voice: "You are not the only man who has had to deal with the loss of a beloved wife. You are not the only one who grieves for a family member gone to the other world. You are not the only one who knows a black emptiness inside that won't go away." The corner of the holy man's mouth quivered as he spoke. He looked away when he was finished to let a sad memory work its way across his chiseled face.

"I don't care if everyone is sad—from here to the end of the world. I don't care. I just want to be left alone."

"I am sorry, my son," Stone-Dreamer said in a resigned voice. "I will see you are not bothered any more."

The holy man started to leave and was stopped by Panther-Strikes's sudden question: "Why did you announce I was dead?"

Blinking his eyes to cast away the harshness of the question, the holy man said quietly, "It was time for the People to know your greatness." He left the tipi without waiting for a response or explaining further.

Before dawn of the next morning, Panther-Strikes awoke from another night of feverish nightmares and walked to the stream. Waiting for him was Stone-

Dreamer; his hands were filled with *inipi*, the rocks used to create steam in a sweat lodge.

"Why are you here?" Panther-Strikes demanded, already knowing the answer. His eyes were fire.

"I came to prepare *inikagapi*—the sweat lodge—for you. I have brought the necessary stones."

"*Goddammit!* I said 'no.' I meant 'no.' Can't you understand that? Go back to your stones and leave me alone," Panther-Strikes yelled and grabbed at the stones, tearing them from the holy man's hands. The rocks tumbled to the ground and Stone-Dreamer studied them for a moment. More than the physical response, he appeared stunned by Panther-Strikes's use of the *wasicun* curse. Without looking again at the young warrior, Stone-Dreamer picked up the loose stones and walked away.

Panther-Strikes watched him, felt no guilt about his rebuke, and then continued his trek to the stream. As he entered the cool water, Panther-Strikes saw an elderly Oglala woman sitting in the scraggly grayness of a young tree off on the south bank. She appeared to be asleep, her carrotlike hands grasping a small bowl of water. The liquid had spilled upon her dirty dress. Why wasn't she with her family in a warm lodge? The question pushed away momentarily the depression that was eating him far worse than any physical injury.

He waded through the stream to the other side. As he approached, she sat up, startled. Her shaking head looked from side to side, but milky-covered eyes told of near-blindness. She spoke in a shrill whisper, her few teeth adding to the strange tenseness she was trying to express.

"Why are you here?" she asked in a raspy voice. "Why do you bring the spirits of my family? Have you come for me? I am ready. There…there, my father! See, my father stands beside you. See?! *Hokay hey*, it is a good day to die."

He was annoyed by her remarks, and his anger quickly

returned. Turning to stomp away, he hesitated, took a deep breath, and, instead, walked over to the old woman. He touched her head gently with his hand to reassure her. She was weaving back and forth rhythmically, from a squatting position, sobbing and speaking incoherently. As soon as she felt his hand against her face, she stopped. Grabbing his outstretched hand, she held tightly, then caressed his palm like something holy. Her death song rolled sweetly from cracked lips. He recognized her. She was Ligfrt-in-Tree, grandmother of a warrior killed by the Shoshonis last autumn.

He kneeled down and asked, "*Unci*, Grandmother, why are you here? Where is your family?"

"O great rider-with-the-grandfathers, my family lies on that hill," she said, and pointed a bony finger in the direction of the funeral scaffolds resting on the gray hill to the south. "I have no one. They have gone ahead of me."

"I see. Where is your family's lodge, Grandmother? Is it Lone Elk's?" He ignored her designation for him. Now was not the time to be angry.

"Y-y-yes…but I—I—I'm not sure which way to… how did I get here?" she said, rocking her body in rhythm with her words. "I remember now. I went to see them… my family…to see if they were all right. Then…I don't remember what…"

"Everything is all right now. I will take you home."

"T-t-there is no home when the ones you love aren't there anymore."

Panther-Strikes swallowed back the gurgling scene of his dead wife and struggled to respond: "Y-y-yes, I understand. It is hard. You must remember that others love you—and worry about you." The words were those Stone-Dreamer had told him the day before. They were tender, but they rang as hollow to him now as they had then. But she seemed comforted by them and he repeated them:

"You must remember that others love you—and worry about you."

Slowly she turned to Panther-Strikes and said, "You are the one who rides with the spirits. Why do you waste time with dust?" For emphasis, she picked up a small handful of dirt and let it dribble through her bent fingers.

"You are my mother, my sister, my grandmother," Panther-Strikes said gently. He smiled wanly to himself. That was something else he had heard Stone-Dreamer say to an ailing woman.

She cried at the words. The old woman did not seem ill, just weary from hunger and loneliness. Her disorientation had kept her from returning to her tipi on the far side of the village. He lifted her and carried the frail woman back in his arms. Men and women came running to see what was wrong as he entered the circle of the village. Minutes later, he was spoon-feeding warm broth to the old woman as others waited outside the lodge.

A crowd of the curious grew rapidly around the tipi. Even tribal leader Black Fire, his mountain man friend, and Stone-Dreamer joined the curious throng. At first the holy man was uncertain of the meaning of this situation. Had his son done something to an old woman in his time of unreachable sorrow? Surely not. His relief was visible even to Black Fire when he realized that his son was helping an old person in need. But the tribal leader thought it was an expression of pride.

"It is good, my friend," Black Fire said with a reassuring pat on the back of the holy man. "You have a great son, worthy of much pride. The grandfathers have chosen wisely."

Stone-Dreamer nodded, unable to speak. Silently, he thanked *Wakantanka* and hoped this was a sign that his son was turning away from his horrible journey of the soul. He had already forgiven him for the hot-tempered encounter earlier.

Squirming through the tightly assembled adults was the youngster Wolf Cub. He got to the front and stood next to Stone-Dreamer. Bouncing on first one leg then another, Wolf Cub could hold back no longer and blurted, "Is she a spirit too?"

Standing next to the boy, Stone-Dreamer answered with a stern voice, colored with a lilt of relief, "She is a tired grandmother who needs caring. Great warriors always watch over those who can't help themselves. You must learn that."

"My father is a great warrior." The boy's words were part challenging and part defensive.

"Yes, he is—and a great leader," Stone-Dreamer said, glancing toward Black Fire, who was near the back of the crowd and couldn't hear them. "As you can see, he is concerned Light-in-Tree was left alone this way. Some young warriors will be sorry for their carelessness. But he will be pleased you are paying attention to our elders. It is a sign you are on the red trail to becoming a warrior."

Wolf Cub looked up at the holy man and grinned at the compliment.

After patting the boy on the shoulder, Stone-Dreamer stepped to the entrance of the lodge and asked, "My son, may I enter?"

Chapter Four

"Yes, but no one else." Panther-Strikes's voice was without emotion.

Inside the lodge, Stone-Dreamer nodded toward his son. "With your permission, my son."

"Of course."

The holy man leaned over the elderly woman and said, "Here, *Unci*, take this. It is good for you." He pushed a small bowl of dark liquid to her lips and helped her sip it.

After she swallowed the bitter medicine, he blew on her stomach four times, set the small red stone of Eyes-of-the-Wind upon it, and prayed in a language unknown to Panther-Strikes. She watched the weakened warrior with slitted eyes and immediately grabbed the spoon out of his hand and began eating on her own. As she ate, Light-in-Tree would occasionally raise her head as if to say something, then return to the broth without speaking. Stone-Dreamer told Panther-Strikes that the woman was alone, her family was killed in the Shoshoni raid. He thought several warriors had been looking after her and bringing her food. Panther-Strikes indicated that she had told him the story of losing her loved ones.

Soon she was resting comfortably on a bed of buffalo robes and trade blankets. The holy man left the lodge to inform the gathered villagers that she was going to be all right. Before they could disperse, a returning scout rode toward Black Fire in a zigzag line, indicating good news.

"*Tatanka! Tatanka!*" the excited scout exclaimed as he drew closer. "A huge herd—across the south ridge! It is as you said, Black Fire. Rides-With-Spirits has spoken with the spirits of the Buffalo Nation and brought back *Tatanka*!"

With a smile splitting his face, Black Fire repeated the news and pointed toward the lodge where Panther-Strikes still remained. Instantly, words of tribute rang out from the gathering: "Aho, Rides-with-Spirits! Aho, *Yanka Is-akib Wanagi*!" "Thank you for caring for the People." "Sing to the grandfathers who ride with our spirit warrior! Sing!" "Thank you for bringing *Tatanka!*" "Praise to all *wanagi*!" "Thank you, *Yanka Isakib Wanagi*!"

They cheered and sang and asked for Panther-Strikes to come out. He did not. Knowing his stepson did not want this adulation, Stone-Dreamer suggested they should be readying themselves for the big hunt. He added that the *tunyan* had sung to him of this herd and that it was a large one. Black Fire nodded his head enthusiastically and the gathering began to break up into small groups who left gaily for their lodges. Soon only the holy man remained. After he was certain everyone had gone, Panther-Strikes came out of the old woman's lodge.

"I—I cannot stay," Panther-Strikes mumbled; his eyes were giazed.

"Why, my son? You are revered by the People. They—"

"That is why, my father," Panther-Strikes said, tears

beginning to trickle down his cheeks. "Every day I am tortured by her memory—and, and…I am not *wanagi!* I can't even see the spirit of my wife! You are the holy one, can't you make them understand? I hear no stones singing. There are no grandfathers helping me. I am just a man. A man without…his wife. Why can't they understand that?"

Stone-Dreamer looked down at the embers of the cooking fire outside the lodge. His eyes stayed there as his words darted toward Panther-Strikes' heart: "I cannot make them see what they do not want to see. Just as I cannot make your heart sing again. But it is my fault they see this way. I told them of what the *inyan* sang and the winds whispered. I helped them see the grandfathers riding with you in the spirit rain battle."

"You told them this?"

"I told them what I saw. Many spirits rode with you in the great spirit rain battle against the Shoshonis, of this I am certain. Our grandfathers were there. And our great-grandfathers. With their best horses. I felt them. I saw them. I believe they came to the spirit rain battle led by Eyes-of-the-Wind—and they came because you asked his *tunkan* to help you. I cannot change that, my son."

Panther-Strikes looked away from the holy man, sighed, and walked toward his own lodge. Stone-Dreamer watched him and tears festered in the corners of his half-closed eyes. He called out in a voice desperate for understanding, "It is a thing for much pride, my son, for all the village. It is worthy of a new name, of great songs. They will be sung at the summer gathering of Lakota so that all might know. You will be remembered by all Lakota!"

Minutes later Panther-Strikes galloped away from the quiet camp, kicking the black horse into a heated run. The holy man stood beside his tipi and gazed at the ever-smaller silhouette until it was no more. He reached into the white parfleche hanging at his hip and withdrew the small red pebble that held the *sicum* of Eyes-of-the-Wind. After examining its surface, he took an elk string and tied it to the stone, leaving a small loop. He placed the loop over his right ear, letting the stone hang as an earring, and went inside the lodge. Passersby were disturbed by the strange chanting that came from the holy man's place. Some said they heard voices of many yet knew Stone-Dreamer was alone. Sounds of animals inside his tipi wandered through the early-evening air, carried along by the sweet smell of burning sage.

That night Panther-Strikes sat alone on a treeless ridge, far to the south of the encampment, watching the stars graze across the great darkness. It was a forlorn place many Oglalas felt was haunted with spirits. He had never been here before, but it pulled him like a thirsty horse to water. Below him, he saw an old cottonwood tree standing alone in a small valley surrounded by the ridge and three parallel hills. Branches pushed in every direction, the imprinted struggles with different battles of wind and weather through its years of life. Even in the dark, he could see the tallest limbs reaching up to touch the sky, matching deep roots that hugged Mother Earth. He studied the black shape, wondering what it was thinking, how it coped with such battles, why it cared to live on.

Depression wrapped around his soul and made it a black void, like the night itself. Loneliness followed, squeezing every emotion from his mind and standing guard against any positive thought reentering. Little about him spoke of Oglala. He had stripped himself of everything tribal, like a man crazed by a fire eating at his clothing. Except for Young Evening's wedding choker, he wore only a breechclout nearly touching his knees when he stood. Two *wasicun* pistols with their bloodstained elkskin lanyards lay on the uneven rock shelf beside him.

Gradually his eyes moved from the stars to the guns and back to the stars, then rested again on the guns. With his left hand, he casually picked up the closest revolver by the barrel. His hand acted independently of his body and his mind. Raising the gun over his head, he examined the cylinder as if to see whether the bullets had mysteriously disappeared since he had loaded them hours before. They were brass-capped, some of his best ammunition. The stiff lanyard dangled against his arm. He switched the weapon to his right hand, cocked the hammer all the way back, and pushed its nose against the side of his head.

He tried to concentrate on pulling the trigger. His sweaty finger nudged against unmoving steel. Something brushed softly against his cheek. There! It came again. Like invisible fingers caressing him. His dulled mind said it was the wind, but the touch came a third time, then a fourth. Finally a fresh thought broke through the black wall in his head.

It was Young Evening! She was here! Beside him! Now! Her spirit was trying to keep him from killing himself.

He dropped the gun and it exploded into the night, driving a bullet into the heart of the darkness. Panther-Strikes looked around for his beloved wife and saw nothing. He took harried steps toward the northern edge of the ridge where he had climbed earlier and saw his black horse standing quietly below, waiting. He breathed deeply and tried to call her name.

"Young Eve—"

His voice cracked and he began to weep. When all the anguish was strained from him, he lay against the cold rock and didn't want to move or think. Like the first tiny bubble in a kettle of water just beginning to boil, an idea began to surface in his mind. Another bubble followed, a bigger one this time, and then another. Soon his entire body was blistered with this idea: It was time to leave the village. Forever.

It was time to forget being a warrior, forget being an

Oglala Sioux. It was time to leave behind Stone-Dreamer, Touches-Horses, and his other friends. Yes, it was time to let Young Evening go, too. That was her message tonight, to let her go on the spirit trail and quit praying for her return.

In the darkness he concentrated on recalling his young life as a white person, but it was difficult. Even the faces of his real mother and father would no longer take shape in his mind. He barely remembered the time when warriors returned with him from a hunt ten years ago. They had found the white man's child wandering among a small garden in search of food. His parents lay dead in the nearby sod house, along with a younger sister—all victims of the white man's disease of cholera. The warriors were fascinated by the boy's feistiness as he attempted to fight them off with a pocketknife. They decided he had the spirit of an Oglala warrior and took him with their hunting party. In honor of his fierce spirit, they named him Angry Dog.

Stone-Dreamer feared the white man's sickness and insisted the boy's clothing and the rest of the things gathered from his family's home be burned—except for his small pocketknife and the Lockhart family Bible. Sensing the *wakan* power within the book, he kept it after purification with the caring smoke from a fire of sweetgrass, the sacred grass that never died. Later, he put both the small knife and the holy book away for safekeeping.

One group of warriors wanted to kill the boy, but the holy man told them he was not to be harmed; the *tunkan* had advised him that the boy was placed there for a reason. Stone-Dreamer had no other children; his late wife had died barren years before and he had never remarried. No one disputed Stone-Dreamer's wishes after that pronouncement—at least, not where he might hear it. Soon the white child was fully accepted by the tribe, for they loved his eagerness, his courage, and his quickly apparent athletic skills. Training in the ways of a warrior were turned over to respected members of the tribe, among them Black Fire, chosen as his second-father, and Bear-Heart.

As a sullen cloud marched defiantly in front of the biggest cluster of stars, Panther-Strikes stood up and shouted into the night, "I am Vin Lockhart! I am *wasicun*!"

Across the night a long, low growl of a mountain lion joined the bitter chorus of coyotes, but his concentration on the future did not allow room for other sounds. He looked down at the ground and saw small stones of many shapes and colors. He grabbed a handful in his fist, opened it, and let the pebbles lie on his flattened palm.

He yelled again, "*Tunkan*, you do not have to sing to me. It is not necessary. I go away. You can sing for another." He clinched his fist again and threw the stones into the darkness.

The morning bird had not yet brought the morning light when Panther-Strikes rode back to the village, quickly entered his lodge, and then left, carrying his tomahawk. He walked swiftly to the silent Ghost-Keeping Lodge where Touches-Horses continued his vigil. This time he did not hesitate, entering swiftly into the sage-smoke-filled tipi. His eyes burned at the touch of the thick, sweet air. A few coals burned enough light for him to see a sleeping Touches-Horses and the two ghost bundles hanging from separate tripods, one for Young Evening and one for Sun Wolf, their father.

Placed at the *catku*, the place of honor, they hung opposite the doorway. The three feet of each tripod were placed at the west, north, and east directions, leaving a southern opening where the ghost bundles hung. In front of each tripod were dishes of meat and cherry juice set in specially dug depressions in the ground. Panther-Strikes knew of the terrible demands made on a family that conducted such a ghost-keeping. Near the exhausted

Touches-Horses, he saw piles of new clothing and utensils that his mother was working on, to be given away on the final day of the ghost keeping.

Untying the choker necklace, Panther-Strikes strode softly to the bundle carrying Young Evening's hair lock and laid it at the base of the tripod and turned away. As he left, he placed his hand lightly on Touches-Horses's head, said goodbye, and left his tomahawk beside him.

An hour later, he came to his stepfather's lodge and asked to speak to him. The young warrior was dressed in his plainest leggings and warshirt; his hair was untied and without feathers; his face was free of any paint. Dangling from his studded belt was a sheathed knife with a pistol nestled inside the wide band.

Around his neck was the choker necklace Stone-Dreamer had given him when he was honored as a warrior by the tribal council. He hadn't worn it since Young Evening gave him a choker on their wedding day. This necklace contained dark-red stones mixed with carved elkbone circles.

The holy man saw the gift necklace immediately as he greeted Panther-Strikes warmly but did not understand its significance. Inside Panther-Strikes remained standing, in spite of his father's invitation to sit and smoke with him. Panther-Strikes looked up at the small hole in the top of the tipi where the smoke from the fire spiraled to the sky. He was silent. His face was pulled with the strain of what he had come to say and didn't want to.

Finally he spoke. "I leave the village."

"Yes, a vigil would be good, but wait—until you are stronger. I will prepare *inikagapi.*"

"No, my father, I must leave the village. You. My friends. I must not come back."

Stone-Dreamer was stunned. He blinked to hold back emotions that slammed against his brain.

"I do not understand, my son," the holy man murmured.

"It is hard to explain."

"Try…please."

"M-m-my father—and you will always be my f-f-father—I must go. I am dead in many ways. I do not have the strength to see my…my wife in death. I cannot. Neither can my heart carry the weight of being seen as *wanagi.*" Panther-Strikes spoke with his mouth trembling and his words mirroring the emotion. He looked straight into the holy man's face as it cracked with disappointment over his adopted son's decision.

"I-I am sorry, my son…if I have done wrong, if my
words have cut your heart, I—I—I only…"

"It is not you, my father. It is that my time to be here has passed. I realize this now. I must find another trail in this life, or I will wither. I am no longer an Oglala warrior. I no longer want to be. It is no one's fault."

He was silent. And so was Stone-Dreamer.

"Yesterday Rainbow Wing agreed to become your lie-beside wife," Stone-Dreamer suddenly said, as if the thought of Young Evening's younger sister would be enough to change Panther-Strikes's mind.

"Thank her for me. But her place is with a man of her own choosing."

The awkward moment brought both men to silence again.

Hesitantly Stone-Dreamer spoke as if his words had no breath behind them. "My son—and you will always be my son—I have feared this day since you came to us as a small boy. I looked into your young eyes and saw courage beyond your few years. You have become a warrior to make any father proud. I wish that I had the power to make you stay—and yet I don't wish it so. If there was a stone with such awesome power, I would throw it into the deepest river."

Panther-Strikes bit his lip to keep from challenging the statement and said, instead, “My heart has been taken, Father. They took it from me when they took her. I must find my heart again. I only know it lies elsewhere. Maybe I will never find it again, but I must look. I prayed you would understand.”

“I understand. But it wasn’t the spirits that took her—nor was it your friends.”

“P-p-please do not speak more of that.”

“When will you leave?”

“My new black horse is ready. A second horse is packed with what I will need. Give the rest of my horses to Touches-Horses and Bear-Heart. Let my brother-in-law choose first. Give my wife’s clothes and things to her mother and sister. I take one robe. Give the others to Light-in-Tree. Whatever else is in the lodge, please give away as you see fit. My shield and coup stick are in there too. You may do with them as you wish. I take my medicine bundle. I do not choose to anger my spirit helper. After I am gone, burn the lodge.”

“B-b-but where will you go, my son?”

“I know not. Except I will become Vin Lockhart. I will become a *wasicun.* I will let the winds guide me.”

“Are you going to let your sweet wife’s spirit wander among us without your love?”

Panther-Strikes cocked his head to one side, then righted it and said, “She came to me last night. She wants me to go; she is ready to leave herself. Early this morning, I went into the Ghost-Keeping Lodge and left the necklace she gave me at her bundle.”

“Did you see Touches-Horses?”

“He was sleeping. I did not wake him.”

“Touches-Horses will take this hard,” Stone-Dreamer said, “for he loves you too.”

“Tell Touches-Horses that I’m sorry.”

Stumbling as he tried to stand, the holy man numbly

asked if his adopted son had enough food for his journey. Panther-Strikes acknowledged that he did. The old man walked slowly to the corner of his lodge where many items of medicine were gathered. He shuffled through the storage of herbs, roots, gourd rattles, feather wands, bones, and stones. Hurriedly, he tossed aside a deer's tail, then a gnarled bear snout, a large piece of dried air from the spirit world and a dried buffalo hoof, until he came to the Lockhart Bible and a small pocketknife, wrapped in white elkskin.

Holding them with both hands to minimize the shaking, Stone-Dreamer presented the Bible and knife to Panther-Strikes and said, "Here, you will need this. The *tunkan* told me long ago you would someday become Vin Lock-Hart again. I prayed this would not be so. The *inyan* said it was soon."

The holy man paused and spoke in halting English, "I—I—I love you, Vin Lock-Hart."

Panther-Strikes took the Bible and the little knife, held the medicine man tightly in his arms, and said, "I am sorry to let you down, Stone-Dreamer. Please forgive me."

"There is nothing to forgive, my son." The holy man returned the hug and squeezed shut his eyes to hold in the emotion.

Both men's eyes were bleary as they stepped apart, the older man aware of the use of his name rather than "father."

"I will pray for the spirits to protect you, my son," Stone-Dreamer said, his face straining with long tear paths. "Here, wear the *tunkan* of Eyes-of-the-Wind—until you have found peace." He pulled the small pebble earring from his ear and handed it to Panther-Strikes.

"I—I—I love you, F-F-Father," the trembling warrior said, placing the elkstring loop over his own right ear.

As Panther-Strikes rode away, Stone-Dreamer could

see *Wakinyan*, lightning beings, talking angrily in the gray horizon. Bad spirits were all around the village, he could sense their presence, feel their wings brush against his cheeks. He hoped his ancestors had not become upset with his son.

"*Hiye haya. Hiye haya. Hiye haya. Hiye haya. Tunkasila*, Grandfathers, I am sending a voice. *Tunkasila*, Grandfathers, I am sending a voice. *Tunkasila*, Grandfathers, I am sending a voice. *Tunkasila*, Grandfathers, I am sending a voice. Hear *Ista Un Tate.* Hear *Ista Un Tate.* Hear *Ista Un Tate.* Hear *Ista Un Tate.* Ride with my son. Ride with my son. Ride with my son. Ride with my son. *Hiye haya. Hiye haya. Hiye haya. Hiye haya.*"

Now he knew why the stones had been silent.

His mind black with depression, Panther-Strikes/Vin Lockhart squinted against the hot yellow sky. The emptiness he had felt in leaving the village had disappeared into fatigue. He was weary, eye-burned, and hungry. Three weeks of hard riding were taking their toll on a body not yet fully recovered from the Shoshoni battle.

Only two things he had decided for certain. First, he had made the right decision in leaving. Second, it was right to become a *wasicun.* After all, that was what he was. A white man. He *was* Vin Lockhart. Maybe there was peace in the white man's world. There wasn't any in the People's world. For a while, he tried again to remember what his parents and his sister looked like, but there was only fuzziness.

The southeastern trail he was following had led him into the white man's Dakota Territory, with its rolling, treeless lands scarred by the white man's iron-horse road and festering with rows of corn and houses made of thick sod. He came across the whitened bones of many dead buffalo and foul-smelling carcasses, stripped of their hides. What kind of man would do this? He decided it must be a trick done by the spirits and rode in a wide circle around them whenever such a thing appeared ahead of him.

A lonely white man's "talking rope" stretched across one long, empty sea of grass. He finally decided to ride under it and was relieved when nothing happened. How strange the *wasicun* were, he thought. They cut down trees everywhere they find them and plant dead ones to hold their magical rope. It would be something he must learn to understand if he was going to be one of them.

Forts and trading depots were isolated blossoms of *wasicun* activity. Long trains of emigrants snaked across the land, seeking the sun behind the mountains. His village had chosen to stay as far away from the "Holy Road," the Oregon Trail, and its endless string of emigrants headed west. In other parts of the untamed country, Cheyenne, Arapaho, and Sioux—including Oglala tribesmen of other villages—were attacking such trains, but he didn't know that.

His tribe avoided contact with white men, stayed away from their forts of trees, away from their smelly villages desecrating Mother Earth. They welcomed any white visitors that might come to their village and loved the sweet coffee, baked goods, and whiskey they usually brought. And worshiped their guns. He considered riding down to a trading post to learn more about how to be a good *wasicun* but couldn't make himself do it.

Occasionally he would pass discarded dressers, trunks, and other heavy items staring up at the sun, waiting for someone to return. They had been left beside the white man's trail to rot, and he wondered why. Once, he also saw a stick placed in the ground close to the discarded furniture, with a second stick tied near the top to form a cross. He recalled that *wasicun* buried their dead in the dirt instead of letting their souls have the freedom of the sky. White men visiting the village had told him of this practice and the presentation of the crossed sticks.

He had no place in mind to go. The direction didn't matter, nor did the destination of the trail itself. It only mattered that he get away from the reason for his grief and the wild stories generated about his connection to the spirit world. Surely, the farther away he got, the less he would be tortured by either. Thoughts of Stone-Dreamer and Touches-Horses had already been locked away. So far, he hadn't been able to do that with the nightmares of Young Evening's death. But yesterday was the first time he had wretched by the side of the trail in a week. Without realizing where his trail was headed, he rode toward his family's old homestead.

To help pass the time and prepare himself for his recent decision to become a white man, he recited, over and over, all of the English words he could recall. Each night he drew out the Bible from his things and thumbed through its pages, hoping they would tell him something. Occasionally he would seize upon a recognizable word and study it for minutes. Flickering like a dying candle in his mind, he saw himself in the corner of a gray place reading a book. Could that be? Where was that place?

On some evenings the holy man would speak to him only in English, using the sparse vocabulary he had obtained from the occasional visits of white men. Panther-Strikes/Vin Lockhart wasn't too keen on the idea because "he was an Oglala"—but he obeyed his elder. He became much more interested in speaking English when he discovered the white man's firearms—even learning when to say "goddammit," based on his father's observations of white men's aggravations.

Although no one knew it, Stone-Dreamer feared what the coming of the *wasicun* meant. Like other tribal elders, he had heard of the battles of Red Cloud, He Dog, and Crazy Horse during the annual summer gatherings of all Lakota—and the growing encouragement to join their crusade. But he had encouraged Black Fire to take another path, to continue living the old ways.

Whenever white men visited the encampment, the young white warrior was included as a host. When his English failed, sign language would prevail. Visitors were not surprised to see a young white man living with the Oglalas; it was not that rare. However, he was curious about the things they talked about or owned. From candles to tin plates, from books to saddles, from gloves to cigars. Most were vague memory wisps from his earlier life.

Once Stone-Dreamer had traded two buffalo robes for a book from a trapper. The holy man gave it to then-Angry Dog, but the youngster had looked at it only occasionally and left the book behind when the village moved. Stone-Dreamer had been greatly disappointed when he learned of his son's carelessness. His forgiveness came quickly when he later discovered the boy ran back to retrieve it. Then he was awake for hours, worrying about what might have happened to a mere lad alone on the plains.

Rolling stiffened shoulders caused his long hair to brush against the red pebble earring. He wiped his glistening brow with the sleeve of his warshirt, too tired to think of anything except eating. Soon he should stop, eat something, and let his two horses rest. The packhorse was tiring; its pack contained his remaining food, blanket, ammunition, and his other pistol. Only a small amount of *pemmican* was left, and some wild bee plants he'd gathered for cooking were packed away too. Maybe he should take the time to track some game.

Ahead, four stilted willows did their best to grab the hot sky. Thin shade but welcoming. More important was the small spring that fed them. A related, lackadaisical stream sought the valley to the south. He paid no attention to what lay beyond the trees, concentrating on the coolness touching his weary body. His eyes stung from lack of sleep and too much sun. His insides ached from the longing to be with Young Evening again, but it was less painful than before. His face glistened with sweat. His mind gurgled with remorse.

Somewhere an owl hooted its own loneliness, anxious for nightfall, when he and his other winged friends would come from the other world and take over this one until dawn. He was reminded instantly of Stone-Dreamer's admonishments that the bird was often a reincarnated spirit. Scornfully, he said aloud that he hoped all the ancestors were watching over him. The black horse pricked his ears to catch the meaning. This was a good place to rest, he decided, and reined the black to a stop.

Behind his warrior horse, the pack animal stood with its head down and tongue out. Dismounting, he leaned against the black for several minutes, letting the ground restore his equilibrium. Both horses drank slowly from the stream, and he did the same. From the tall grass to his left came a small lark. The gentle sight triggered barely-locked-away memories.

Young Evening had become fascinated with a similar bird on one of their first walk-outs together. She had called and the bird had flown to a sapling near her. She sang to the tiny thing as he watched in amazement. Without warning, this sweet memory was ruptured into the staggering scene of her awful death. The bitter picture came like an unseen hawk down on the tiny lark. He splashed water on his face, trying to cool his mind from the torturous remembrance.

Suddenly nerves along his back sprang alive. He jumped up and looked around. His eyes were wild with discovery. He knew this place! He had come here as a small boy with his real father. No, that couldn't be! Surely his mind was playing yet another cruel trick. He had been a mere boy when he was taken from the place and had never come this way again. It couldn't be, but it was. Yes! His family's home was close. It had to be. He sensed a connection to the land that he hadn't felt before.

Stumbling over a downed tree, he raced past the willows to the edge of the upslanting land. Shadows lashed at his face as he ran. Panting for breath, he finally stood and gazed out upon a valley dotted with *wasicun* sod houses. White man's plants covered sections of the land, pushing against dense, matted soil. An occasional windmill stood defiantly. He did not know what they were but decided they were some kind of *wasicun* tipi.

This small stream meandered through the green. There! There was the Lockhart family house! He was certain of it. The grayish-brown sod structure looked unchanged, row after row of carefully cut bricks of matted sod composing the structure. Two windows faced the front along with the doorway. Tree limbs were weaved among the rafters, supported with dry grass and laden with large sod blocks. The house seemed smaller—and so did the valley. Occupied with more similar houses and more crops, maybe that's what made it seem smaller, he thought. His hunger was gone. So was his weariness.

He raced back to his horses, a new energy spinning through him. Kicking his right leg over the black mustang's back and squeezing his legs brought the mount into a smooth lope. Thirty feet from the squatty willows, three man-sized, pointed rock formations stood like an entrance to the valley. "*What would Stone-Dreamer think of this inyan*?" he said aloud. He remembered thinking they looked like giant knives cutting into the sky. He remembered a time long ago…

"Daddy, are those knives from giants?" the nearly-eight-year-old Vin Lockhart asked his father, looking toward the rocks while they took a break from plowing.

Josuah Lockhart puffed on his pipe and smiled. "Well, maybe so, Vin. They sure look like it, don't they?"

"You think I'll be old enough to have a knife someday?"

"Well, sure, Vin. When you're old enough."

"When will that be, Daddy?"

The young warrior reined the black to a harsh stop. Nervous sweat blossomed on his forehead. He nudged the horse forward again. That was the first time he had thought about his real family in years. Nothing was moving around the open spaces of the small house as he approached. The sun was high on his shoulders. It must be the white man's midday mealtime. Thin tendrils of smoke stuttered from the sheet-iron pipe protruding through the grassy roof. Definitely someone was living there. He thought the roof looked new; at least its grass was green. Pots of geraniums accented the front doorway.

He could see laundry stretched out to dry on bushes next to the stream thirty yards to the south and remembered his mother doing the same thing. A sturdy lean-to shelter housed the new family's big animals. He didn't recall it. He could see the backend of a *wasicun* wagon behind the lean-to, a dozen chickens scurrying about. A gray barrel for collecting rainwater stood stoically at the front corner of the house. As he rode closer, memories rushed to meet him. He was running across the roof, and his mother was yelling at him from inside the house, "Get down from there, Vincent, you're getting dirt all over everything!" He could see his mother, in a gunnysack apron, standing on the same porch waiting for him to come down. Her face became that of a brown-bearded man in dirty overalls and a faded red shirt, holding a shotgun.

"What can I do for you, stranger?" the stocky man asked. His words were neither friendly nor threatening. Just cautious. He stood a few steps beyond the closed door with his legs spread apart and the gun cradled easily in his crossed arms. His hair and beard were dotted with dirt; sweat had pasted strands to his forehead. He had obviously just come in from working the field and not yet washed up.

Panther-Strikes/Vin Lockhart swallowed and said, "I Vin Lockhart. Long time back, I live here. My mother, father…sister die here."

"I see," the bearded man replied, frowning. "What did you say the name was again?"

"I Vin Lockhart. Father, Josuah Lockhart. Mother, Mildred Lockhart. Sister…Alice Lockhart."

"Yeah. That's them all right," the man said. "There's some markers out back. For all four of them. Didn't know 'em. We came here five years back. I imagine the Robertsons would 'member 'em, though. They've been here since afore the War." He paused and added, "We dun came by this place legal-like, ya know. Put in the time and the upgrades. Yessir, it dun be ours now. Got the papers if' n ya'd like to see them."

Vin Lockhart did not know what the man was talking about, except the first part sounded like he knew where his family was buried. Muffled scuffling of feet accented by a few garbled words followed. He could hear a woman's voice, followed by the chattering of two boys. The man turned sideways, pushed the door open slightly, and yelled in, "He's looking for the Lockharts. Says he's one of them. Yeah, I'll show him."

Walking toward the west side of the home, the man waved his arm and said, "Follow me, mister. I'll show you the graves. My wife, she puts flowers on 'em ever' so. Says she figures someone would do it for us if we didn't have no kin around. She's like that, ya know."

The young warrior studied the simple home and the memory of his eighth birthday flooded over him. His mother was fixing a special meal just for him. She was working over a cast-iron Franklin stove that needed constant stoking. It also provided the only heat for the one-room house. Her face was merely white light, but her voice was warm and loving. Her carefully guarded sack of flour was opened.

"Vincent, supper is special because it's your birthday. My fine son is eight years old, and look at you, so strong and tall," Mildred Lockhart said, and smiled at her young son.

"What's it going to be, Mother?"

"Oh, that's a surprise. But I will tell you it ends with doughnuts a young fellow I know likes!" She ruffled his hair and kissed his forehead. With a twinkle in her eyes, she added, "I think your father would like to see you."

"What about? I finished my chores."

She smiled and said, "I don't know. Go and see."

His father was in their main room, sitting in a rough-hewn chair made from a split log and smoking his pipe. The floor was dirt, packed hard and swept clean. A cupboard made from two crates sat in the far corner. His little sister was playing with a handmade doll constructed from an old sock. The shutters on the windows were closed, but a few aggressive beams of fading sunset managed to get through. Their lone coal-oil lantern was doing its best to fill the room with yellow light.

"Mother said you wanted to see me," young Vin Lockhart said, an implied question in his voice. He was certain all of his chores were done.

"She did, did she?" he said. "I wonder why."

"I don't know. I told her that I had finished my chores. I have, Father."

"Yes, I know that—and they are done well," Josuah Lockhart said, leaned to the side, and lifted a small item wrapped in brown paper from his pocket. "Oh, I'll bet this was it. Here."

Young Vin Lockhart's eyes lit up. It was a pocketknife! The same knife Stone-Dreamer had returned to him along with the family Bible. Six months later, his family was dead.

"Say, are you coming or not?" The farmer's question broke his daydream and the young warrior nodded.

Rounding the side of the sod house, the man pointed in the direction of four wooden boards growing from the long grass twenty yards away. Vin Lockhart glanced at the man, nodded his appreciation, and walked toward the graves. His two led horses walked slowly behind. The warrior's legs were so empty, he thought he was going to have to crawl to get there. Each step was like he was in deep water. The broad flaps of his leggings tailed behind his feet like a special covering.

A flock of yesterday's images, long forgotten, flew across his mind. Helping his father dig a pit for storing potatoes and other root crops during winter. Weeding his mother's "tonic" plants of butterfly weed, sweet flagroot, and boneset, plants Stone-Dreamer also used to heal. The smell of lye-and-ashes soap that was always close to her.

He saw his father plowing the field to his left with a pair of dark brown mules. Vaguely he remembered men cutting bricks of sod to make a neighbor's house. He and his sister searching for buffalo chips, dried corncobs, and sunflower stalks for firewood and placing them in a large gunnysack. Both of them helping their mother with mulberries and getting their little hands and laugfring faces stained with purple. There was the Christmas when he received a knit cap and an apple—and they sang songs with their closest neighbors. Saying a prayer each night: "Now I lay me down to sleep, I pray the Lord my..." The rest of it was gone.

He remembered cutting up potatoes for breakfast, dinner, and supper. It seemed he was always cutting up potatoes. Watching his father add runners to a wagon box so they could slide across the snow. His mother sewing on one of his father's old shirts so it would fit him after he outgrew his own. Milking their lone cow. Twisting hay for fuel when everything else was gone. Fixing harness. Reading a book, one of three, in the house. Finding honey in an old hollow tree and helping his father bring home the wonderful sweetness in a washtub. Finding a nest of prairie chicken eggs and being the hero of the family. His father's hand on his shoulder. His mother's hug at night. His sister's teasing laugh.

Chapter Five

Vin Lockhart walked slowly to the weather-beaten stakes and read: "Josuah Lockhart—Father & Christian, Died 1855," "Mildred Lockhart—His Loving Wife, Died 1855," "Alice Lockhart—Daughter, Died 1855"—and "Vincent Lockhart—Son, Died 1855"! Whoever buried his family must have thought he, too, had died and the body pulled away by animals or worse. He didn't remember kneeling beside his mother's grave marker, but he was. As his knees hit the ground, his mind was taken to her bedside ten years before.

"V-V-Vincent, l-l-love you," Mildred Lockhart said from her bed. She was pale, too thin, and knew she was dying. He did not.

"I love you too, Mother. When will you and Daddy be able to get up?"

"I—I—I don't k-k-know, my s-s-son. S-s-soon," she whispered, and coughed so violently her body rattled uncontrollably. "I think you s-s-should go s-s-stay with the

R-Robertsons for a few days. W-w-would you like that? I love you…"

His next memory was of being found by three Oglala warriors in the garden. Guilt jolted him. Why was he the one spared? Why not little Alice? Or his mother? Or his father? Why were any of them taken? Why was his beloved Young Evening taken? He whispered, "*Wakan-tanka unsimala ye*—Great spirit, pity me. Hear the unworthy…you know me as Panther-Strikes. Tell the spirits of my mother and father, and my sister, that I loved them. Thank you for letting their memories walk again through my soul."

Behind him, standing next to the house, a plain woman had joined her husband and whispered something into his ear. He frowned and said something back. She shook her head negatively and insisted.

"Ah, Mister…Lockhart, we'uns are 'bout to set to the table for some dinner. Would you like to join us? We're the Kissels. I'm Walter. This hyar's my wife, Mary."

It took a few seconds for Lockhart to realize that he was the one being addressed. His shoulders rose and fell, and he stood, his body trembling with unexepected emotion. Without turning around, he said, "I go now."

"Oh, please stay," Mary Kissel said with genuine warmth. "We don't get a lot of visitors here. I'm sure you'd like to see…the house. Are you a relative of the Lockharts? Of course, we didn't know them."

He looked at her, and she smiled in spite of herself. Her face betrayed her newest concern upon seeing him full-on. Before her was one of the wildest-looking men she had ever seen, armed with pistol and knife, garbed in fringed buckskin leggings and shirt. Only a long piece of buckskin, hanging from his wide belt, covered his genitals. That idea sent a tickle through her mind. Strands of his long brown hair teased across his chiseled face by the gentle winds. He was young, yet hardened.

Certainly he was as wild-looking as those Cheyenne that had ridden through the valley last spring, killing their neighbors, running off their horses, and burning their cabin. My God, he even wore an earring—-or whatever that little pebble thing was behind his ear! Was this man an Indian? Surely not, but his dress was like that of a red savage. His response was as upsetting as his appearance, yet she was drawn to him.

"I son. I…Vin Lockhart. Vin-cent Lockhart," he said, finding a little more familiarity in the name, and pointed at the grave header with his name.

Her eyes widened, and she gasped, "Oh…oh my! I …how can that be? I don't understand. You don't look like a…" She didn't complete the sentence. Something about him made her stop.

Lockhart frowned, searching for the right words, and explained, "Father, mother, sister die here. No me. I go with Oglalas. Someone think me dead, maybe so."

"I see," she heard herself saying, but bit her lower lip. "Please stay, Mr. Lockhart. We would like that."

His strange use of words, their biting cadence, made her wonder if he was foreign. Certainly he was not a poet, she thought and smiled faintly. He nodded approval and walked toward them, his horses bobbing their heads in an easy rhythm. Walter Kissel took the reins and led them to the lean-to.

"I'll see they git some grain—and git watered," he said, looking at his wife for approval. She was already chatting with Lockhart as they entered the house.

"Vincent Lockhart, that's such a nice name. I knew a Lockhart family back in Indiana, before we moved out here. I wonder if they were relations of yours?"

Lockhart smiled, not knowing what she was talking about. The inside of the cabin seemed smaller than his dim memory recalled. Earthen walls seemed grayer, packed with sand from the creek bank. He saw his father's chair and a short gasp cleared his clenched teeth. No other signs reminded him of his long-ago family except the large Franklin stove, with its cast-iron pipe cut through the roof, providing warmth and a place to cook. The floor itself was now partially covered with a light brown rug torn at one end, and two walls were covered with old newspapers for wallpaper. He remembered an occasional snake dropping from the sod roof and smiled.

He walked over to the southeast corner, bent over, and touched the warm ground. It was here that he had sat to read in the evenings. His memory had not been wrong. He tried to remain calm and let the energy of this encounter settle within him. He didn't feel happy, yet he didn't feel sad either. It was just—different. This was not really home. Home was the warm lodge of Stone-Dreamer.

The Kissel family stood near the large table dominating the center of the room and watched him without comment. Walter Kissel held the smallest child in his arms; his shotgun stood against the wall only a step away. Mary Kissel held the hands of the two oldest boys, squeezing them whenever she sensed either was about to say something. This strange man, now in her home, appeared to be a violent man by his dress and weapons. Yet something told her he was gentle inside and one whose soul had been deeply wounded. That feeling kept her comfortable with his raw presence.

Without intending to be, she also found herself attracted to this stranger. Once she had been a handsome woman, she told herself, but this hard land had sucked away most of that beauty. When he looked at her, his eyes cut deep. That frightened her, because he might see the murmur of passion toward him within. She sighed quietly and her breasts moved. She blushed, but secretly wished he had seen the movement. For an instant she let go of her son's hands, brushed her hands along her shoulder-length hair, then retook their grasps. She was glad her hair was down and not braided in place, like she usually wore it. Her hair still looked young, she thought.

Lockhart only noticed sunlight reflecting from the glass pane in the front windows to his right. He walked toward them, puzzled by what he saw. He had never seen glass before; the windows had simply been shuttered when he was a boy here. His fingers slowly reached out to touch the invisible shield and jumped back in surprise. Invisible stone! A *wasicun* mystery! Stone-Dreamer had such a *tunkan* that came from the spirit world. This must be more of the same.

"Is everything all right, Mr. Lockhart?" Mary Kissel asked.

Lockhart ran his tongue along his lower lip and tried to think. These were obviously a *wasicun* holy man and woman. He must be careful. Oglalas were keenly aware of the power of a woman and he had been taught of their special place in the world. During menstruation, a woman even slept in a separate lodge to avoid her presence crippling her husband's medicine. Anytime a woman touched a warrior's medicine or his weapons, it could lessen his strength in war. After all, it was White Buffalo Calf Maiden who had brought the four virtues and the seven sacred ceremonies to the Lakota nation. *Aiiee*, he thought to himself. His parents would be pleased that their home was being lived in by holy people.

He turned around and smiled warmly at her. She blushed again.

"Dinner is ready, Mr. Lockhart," Mary Kissel said quietly.

At the planked table, Lockhart took a seat with the two adults and three boys of various ages. He remembered what chairs were for but settled into his chair with his legs spread widely apart like he was mounting a horse.

Immediately Walter Kissel introduced his three sons:

"This hyar be Jacob, named after his grandpaw on Mary's side. An' this be Thomas. He's eight…"

"I'm eight and a half."

"Right, eight and a half." Walter Kissel chuckled and continued. "An' this be the youngest. He be Jeremiah. He's only two. Don't talk much."

"I Vin Lockhart."

"Are you a Injun, mister?" the oldest boy, Jacob, asked.

"Jacob, mind your manners!" Mary Kissel admonished.

"But he talks funny."

"That's enough, Jacob."

Vin Lockhart didn't respond. Mary Kissel asked her husband to lead the grace; Walter Kissel bowed his head and folded his hands. Lockhart watched, and the process seemed strangely reminiscent. He did the same. The two oldest boys watched him with their eyes partially opened as they recited the poetic prayer.

"God is great. God is good. Him we thank for daily food. By his hand we all are fed. By his love we all are led. Amen."

"Amen" sounded vaguely familiar to him. After the recitation, Mary Kissel stood and walked around the table, serving portions of boiled pork, wild greens, and chunks of corn bread. Lockhart's plate received the largest portions, and Walt Kissel frowned at his wife's distribution. From a wooden pail she poured a weak cider into tin cups and distributed them. Lockhart looked at the food before him. He much preferred the stronger aroma of buffalo meat.

As the others began to eat, Lockhart looked at the food, cut off a small piece of steak, and stood. He held it chest-high with one hand cupped beneath the other and walked outside. The Kissels stopped eating and watched in surprise.

"What's he doing, Mother?"

"Doesn't he like our food?"

"Shhh, he'll hear you," Mary admonished, uncertain of the young man's intentions. "Walter, go see if he's all right."

With a groan, Walter rose and headed for the door. He stopped a few feet in back of the entrance and watched, providing a running description of Lockhart's tribute of the first morsel of food to the Great Powers, without realizing that's what he was watching.

"I don't know what he's doing. First he holds it up in the air, then down at the ground, and now he's moving around in a circle. He stopped, four times. Now he's tossing it. Oh, here he comes!"

Walter scurried to his seat as Lockhart reentered the house and realized the family had been watching him.

Lockhart frowned and said, "First food to *Wakantanka.*"

"To what?" the oldest boy asked.

"Never mind," Mary said. "Thank you, Mr. Lockhart, we've just never seen an Irish prayer before. Thank you for explaining it."

He nodded and sat down. With his fingers he tore a piece from the pork and brought it to his mouth along with several strands of green vegetable. He heard a chuckle, then another, and stopped. The family was staring at him. What had he done wrong?

"Hush, boys," came Mary Kissel's command.

"But, Maw, he's eating with his fingers!" Thomas giggled.

Lockhart swallowed hard. How stupid could he be? He had seen *wasicun* eat with their metal sticks before. He should have remembered.

"I forget. Please forgive. Long time not use," he explained, returning the food to his plate, wiping his fingers on his leggings under the table, and gingerly picking up a fork. It felt awkward.

"Oh, that's quite all right," Mary Kissel replied, and

returned to her own food. She tried to hide her own smile by looking down at her lap.

Walt Kissel grinned and said, "Seems like a right handy way to eat, come to think on it." Mary's elbow stopped him from elaborating further.

The meal tasted different but good. Lockhart hadn't eaten well for several days. As a precaution to making further social errors, he kept his eyes on the others while he ate. He watched them spread a thick yellow substance over their pieces of corn bread. It looked inviting. He decided not to risk such a task and make himself look foolish again. But his two heaping spoonfuls of sugar into his cup of cider caught all of their attention again. No one said anything, but the two older boys looked at each other and giggled. No one talked during the meal, as was the custom of most western people. That pleased the young warrior because he couldn't eat and concentrate on all of the strange words being thrown around.

When he was finished, Lockhart said, "Thank you, Mary Kissel. This good. Long time no eat."

She smiled, took away his emptied plate, and replaced it with a smaller tin plate holding a large slice of dried currant pie. "I hope you like it."

"My Mary's the best pie maker in the valley," Walter Kissel said boldly.

"Now, Walter, let's not be bragging in front of our guest," she admonished, but she obviously enjoyed the compliment.

Lockhart waited for the others to begin eating their pie and followed their use of forks. It was a clumsy procedure, but he kept a too-large piece on his fork with his fingers as he shoved it into his mouth. The taste was wonderful. He tried to say something with a mouthful and the boys laughed again. After gulping cider, he said, "Mary Kissel, that good. Real good."

She blushed and said, “Oh, it’s nothing really. I thought the crust got a little overdone.”

“It good, Mary Kissel.”

The oldest boy said, “I think you’re a Injun. You sure look a lot like one.”

“He sounds like Grandpaw Kissel,” the middle boy chimed in.

“Your grandfather came from Germany,” Walter Kissel said. “He spoke German until he was twenty.”

Mary Kissel was inclined to agree with her sons but said, “That’s not polite, boys. Mr. Lockhart is a fine white man. Probably, he’s come from trapping in the mountains and has been alone for a long time.”

“Bet you’re right, Mary. That right, Lockhart? You a trapper?” Walter Kissel asked, lighting a pipe he had just placed between his teeth. “Them beaver holdin’ out up north? Heard tell they’s gittin’ thin.”

Lockhart frowned, understanding only the words “trapper,” “north,” and “beaver.” He studied the man’s mouth, hoping for more words to come so he could catch a few of them.

Instead the middle boy asked, “Where’d ya git them neat Injun pants?” His mother shot him a look that took the eagerness out of his face.

“I live with Oglalas. Family die here. I boy. Live with Oglalas. Be warrior. Now be *wasicun*,” Lockhart said as an explanation of his situation. It wasn’t really an answer to the boy’s question, but it sounded like one. He just thought they deserved to know his intentions after treating him so well.

“Oh my gosh, Mary, this poor man was captured by Injuns—when he were nuthin’ but a boy!” Walter Kissel blurted. “That’s what them Oglalas is. Mean red savages. The worst. Them an’ the Cheyenn-ees. They’s the ones bin a-killin’ white folks. He’s a mighty lucky man to git slipped from that bunch o’ heathens. Yessur.”

Mary's hand went to her mouth and tried to hide the escaping concern. "You poor man! How awful. All these years—and you've just escaped. What an ordeal you've been through. Forced to live with those ungodly savages. Oh, I can't even bear to think of it."

"Maw, that's why he talks so funny,'' the oldest boy whispered.

Lockhart did not understand the conversation or its intent and thought they were simply being nice to him. In the best English he could muster, he stood and excused himself: "I go now. Give thanks to you, Mary Kissel and Walter Kissel, for good food. For kindness. For to see… my family long time back."

"Oh, you're so welcome," she said, tears welling at the corners of her eyes. "Where are you going? You have no family, oh my—"

"Now, Mary, the man has things to do," Walter Kissel interrupted, afraid his wife was going to ask this stranger to stay with them. "Lockhart, do your horses need oats for the trail? I could spare a bucket."

"Oats? Food for horse?" Lockhart asked. "Yes. I trade."

"No need to pay, Lockhart," Walter Kissel said, catching his wife's negative motion. "Jacob, run and get Mr. Lockhart hyar a sack full of oats. Be quick about it."

"Yes, Paw."

"Oh, I almost forgot," Mary Kissel said, touching her hand to her cheek. "Mr. Lockhart, I've got something for you. Please…wait."

She immediately left the table, disappeared behind the bedroom curtain, and returned a few minutes later holding a small, wooden box, a black frock coat, and a folded gray shirt. She laid them on the table, disappeared again, and brought back a pair of worn black boots and a wide-brimmed, flat-crowned black hat. She held the boots by their calf-length tops and placed them on the dirt floor near his mocasined feet. She continued to hold the hat.

"Here are the things we found when we came here," she said softly. "I imagine you would like to have them. I'm sorry it's not much, but it's all we found. They're your family's things. I've kept them put away—for just a day like this."

She handed him the box first and he began to look dully through the captured treasures, not certain what to expect. He lifted a brown, faded daguerreotype of his mother and father on their wedding day. He studied the images for several seconds. The faces missing from his daydreams were there. His finger traced them as his mind observed the lost pieces, before returning the photograph to the box.

He wasn't aware of his deep, slow breathing, but Mary Kissel was and watched him tenderly, holding the coat and hat to her bosom. She wanted to hug this strange man and tell him it was all right to cry, but she knew she couldn't. There was also a dirty sock doll, a thimble, and a leather belt nearly severed where the buckle had been placed for so long.

The last thing in the box was a pale-blue-and-moss-green stone pin, one of his mother's few pieces of jewelry. She wore it on special occasions, like Christmas. He remembered how she loved the simple pin and rubbed the stone with his thumb, trying to recall more. Surely this was a sacred stone, like the ones Stone-Dreamer owned, and he hadn't realized it as a child.

"You are good woman, Mary Kissel," he said, looking into her eyes.

For an instant, her gaze locked on his and danced with him. She shyly glanced away, then looked up and held out the hat. His father's. He knew it instantly. The image of his father standing tall filled his mind. He put the box down on the table. His mouth quivered. He took the hat and placed it firmly on his head. He had never worn a hat of any kind before. It felt funny, but his smile was broad; his eyes fought the emotion of the moment. Then he picked up the black frock coat.

"Try it on," Walter Kissel suggested, waving his arms for further encouragement. Lockhart stared at the coat and slowly placed his right arm into the sleeve, then his left.

"Oh, it fits nicely," Marry Kissel said, helping him into the garment.

Lockhart stared down at himself, ran his right hand along the left sleeve, and pulled on the lapels. His father!

"Reckon them boots'll fit ya ri't fine. They's got years in 'em, I figger. That flannel shirt'll go sum too," Walter Kissel observed. Mary Kissel's quick glance said the man had wanted to wear them himself at one time. Lockhart decided not to try either for the moment. It was enough to wear his father's coat and hat.

"Gifts for you," Lockhart said, and walked toward the front door, carrying the box with him. He tugged awkwardly on the brim of the hat.

They watched him go unsure of what he was doing. In minutes he returned without the box but his hands filled. Without speaking, he handed Walter Kissel the extra pistol from his pack and a small pouch of bullets. He gave the oldest boy a bone-handled knife in a beaded sheath; his childhood pocketknife went to the middle boy and an eagle feather was handed to the smallest child, who proceeded to wave it vigorously. To Mary he presented a dark-red stone and elkbone choker necklace; no one noticed that he had taken it off while he was outside.

"Oh my, it's beautiful," she exclaimed, and held it to her neck for everyone to see. Walt Kissel held out his hand for the warrior to shake. Lockhart was familiar with the white man custom and gripped it vigorously.

"We thank you, Lockhart. That's mighty kind o' ya. Sure didn't need to," Walter Kissel said, and smiled.

"That's a mighty fine six-gun. Come in mighty handy fer varmints 'n' sech."

"Thank you, sir," Jacob chimed in. "That's the neatest thing anybody's ever given me. Ever! Wait until Bobby Cabe see this! Him an' his ol' sheath knife. He'll be green with—"

A hard knock on the door stopped their conversation. Walter Kissel looked at Mary and then moved to open it. Outside were eight men armed with rifles and shotguns, neighbors of the Kissels. Walter Kissel was surprised.

"Why, good day, men. What brings you to our place? Is everything all right, Axel?"

Axel Garrison, the tallest of the group, a plank-thin man with a stringy mustache and a too-big suitcoat, cleared his throat and spoke authoritatively: "Clement saw an Injun ride in to your place an' we came as quick as we could. I prayed to God you'd be alive when we gpt here. You're a brave man, Walter Kissel, and you too, Missus Kissel. I see you've been able to stop the savage—"

A thick-necked man in a bowler hat and a dirty coat interrupted: "Walter, we'll take it from here! There's a willow over a piece strong enough to stretch his miserable red neck. We'll leave him there, swinging in the wind, so all the other red devils will know not to come where Christians live."

"Yeah, step aside an' we'll give this red devil what he deserves!" yelled Clement Matthews, a fat-jowled man with a foot-long, reddish beard and a heavy belly. He stood in the middle of the group. He swung his rifle back and forth to reinforce his emotions. The men on either side of him watched his gyrations uneasily.

It was Mary Kissel who spoke first, rushing to her husband's side, her face flushed and her eyes brittle with annoyance: "Thank you for your concern, Mr. Garrison. But Mr. Lockhart is our friend. He is visiting us. And he is definitely *not* an Indian, he is a fine Christian. We bid you good day."

The gathered men were amazed—and disappointed. They had whipped up their courage on the ride over, each man secretly happy about the favorable odds they would face: one Indian to eight of them.

"Then how's he come to be ridin' an Injun pony with a Injun rig, by God!" Clement Matthews said defiantly. The farmer to his immediate right watched him continue to wave his gun, then pushed it toward the ground. He gave the farmer a dirty look but left the gun pointed downward.

It was Walter Kissel's turn to speak: "Lockhart hyar is a trapper, Clement. He's been way north o' hyar. All the trappers go Injun, ya know that." He was proud of his slight deception and couldn't keep from grinning. Mary Kissel's frown stopped it.

The former glared at Matthews as if he were an idiot for ever assuming anything else. He turned and headed for the horses held by a member of the group.

Clement Matthews stuttered his apology to the others: "H-how was I to know? I saw his, his outfit an'…an' he looked like a Injun. H-h-he wasn't wearin' no hat or coat, I swear it. How was I supposed to know?"

No one answered as they followed the first farmer to their horses.

Garrison touched the corner of his narrow-brimmed hat and bowed slightly before responding. "We're sorry to have bothered you, ma'am. I hope you understand our concern. What with those red devils from last spring, we thought—"

"I know what you thought," she interrupted. "Now please, excuse us."

"Yes, ma'am." His reply was spoken to a closed door.

Walter Kissel stood looking at it, not certain what to do next. Mary Kissel immediately spun around and went to

Lockhart. She took both of his hands in hers and held them in front of her.

"I am very sorry for that, Mr. Lockhart. Our friends are sometimes not very kind. They mean well, I suppose. Please don't let this spoil your return," Mary Kissel said, her eyes searching the young warrior's tanned face.

"Mary Kissel, you fine woman. It is not a problem."

She was certain he didn't really understand what the men were intending to do. A shiver ran up her back and she flinched. For an instant she thought he was going to kiss her. Part of her wanted it; part of her feared it. Instead, he pulled his hands away and placed them on the shoulders of the two oldest boys.

"You give honor to Mary Kissel and Walter Kissel. Mother and father."

"Y-essir," they both answered timidly.

Minutes later Lockhart rode away from the sod house, waving at the Kissel family, who stood watching him. Across his saddle was a sack of food Mary Kissel had insisted he take, in spite of her frowning husband. The sack of oats had been added to the main pack, along with the special box, boots, and shirt. Almost an hour went by without his being conscious of where he was heading. He felt very alone and depressed. The house had long disappeared from view. For an instant, he almost turned around to ride back to the Kissels' house, but he realized that didn't make any sense. They had been nice to him, but they wouldn't be happy to have him stay. He wasn't family.

Defiant slopes of gray rock, dried-out buffalo grass, and weaving sagebrush lay in front of him as far as he could see. Like a song, the hooves of his mustangs made soft pushing sounds in the trail-beaten dust, followed by loud clacks on the sun-baked red clay. Softly he repeated, "I am Vin Lockhart. I am Vin Lockhart. I am Vin Lockhart," to the rhythm of his horses' hooves. The name wasn't him; he was still Panther-Strikes, the Oglala warrior. Lost in his sorrow, he rode on, uncaring, and the days churned away as he headed southwest. Without realizing it, he rode into the white man's Colorado Territory.

Snowy peaks began to look down upon him as he sought a peace that swirled somewhere ahead of him. He wondered if Stone-Dreamer had ever seen so much stone. He decided the holy man would certainly know of this place and probably would be listening to the stones singing now if he were along. Such great stones must surely sing louder than mere pebbles, he thought. Then the idea depressed him. If this were so, why couldn't he even hear these great stones?

So far he had met no one on mis part of his lonely journey, red or white. Since leaving the Kissels, he had passed several strange-looking, wooden structures built near rivers and mountain waterfalls. White men were there, staring at pans and shoveling dirt into long wooden troughs, but he hadn't mustered up the courage to meet them. Their strange behavior was puzzling and made him uneasy, so he rode on, avoiding being seen by any of them.

Finally he rested within the safety of a squatty knoll, a near-black arm of stunted cedar and jack pines that connected with lodgepole pines ringing triumphant mountains. After eating a meal of a raw potato, soda crackers, and water, he lay down on his spread-out buffalo robe and laid out the few things of his family to once more inhale their simple memory wisps. His father's hat lay at his elbow as he held the wedding photograph in his hand and studied it.

A sound behind him! He swung around with a cocked pistol in his right hand. The photograph floated toward the earth. Standing twenty feet behind was a baby elk calf. The wobbly animal looked at him, then began squealing. The mother elk appeared from the trees and nudged her infant back into the darkness, giving the warrior a scornful look as she did. He tried to smile at his overreaction but couldn't. He stared at the daguerreotype on the ground, then at the pistol in his hand. A sigh followed the flicker of a thought about joining his white family and Young Evening. He didn't remember falling asleep.

A feeble morning sun had not yet cleared the peaks and he was in the saddle. Sleep was its own struggle, and he had finally given up on resting and decided to go on. In a dull stupor, he rode beside an arctic meadow crouched between towering mountain slopes. The uneven slopes on three sides were draped by the purple shadows brought by the cracked cliffs above them.

To his left was a thick stream that went wherever it wanted across the flattened land. Out of sight, he could hear the roar of waterfall, and at the edge of a band of aspen and dwarf willows, he saw elk feeding quietly. He crossed through a dry streambed and through a cluster of cottonwoods, then turned alongside a riverbank that pushed through the foothills as far as he could see. Ahead a strange gray shape in the water became a wooden cradle. What is this for? he wondered, and decided to ride closer.

"That's far enough, my friend—unless you care to have your head separated from your shoulders."

Vin Lockhart reined in his horses, angry at riding into a *wasicun* trap. A shadow turned into a skinny, red-faced man with a sawed-off double-barreled shotgun. Shortened in both the barrel and stock, the strange man held it in one hand, like a pistol. At close range, it was an ugly weapon. This sunburned man didn't look anything like the white trappers and mountain men who had passed through the village from time to time. Not at all.

This must be a *wasicun* shaman, Lockhart immediately decided. Far from the gathering of whites, he was talking to the great stones alone. Lockhart couldn't help staring at the man's wild and wispy beard that looked like someone had pasted on fake strands of pink and red. The scattergun-toting stranger wore a coat that had once been dark blue and pin-striped, covering a faded, but white, buttoned-to-the top shirt. His pants were just as clean and just as faded. His hat was a derby with a hole in the top.

Later, Lockhart would discover that the man washed his clothes every day in the stream after working on the sluice, no matter how cold it was. Right now the man's bloodshot eyes, staring at him through wire-rim glasses, searched the young warrior for answers. Lockhart had never seen anyone wear spectacles before; he thought they must be magic, and it made him even more wary. He knew the dangerous things Stone-Dreamer could do if provoked. There was that tale of a warrior who disappeared from his lodge one day and was never seen again, after questioning the holy man's ability to talk with the spirits. Lockhart didn't know the warrior; it had happened before he was brought to the tribe.

"What are you doing, snooping around my claim?" the strawberry-toned stranger asked, waving the shotgun to demonstrate his seriousness.

Lockhart didn't understand the question and said so in halting English: "I not know…asking."

"What? Are you an Indian? Well, howdy-do! You've got britches like an Indian, but that's no Indian hat. And more of a Sunday-go-to-meetin' coat, it looks to me. Your hair and eyes aren't Indian either." The stranger spoke rapidly, with a nervous twitch to the left side of his face. "Say, is that an earring you're wearing! What the heck are you? Speak up, young man. Are you a road bandit? A red savage? A rogue looking to steal a man's poke?"

"I Vin Lockhart."

"Lockhart. Vin Lockhart. No. Never heard of you. What are you doing out here? Don't get many folks just passing through, you know. Except that pair a month ago. Boy, were they something! Had a cart to carry their things in. Thought the gold would be lying around just for picking up," the prospector rattled on in his distinctive voice.

"Don't know what happened to them," he continued after only a short breath that barely disconnected his sentences. "Fed them a meal and sent them on their way. They didn't have a clue about prospecting for gold. Thought the stuff would just be there lying on the ground, waiting for someone to pick it up. Say, have you got the gold bug too? Most folks have given up on that, you know. Silver's the big thing around here now. Three big silver mines within ten miles of here. Nobody else has found this place, though. Not a one."

The young warrior, Vin Lockhart, watched the man's mouth move with fascination. It seemed to match the constant movement of his fingers along the barrel. He had never heard any person, white or red, talk so much in such a short amount of time. It was a holy man's chanting, for certain, he decided. The strange man's reedy voice had a fascinating rhythm, sort of like someone singing. In addition to not looking like other *wasicun*, he didn't sound like any Lockhart had listened to when they visited the village. Their voices were grunts and growls, like buffalo and panthers; this *wasicun*'s voice was like a bird singing. He didn't sound like the Kissels, either, and they were holy *wasicun* too.

"I ride. No place to go. Just ride."

"Drifting, eh?" The sunburned man grinned, revealing a gap between his two front teeth, and lowered the sawed-off shotgun. "Well, I know that way, that's for sure. Did it in '56—or was it '57? Quit teaching and just took off. Boy, was I green!"

The young warrior kept his hands up and away from his handgun. This appeared to be a different kind of white shaman than the Kissels, and he didn't want any of his movements to be misunderstood. Especially when he wasn't certain about what the man was saying. A holy man could call down upon any manner of evil. It didn't make matters any better that he had never seen a weapon like the one the skinny prospector held. He decided it was a magical gun only a shaman would be privileged to carry.

"Well, get yourself down from that horse. Breakfast is about ready. Hope you like fried raccoon. The rascal was nosing around camp for at least a week, so I made a trap and nailed him. Quite a contraption, if I do say so myself. Newton thought it was marvelous. Yeah, fried raccoon, that and some strong coffee and lots of beans," the prospector said, and spun on his heels to return to his camp.

He stopped, turned back, and added, "My name's Desmond. Desmond T. Crawford. You can call me Crawfish. That's what my friends used to call me back in the States. Got used to it."

The young warrior thought a crawfish was a strange spirit helper for a man, but he allowed that he didn't know anything about *wasicun* holy men.

The left side of the prospector's face twitched again as Crawfish smiled and said, "I'll introduce you to Newton a little later too. Of course, he isn't much help. Mainly he's a good listener. Has some funny opinions sometimes, though."

"Newton? Where Newton?"

"Oh, he's around here somewhere."

Lockhart didn't like the idea of not knowing where another white man might be. His eyes quickly searched the gray terrain but saw nothing. He could almost feel a rifle pointed at him from somewhere. Where? It made sense, he thought. A man couldn't be too careful in a country like this, and keeping one man out of sight while the other measured up a stranger was a good way to stay alive for another day. However, if Newton or Crawfish wanted to shoot him, they would have already done it, Lockhart realized. Still he would watch for signs of the missing man.

If something did happen, it would help to know where the bullets would come from.

"Say, you're not packing any sugar, are you? I sure do miss my sugar. Newton says it's silly to miss something like that, but I do."

Lockhart blinked away his distraction and said, "Aiiee, yes, I have sugar."

A small amount remained in the foodsack Mary Kissel had provided. The original provisions on his packhorse were down to a little *pemmican* and wild edible plants he had found.

"Well, holy wishwash, bring it on, bring it on! Haven't had any sugar for...let's see...What month is it? Gosh, I'll have to ask Newton. He usually remembers things like that."

Eager to please, the young warrior quickly found the sugar in his pack and handed the small sack to the prospector. "Here. Sugar. Good taste. Put in black water."

Crawfish accepted the small sack and stared at the young stranger for an instant before asking, "Won't be the first time my mouth's pushed me square into trouble—but you sure talk like a man who's spent a lot of time around Indians. You dress like one, sort of. No offense, just curious about who I'm eating breakfast with, that's all."

Lockhart nodded and tried to explain, using his limited English as best he could, about his life with the Oglalas and what had happened to him. He told of the death of his wife, his decision to leave the village, his unexpected discovery of his real family's old homestead and the few family things the Kissels had saved. He didn't mention Stone-Dreamer, Touches-Horses, or that the tribe thought he had been helped by spirits in a recent battle.

Crawfish's eyes widened as he pieced together the story coming jerkily out of Lockhart's mouth. His conclusion was that the young stranger had been captured by Indians and had escaped. The young man's wife had been killed by them! "My God!" he mouthed, but no sound came with it. He had read horrible stories of Indian atrocities to white people. Awful things about taking scalps, burning victims alive, gouging out their eyes, raping innocent women, and bashing in the heads of children. All manner of gruesome things. This poor young man had survived all of that!

"Holy mother of God, my friend! I didn't realize! I'm sorry, I just didn't realize! My God, what have you been through? Come and sit down. There are no red devils around here, I assure you. You're safe here, Vin."

Chapter Six

Together they walked back to Crawfish's camp with Lockhart leading his two horses. The thought of a hot meal was strong in the young warrior's mind; curiosity was burning up the prospector's.

"How long were you with those red devils?" Crawfish asked, twisting his head back and forth to remove the night's stiffness, and waving his left arm. His right hand held the sawed-off shotgun at his side. When there was no immediate response, he tried a slightly different version, figuring his new friend knew a limited amount of English: "How long were you with those *Indians*?"

"I with…Indians? Ah, yes, *wasicun* word for the People," Lockhart said. "You ask how long I with Oglalas?"

"Yeah, if you don't mind my asking. It must have been awful, son. I'm really sorry."

"I…eight. Eight summers, Oglalas find me. I young boy. Stone-Dreamer father to me. He holy man. Talk with stones. Stones sing to Stone-Dreamer. Much strong medicine."

"Ohmygosh! That's a long time, Vin. My God, what awful things you must have had to go through. Lordybe, all this time." Crawfish shook his head as he spoke. "I'm surprised you remember any words at all, being around only Indians all this time."

The bay packhorse jerked back on the lead rope, and Lockhart turned to see what the matter was. His horse had just seen the prospector's mule grazing on the other side of a thin row of trees ten yards away, and was frightened by the strange-appearing animal. Lockhart reassured the nervous animal and returned to the fascinated prospector.

"Stone-Dreamer make me use English. White men visit. I talk for tribe. Use English. Father proud. Learn much words from white men. 'Goddammit.' 'Son-of-bitch.' 'Tobacco.' 'Buffalo.' Much words."

"I see." Crawfish frowned, rubbed his chin with his left hand, and asked, "Didn't the white men, uh, try to get you away?"

"I no understand."

"Didn't they help you to escape? You know, didn't they help you run away from the Indians."

"I here. I Vin Lockhart," Lockhart answered, unsure of what Crawfish was asking.

The red-faced prospector scratched his cheek, which was twitching, and looked away. "What's that, Newton? Yeah, what the hell do I know about Indians? Never met one…well, there was that old Indian in town once. And he—oh, never mind."

Lockhart spun in the direction that Crawfish spoke but saw nothing, so he studied the camp as they approached. Everything was tidy around the small open area with a slatted hut that served as Crawfish's living quarters. Lockhart could see a cot inside the small structure, a woodstove, a rifle, and a stack of magazines. An equally high mound of books stood beside a small table. Only the cot, the rifle, and the books made sense to him. Lined up next to the hut were pans, spiked hammers, buckets, and other mining tools. An early slice of sunlight spat brightness from a gold pan.

It seemed logical to Lockhart that a holy man would have such odd-looking things. Most likely they were for various *wasicun* rituals. A water barrel with a convenient spigot squatted on the north side of the sturdy building. Next to it was a cast-iron Dutch oven and a keg of vinegar. Snapping in the morning breeze was a shirt and trousers on a rope tied to two ancient willows. All appeared strange and mystical to the young warrior. This was truly the world of a great white shaman.

Definitely more powerful than the Kissels, he told himself. He must be careful not to anger this unusual man-creature. On the other side of a thin row of trees ten yards away was the grazing mule. No signs of the Newton fellow were anywhere.

Questions about Lockhart ran through Crawfish's mind, but he could hardly keep from smiling. It was wonderful to have someone to talk to after all this time. He had actually forgotten how truly alone he was. Even with his stilted English, Lockhart's voice was like pure music to his ears.

"Vin, let me get this straight. I been out here so long my mind doesn't always work so good," Crawfish blurted as they neared the cooking fire. "You were living with these Indians, these Oglalas, right? They were…ah, good to you. They were…your friends. Right?"

"Yes, much friends. I leave Oglalas, be white man."

"Well, I'll be hornswaggled. Heard about folks like you, but I never thought I'd meet one. I'm real proud to know you, Vin Lockhart," Crawfish said, and motioned for the young warrior to sit down by the fire.

As he squatted, Lockhart gpt up the nerve to ask, "Is crawfish big spirit helper?"

"A what?" the prospector asked, his thin eyebrows jumping up and down in syncopation with his arms. "Oh, I get it. Indians name themselves after animals, don't they? Well, sure, why not."

Lockhart nodded with the satisfaction that he had assumed correctly. Crawfish laid his gun on the ground and dished up two plates in an exacting manner. He measured the width of both portions of beans with an extended finger to make certain they were equal. The young warrior Vin Lockhart studied the camp as he waited for Crawfish to carefully measure out the portions. Crawfish added a fat slice of sourdough bread dripped in sorghum molasses.

Lockhart wondered if the unseen man had already eaten.

"Here you go. Hope you like it. The beans are mighty hot, so be careful," Crawfish said, handing Lockhart a filled tin plate and a knife and fork. He supported his warning by placing his fingers close to the beans and then shaking them as if they were burned.

Lockhart looked at the food, cut off a small piece of steak, and stood. He held it high with one hand cupped beneath the other. A whispered tribute to *Wakantanka* followed in seven separate directions. He tossed the morsel into a cluster of long grasses wandering along the southern edge of Crawfish's camp.

"Hey! You haven't even tasted it!" Crawfish exclaimed, pointing at the thrown morsel. "Newton thinks I'm a heck of a cook. At least he never complains."

Lockhart frowned and said, "First...food to *Wakantanka.*"

"What?"

"First food to *Wakantanka.* Ah..." Lockhart struggled

to find the right words and remembered the Kissels' table blessing. "God great. Amen."

"Oh. Sort of an Indian prayer. I see. That's nice. Something they taught you, I guess. Should do more of that myself."

"*Wasicun* pray…God great, God good…"

"Oh yeah, I remember that one. Nice idea, praying," Crawfish said, and shoveled a forkful of beans into his mouth. He stopped. Lockhart was watching him with a puzzled expression on his face.

Crawfish quickly swallowed the beans and said, "Huh? What are you staring at? Oh, you want me to pray now? Well, why not."

He closed his eyes and clasped his hands together, at first forgetting the spoon, which was trapped in his intertwined fingers. He opened his eyes, frowned at the utensil and put it on his knee, then slowly recited, "God is great, ah…"

"God good."

"Yeah, that's it. God is good. Him we thank for daily food. By his hand we *were*...no, wait, no, I'll get it. Let's see, ah…by his hand we *are* fed, yeah, that's it. By his hand we are…led. Yeah, it rhymes, you see. Uh, Amen. Yeah, Amen. Sakes alive, I did it! First time in a long spell, I'm sorry to report, Vin. Almina and I, we used to say grace together before every meal. Mighty nice, come to think of it. Makes me think of her, yessir. Long time ago, it seems. Like another world that didn't really exist, except in my dreams."

"Amen," Lockhart answered, and began eating, being careful to use the fork and knife Crawfish gave him.

Beans were a new taste to him and he wasn't sure that he liked them, but the meat was good and the sweetness of the molasses was wonderful. *Wasicun's* black water was good if plenty of sugar was added, and he poured it into his hot tin cup from the small sack. During the meal Lockhart found himself liking this strange man and becoming comfortable around him.

Crawfish was more than eager to talk, in between bites. Lockhart noticed that the man smelled every bite of food before it reached his mouth and decided it was a ceremony. Immediately the prospector explained that he was prospecting for gold and using a "long torn," a wooden sluice box, to help sift through more sand and grit faster. It was called "placer mining," and he was looking for pieces of gold, from flakes to pebbles. The precious pieces were brought downhill by the mountain streams after erosion broke away its support.

With his eyes flashing and his arms waving, Crawfish said, "You know, the richest placers are usually found in foothills like this one. Yessir, they are. The river slows down and drops what it was carrying. This one is a good one, Vin. You just have to know what to look for. The river's like a woman, you know. She gives you signs if she's willing. Like, right here, the river slows down, so she drops whatever she was carrying. But most folks will never notice, Vin."

He took a bite of beans and meat and continued talking with his mouth full. "Why-shoot-me-in-the-foot, I've been at claims that wouldn't pay twenty cents a pan. And that's working at it hard. All day long, butt-deep in cold water, pulling out pan after pan of sand. Fifty or sixty a day. That's a hard way to make money. Not like the stories you hear, that's for sure."

Crawfish stopped, put his right hand to his lips, and looked around as if to see if anyone was listening. Satisfied, he whispered, "Vin, this claim opened up to me with panfuls of fifty dollars a pop. No sir, I'm not lying. It's thick with the stuff. Best I've ever seen. A long string of pockets of the stuff. That's why I built the sluice. Never seen a spot like this before. Heard about them, but didn't think I'd be so lucky."

Proudly he stated that this was his eighth placer claim and, likely, his last. He expected the young warrior to ask why this was going to be his last, but no such question was uttered. Lockhart continued to eat, with no apparent response in mind.

Shrugging his shoulders and looking away, Crawfish said, "Well, Newton, I don't think he knows that much English, do you? He seems like a nice fellow, though. Yeah, me too."

Lockhart swung his head in the direction Crawfish was talking but saw only the shadow of the trees. That's it, the young warrior realized. Newton was a spirit. Crawfish turned back to Lockhart and asked where he was going, speaking much more slowly than he had been. The young warrior shrugged and pointed at the trail he had been following. Crawfish was silent. The quiet seemed even longer to Lockhart after listening to the man's high-energy, and seemingly endless, monologues.

Crawfish chewed on the fingernails of three fingers, examined them, and said, "Vin, I make fast decisions. They aren't always good ones, but they're fast. Here's a proposition for you to consider. I could use the company—and the help. Why not stay for a while? You can help me with the claim and the hunting. I'm not so good with that. I'll give you a fourth of everything we take out—and I'll teach you English to boot. Before I wandered out here, I used to teach school. Be kinda nice to do it again. How's that sound, Vin?"

The young warrior cocked his head to the side and said, "You ask I work for you? You teach me good English. Is that right?"

"Yeah, that, and a fourth of all the gold we take out of here—from here on out. I've already fished out at least two thousand dollars' worth from that river bottom. Of course, it'll play out before long. But it'll do us both real fine in the meantime. I'm not greedy. The company will be welcomed—and so will a strong back.''

"What Newton think? Will he…like?"

Crawfish cocked his head to one side, rubbed his chin, and said, "Yes. Yes, Newton will be happy."

"I do this."

Crawfish was a little surprised his offer was accepted so quickly. "Great. After we clean up the dishes, I'll show you what it's all about. You might change your mind. It's hard work, that's for sure." He paused, looked away, and said, "Yeah, that's a good point, Newton. Vin, are you good with that six-gun?"

Lockhart spun his head in the direction Crawfish looked but saw nothing, and he answered, "I have two gun, rifle and pistol."

"I meant—are you good with them? Uh, can you shoot good?"

"I kill ten and ten Shoshoni by lonesome."

"Boots 'n' saddles!" Crawfish said, chuckling again and slapping his thighs with both hands. This time the right side of his face twitched only twice. "You keep that iron handy. I always worry about somebody coming up on me while I'm working. That's why I was so hard on you this morning."

"You good man, Crawfish. I see why Newton like you."

"Well, that's mighty nice to say. It's good to have you here, Vin. Haven't had anyone to talk to for a long spell. Except Newton, of course. Gets black fire lonely, man, I'll tell you."

"When meet Newton?"

Crawfish smiled, pointed to his head, and said, "Newton's right here. Nowhere else." He stared at the young warrior to see how he would react

Lockhart frowned and responded, "My Oglala father—Stone-Dreamer, he holy man. You holy man."

"Holy man? Naw, not me. Shoot-a-good-lamb, you

heard how rusty my praying was. Mostly I just read the books and magazines I've got here. Maggie-might-be, I can recite half the stories sentence by sentence. I really like reading Tennyson, though. Oh my, I'll tell you, that fella can write a fine poem. Have you heard any of his poems? No, I suppose not. Boy, you'd really like 'Charge of the Light Brigade.' I'll read it to you one of these nights. Say, you don't have any books with you, do you?" He paused, and Lockhart's mind caught up with the last question.

"I have Bible. Bible with names of white mother, father, sister. My name, Vincent Lockhart, in Bible."

"Sounds like your family's good book, all right, by golly. We'll have to talk more about that. But not now. I'm figuring you'll have me doing a full-fledged church service before long."

After the breakfast dishes were carefully washed, dried, and placed back in the camp box, Crawfish brought out a half-filled pouch to show Lockhart what he had been collecting. He opened it so Lockhart could see the collection of gold nuggets, chips, and flakes inside.

"Look at that, will you? Gold. Twenty-four karat beautiful. And there's a lot more where that came from, I tell you. I've really found it this time."

"Gold?"

"Yeah, gold. Isn't that something to see!"

"Gold, white man spirit stone? Much power. *Tunkan*?"

"Power? Well, I suppose you could say that. It sure does make men—white men, anyway—do some strange things to get it. White men use it to buy things."

"I have spirit stone of white man."

"Yeah, you will. A fourth of what we take out," Crawfish said, not understanding, holding up four fingers, then one, to reinforce his offer.

"*Wasicun* spirit stone—in pack."

Crawfish eyed Lockhart suspiciously. Had he misjudged

this young man? Was this a way of saying he was going to rob him? After all, what did he know about Indians. He'd never met one. Just the newspaper stories about their vicious attacks against white men. And this young man had been living with savages for a long time. Certainly he looked like one. Crawfish stepped back, holding the pouch close to his chest with both hands. His mind ran to the sawed-off shotgun lying on the ground a few feet from his cooking fire.

Without another word, Lockhart walked toward his packhorse and Crawfish walked briskly toward the weapon. Lockhart quickly returned with the blue-and-green stone pin in his hand and saw the shotgun in the prospector's right fist, resting at his side. Lockhart was puzzled. Had he misjudged this skinny man with the never-ending words? Where was this Newton? Was that why he was still hiding? Did Crawfish talk to him with only his mind, as Stone-Dreamer sometimes did with the stones?

Crawfish asked tentatively, "What's in your hand?"

"I show *wasicun* spirit stone. *Tunkan.*"

"Where do *you* plan to show these stones?" Crawfish's voice was edged with fear, but he made no attempt to raise the shotgun.

"I show you," Lockhart said, frowning and trying to anticipate Crawfish's next move. Was the man going to point the holy gun at him? Was this a *wasicun* trap? Was Newton closing in behind him? He stopped and raised his left hand, opened it to reveal the pin. His right hand was poised to grab the pistol in his belt.

"I show you spirit stone. Big medicine. My mother."

Crawfish's face broke into a wide, lopsided smile, and he said, "Oh, chicken-and-noodles, I get it. May I see this — spirit stone?"

"Yes."

"Well, great. Let's take a look," Crawfish said, laid

down the gun where it had been, and walked toward Lockhart.

Lockhart handed the tiny decoration to Crawfish as if it were more precious than any gold nugget ever found. Crawfish sensed the importance his new friend attached to the piece of jewelry and held it carefully as he examined the dress pin. Light passed through its swirls of blue and green and Lockhart smiled proudly at the beauty.

"That's beautiful, Vin, really nice. That's a fine piece of agate. Yessir, moss agate. Real nice," Crawfish said without looking up.

"My mother. Spirit stone," Lockhart reinforced, then a dark thought passed over him. "*Wasicun* sickness stronger."

"Well, I'll be a one-eared horntoad!" Crawfish laughed. "You sure do have a spirit stone. It's beautiful. I'll bet your mother loved wearing it."

Lockhart nodded and said, "I work for English. Learn to speak good. Read books?"

"Yes. English," Crawfish said. "That's worth more than all the gold in the world, isn't it? Sometimes I forget that. Come on, my friend, the day's a wasting."

The next half hour was spent gathering what Crawfish wanted to take to the claim for working. He talked mainly to Newton, commenting for or against the need of every item as he and Lockhart came to it. They finally trudged off with two shovels, a large pan, a can, two tin cups, two large potatoes for their midday meal, two rifles, and the sawed-off shotgun. Lockhart would discover that this systematic selection—and the choosing of the same items—occurred each morning. An hour later, Lockhart and Crawfish were shoveling river silt and rock into the slanted trough capped with a shallow hopper.

A late-June sun had propped itself on top of the mountain peaks and was happily shedding sunshine down upon them. The prospector showed him where the most likely parts of the river silt would yield treasure. He called it "a pay streak" and said, fortunately, that it ran only a foot or so under the river's bed. He explained that gold was heavier than sand and silt and could often sink into a riverbed a long way.

"I've seen men go in and dam up the whole stream so they can dig far enough down to get at the pay streak. I've heard a few old-timers say they've seen it sink ten feet down. No such problem here, my boy, nosirree. We've just to keep at it. Scooping and looking. The river's a real lady here. Just keep stroking her and she'll open up to you."

Like a clock, Crawfish would stop shoveling every hour, on the hour, and pan through the heavy sediment left behind. Lockhart would watch him flip each pan in a slow, ritual motion to wash unwanted silt over the rim. Ten minutes later he would run his fingers carefully through the remaining sludge. Gold of any size and shape was removed with his knife and placed in a waiting can. Tonight he would move the findings to a pouch.

Usually offhand comments followed his bottom-of-the-pan discoveries, like "Would you look at that, Newton," or "Newton, that'll buy a half a carriage. Yessiree, that one right there. Of course it will. You know that."

Each time he heard the name, Lockhart would turn around to see where Crawfish's friend was. And each time no one was there. He was certain now that Crawfish was talking to his shadow. It must be one of the spirits Stone-Dreamer had often mentioned. He should have known! All holy men talked to the spirits—and saw them where ordinary men did not. Crawfish's careful panning process reminded Lockhart of his adopted father's methodical healing ceremonies. He wondered if this white holy man could summon the winds like his adopted father could, or heal a sick child, or talk to the meadowlark.

After they filled the trough again, Lockhart shed both

his coat and his buckskin warshirt. Dropping them beside their nearby guns, he watched the prospector search intently through the gathered soil. White men were strange, he thought. This was not the work of a warrior. And no man had the right to tear up the river or eat into Mother Earth. Never had he seen so many rocks in one place before, and he knew it was sacred ground. How dare the *wasicun* show so little respect to the ancient people, the *inyan*, he thought, and wondered how many sacred stones were among the piles of mud and rock. If he could hear the stones, he was certain they would be crying. Lockhart wasn't sure he wanted to be a *wasicun* if this was the way they spent their days.

All the white men he had seen previously were hunters and trappers, more like Oglalas. They were definitely not like this. Perhaps a white sacred man does different things than a white warrior, he reasoned to himself. After all, Stone-Dreamer did not hunt and did not go on war parties. Crawfish's concentration broke and he realized the young warrior was watching him. The eccentric prospector was drawn to the matching set of scars on both sides of Lockhart's chest, as if someone had created a purposeful pattern.

He couldn't resist asking, "Those scars on your chest, are they a battle wound? There. Scars? Ah, fight?" He acted out, drawing a bow and swinging a knife to support his question. "Did they torture you once?" The last question bolted from his mouth before he could think about it.

Lockhart said, "I know 'fight,' 'scars.' " He looked down at himself and touched the scars with both hands before he spoke: "*Wi wanyang wacipi.* Sun dance. Time all Lakota...the People...come together. Happy. Much fun. Sacred circle. Sun dance pain bring strong medicine to village. They pick much good warrior. Me. Great honor. Father proud."

While Crawfish frowned and tried to fathom what the

ceremony was all about, Lockhart did his best to explain how the dancer's chest was pierced and tied with rawhide ropes that were attached to the sun dance pole. Without food or drink, the warrior danced and gazed at the sun from dawn to dusk, until the flesh was torn through and he was released. The dancer prays for his village during this agonizing ceremony. For extra weight, buffalo skulls were often tied to the other end of the thong and dragged around the circle. His sentences were staccato bursts of a few words in between pauses to think of more, but they painted bright pictures.

Crawfish blinked and absorbed the totality of the anguishing performance his friend had just described. "Rattlesnake milk 'n' cookies! Sure sounds like torture to me, Vin! Are you sure these were your friends?"

Lockhart didn't respond to the question and said, "Now learn white man ways. You teach?"

"Well, there sure isn't anything like that to learn," Crawfish said. "Heck, there's no reason we can't improve your English while we work. Repeat after me. Shoveling dirt is hard work." He chuckled.

Lockhart stared at him.

"S-s-shoveling dirt is har…d…"

"Work."

"Work."

"Say it again."

"Say it again."

Crawfish broke out laughing and dropped the pan. He leaned over and retrieved it and said, "Shoveling is hard work."

"Shoveling is hard work."

"Good," Crawfish said. "That is a shovel in your hands." He pointed to the tool, "Shovel," and then to Lockhart's hands, "Hands."

"Shovel. Hands. I know 'hands.' " He repeated, "That is a shovel in your hands."

Crawfish smiled and pointed again at Lockhart's hands. "Ah, *my* hands."

"I understand 'my.' That is a shovel in my hands."

"Good."

Crawfish refilled his pan and began swishing away the unwanted soil. He licked his chapped lips and said, "Vin, say 'This is gold. We will be rich.' "

"This is gold. We will be rich. This is gold. We will be rich."

"Good. Good." Crawfish was particularly pleased the young warrior didn't lead off with "Vin, say."

"Good. Good."

The prospector laughed again. If he was at all nervous about having a stranger so close to his claim, it didn't show. He only looked like a lonely man happy to have company. After pouring moist gold pieces into the pouch, the sunburned prospector pointed to an eagle hovering over the river, searching for dinner. He straightened and placed a hand on his back to ease the pain. As he waved toward the eagle, he said, "Eagle. An eagle flies over us."

"Eagle. A…An eagle flies…us."

"An eagle flies over us."

"Eagle flies o-ver…us."

"Hey, that's good."

"Hey, that's good," Lockhart repeated, and grinned, knowing what he had done. Then he paused and said, "*Wambti.* Eagle is…between *Wakantaka*—and man. Eagle flies to *Wakantanka*, takes words of man—with him."

"Hmm, that's nice. Is that why eagle feathers are so important to you fellows?"

Lockhart stared at him, not understanding. Crawfish shrugged his shoulders, pointed toward the shovel in Lockhart's hands, and said, "Shovel. I dig with the shovel."

"Shovel. I dig with the shovel," Lockhart repeated, and began throwing more sand into the trough.

On the next panful of sludge, Crawfish withdrew twenty-five thick flakes and eight pebbles. He put one of the small chunks to his mouth and bit down on it.

"Vin, bite down on this nugget. If you ever have a doubt about it not being gold, bite it. There's nothing so soft. Bite. Yeah, bite. See?" He imitated the biting process. "Don't try to eat it, Vin. It's rock. I just wanted you to see how soft it was."

Lockhart handed him back the gold, wondering at the significance of the act of putting it in his mouth. As a youngster, Stone-Dreamer had taught him the value of putting a pebble-friend in his mouth to end thirst or to calm worry. Placing *tunkan* in a sick person's mouth would heal certain illnesses. Was this a special *wasicun tunkan* ceremony? It must be. He tried to recall Crawfish's specific actions when he gave the gold to him; that would be a part of this gold *tunkan* ritual. Of course, he realized only a *wasicun* shaman could conduct such an activity. Still, it was good to pay attention to the details and learn about becoming a white man.

"Well, what do you think?" Crawfish asked. "I'm waiting with bated breath."

Lockhart stared at him, bewildered, and asked, "You put bait in mouth? Why you do this? For birds to come?"

Crawfish's eyes widened as an explosion of laughter hit his entire body. He doubled over, tears running down his face. He tried to explain the phrase three times before he could manage to do so without breaking into laughter again. Finally he took a deep breath and said, " 'Waiting with bated breath' is an expression, Vin. It means that I am eager, or impatient. Yeah, like I can't wait to hear your opinion about the gold."

Lockhart frowned and said, "Why bait?"

"This 'bate' isn't spelled the same as 'bait' for animals."

"Oh. Are there much English where words not same?"

"Yes, there are. Ha, like 'there' and 'their.' Ah, 'you,' 'ewe.' 'Main' 'n' 'mane.' Lots of them. I'll teach you all those differences."

"Good. I shovel."

Midway through the morning, a remembrance of Young Evening quietly entered Lockhart's mind and settled there. It was a sweet time recalling the two of them walking among the trees, hand in hand. Without warning, her face suddenly turned into a skeleton and he yelled out, dropping the shovel. Crawfish glanced at their rifles lying against a rock outcropping but grabbed for the sawed-off shotgun strapped across his back in a handmade quiver. He yanked it free and swung the weapon back and forth to spot the problem. When he saw nothing, Crawfish turned to Lockhart, who was sweating and pale.

"What's the matter, Vin? What did you see? A grizzly? Are you all right?" Crawfish grabbed Lockhart's forearm with his left hand, and the young warrior jumped. "Hey, it's all right. It's all right. Easy now."

Lockhart squinted to push away the awful picture burning in his mind. He shook his head and immediately went to his knees.

"I sorry. Will dig—with shovel. See bad thing…inside. My . . . wife. She ., . . she . . . she dead. F-f-face gone."

"Oh, I understand. Had a few of those nightmares myself—in the middle of the day—haven't I, Newton," Crawfish said. "Let me get you some water. We need a break anyway."

The prospector brought fresh water from the river in tin cups and they sat beside it to drink. Winding its way across the foothills, the river's gentle bubbling song was comforting. Crawfish began talking about his late wife to help his young friend regain his composure.

"I know all about losing the one you love," he said. "Now take Missus Crawford, God bless her soul. She was a handsome filly back when we first started courting. Oh, man, I tell you, she could stop a man's heart with just a look. And smart? Lordly, she could outspell any man in four counties. Almina Johnson she was then. Wish you had known her, Vin. You two would have gotten along real fine, I know it."

Lockhart nodded. He thought Crawfish was talking about a woman and guessed he was doing it to help him feel better. Most of the words, though, were a blur of high-pitched sound. It was difficult, sometimes, to concentrate on the words when the man's hands kept jumping around.

"Well, sir, she wouldn't have nothing to do with me at first. I mean, nothing. Why, she'd cross the street, getting all muddied up, just to get away when she saw me coming. Now, I was a mite better-looking than I am today, mind you. Of course, I wasn't a handsome lad like yourself. No, no way. Well, I figured she hated me something fierce, so I finally asked her best friend—Judith Cross—to go on a carriage ride with me instead. And you know what?"

"I not know."

"Well, of course you don't," Crawfish said with a chuckle. "Well, when I go to the Cross homestead with my old buckboard...shootykaboom, out comes Almina, smiling like nothing at all was wrong. God, I miss that woman."

Lockhart watched the strange man blink back the tears that wanted to follow his words. Crawfish swallowed the emotion by squeezing his mouth with his right hand and said, "She died of tuberculosis. Tuberculosis, that's what the doctors said. They didn't know anything to do. Tuberculosis! Wonder what your Indian friends call it. Blackest moment of my life, Vin, I swear to God, blackest moment of my life. And not a day goes by that I don't think of her. Sometimes they've been pictures like the one you just saw. Whooie, goodbye sanity. Isn't that right, Newton."

The young warrior spun his head in the direction Crawfish was looking but saw nothing but a long row of pine trees. He was absolutely sure of it now: Newton was a spirit. Maybe the spirit of the woman Crawfish was talking about. Lockhart understood she was dead—and that he loved her. After a few minutes, he told Crawfish again about Young Evening's death, the revenge battle that followed and the tribe's decision that he was helped by spirits. Crawfish listened and tried to comprehend what his new friend's life had been like. Without waiting for questions from Crawfish, Lockhart began to talk about his young life with his real family as best he could recall. Crawfish realized that the young man was trying to talk about these days as much for himself as for Crawfish. Lockhart repeated the story of his discovering the homestead and being given family items that had been saved all these years. Crawfish still wasn't fully convinced his new friend hadn't been mistreated by the Indians and had finally escaped from their evil.

"So that's where you got that coat and hat," Crawfish said with a lopsided grin, trying to make his friend feel better. "It's a good thing your folks didn't leave a dress behind instead. Or a fancy top hat."

Lockhart frowned, and the prospector wasn't certain if the joke was not understood or just not liked.

"You ready to work again?" Crawfish asked, motioning toward the sluice. "There's no hurry, mind you. That river's a real fine lady, like I said. Her gold is going to wait for us. I'm just asking."

"I work now."

"Yeah, yeah, Newton, I know. We can talk while we pan. Yes, there's a lot to learn from this new friend."

This time Lockhart didn't look to find Newton; he only

smiled. The rest of the day went swiftly, with both men sharing stories. The red-faced prospector told about Denver City, the boomtown growing from the riches of gold and silver. Lockhart was amazed at the description, even from the handful of words he understood. It was difficult for him to imagine such a gathering of white people. He tried to explain his life with the Oglalas and their spiritual relationship to the world around them. Crawfish told about his past as a schoolteacher in Ohio. Lockhart told of his Oglala father being disappointed in his not receiving a stone vision or hearing the stones sing.

Crawfish talked about Almina; Lockhart talked about Young Evening, Stone-Dreamer, and Touches-Horses. Crawfish gently corrected his young friend's English as they worked, and Lockhart eagerly absorbed the suggestions. He tried to explain about the tribe thinking he was helped by the spirits, and why he finally had to leave. Neither quite understood the other on most subjects, but both enjoyed the company and the sharing.

That night Crawfish cooked a stew of venison meat, wild onions, and potatoes. Some of the Kissels' cornmeal became fried corn bread. Lockhart thought the meal's preparation seemed to take forever, but Crawfish had to make certain everything was just right. The venison was the result of nimble hunting by Lockhart.

After the kill was made, the young warrior prayed silently over the dead animal, then carefully placed the four hooves in a sack made from the removed skin. Paying no attention to the prospector, he stood and held the bundle in outstretched arms toward the south, murmuring something Crawfish couldn't make out. The bundle was placed in the crook of a nearby tree and four small pouches of tobbacco were added to the closest limb.

It was a fascinating thing for the prospector to watch, and he held his tongue for once. However, he did remember to say grace, repeating the prayer from breakfast.

Lockhart attempted to recite it with him. Crawfish smiled to himself and wondered if anyone would believe that a red savage, or at least a warrior who lived with them, would be leading a white man back to religion. With supper over, the prospector brought out a small framed daguerreotype of himself and his late wife on their wedding day. He handed it reverently to Lockhart. Touching the glass protecting it, he turned the frame over in his hand to see the other side. This was more invisible stone, he decided. The *tunkan* of a *wasicun* shaman.

Crawfish watched him and said, "That's me there—as a young man. And that's Almina. I told you she was beautiful. That was our wedding day. Oh, what a glorious time it was. Yes, it was. Almina, I love you."

Lockhart watched him intensely, trying to make out the meaning of each word. He handed the photograph back to Crawfish and walked over to his own unpacked things. From the Kissels' small wooden box he took the daguerreotype of his parents and brought it to the prospector.

"My mother, my father. Long back."

Crawfish studied the photograph and said, "They were a handsome couple, Vin. I'm very sorry you lost them."

"*My* sister. She gone spirit world. You have what you call this…shadows of mother, father?" Lockhart asked, pointing at the faded images.

"It's called a photograph, Vin," Crawfish replied. "No, I'm sorry I don't. Didn't know my father. My mother died twelve years ago. God bless her soul."

"I sorry no mother, no father. No…photograph."

"Ah, no, it's all right. It's a…well, forget it," Crawfish said. "Say, I've got some cigars—would you like one? Cigar. Ah, tobacco? Smoke?"

"Yes, I like smoke."

Crawfish smiled and nodded. He jumped up and returned with two cigars. Lockhart placed the tobacco in his mouth, took a stick from the dying fire, and held it to the cigar seven different times. Crawfish was intrigued and held his cigar without attempting to light it. After the ritual lighting, Lockhart stood and blew smoke to the four directions, the sky, the earth, and the eagle. Crawfish watched his young friend perform his adaptation of the sacred medicine pipe ceremony, taught by Stone-Dreamer, with mild amusement.

"That's a lot of doing for one cigar. What is all that?" Crawfish asked, mimicking Lockhart's ritual to help explain his question.

Lockhart held the cigar in his hand for a moment and the prospector thought the young warrior was going to be angry. Finally Lockhart said, "Man talk truth when smoke. Ask winds, sky, and mother earth…hear me. Call on eagle to take words to *Wakantanka*."

"Well, a cigar making a man speak truthfully might depend on the man, Vin. Do you mind if I try that…ceremony? I kinda like it," Crawfish asked. "Ah, may I send words to…*Wakantanka*?"

"Yes. They listen."

Crawfish repeated Lockhart's smoking ritual with mechanical movements, talking to himself as he did, and looked away. "See, Newton, I can pray in Indian now. What do you think of that? Why is that different from a white man praying? Pagan gods? Well, I think we've got a lot to learn from our young friend here. Yes, you too."

He turned back to Lockhart and said, "Ah, is *Wakantanka* one god? Ah, one…spirit? Three?"

"*Wakantanka*…all."

"All?"

"*Wakantanka*…winds, *skan*, ah, sky, earth…ah, moon," Lockhart said and stopped, trying to think of the words. "Yes, lightning. *Wi*, Sun. Ah, yes, *inyan*, stone. More *wakan*. More…mystery. Not know all words."

His furrowed brow reinforced the difficulty of finding English words for his thoughts. He wasn't eager to go back to the Oglalas in his mind but accepted the mental task as a part of their growing friendship.

"So *Wakantanka* is really all of the natural phenomena.

"Fe-nom-e-nom…ah? Holy man word?"

Crawfish smiled and answered, "Phenomena. It means all of the unexplained things in nature. I don't suppose that helps either, does it?"

Lockhart frowned but said nothing. He drew on his cigar and let a white trail of smoke encircle his face and disappear above him. Crawfish watched him mouth the pronunciation of "phenomena."

Crawfish moved his cigar from the right side of his mouth to the left and changed subjects. "What were you doing with that dead buck earlier? Praying to *Wakantanka*?"

"No. I thank spirit of *tatica*, deer. He brother. He give life so we eat."

"Never thought of it that way before. I like that."

"Oglala say…all living things are one family. That why circle sacred. *Mitakuye oyasin*," Lockhart said.

"I was going to tell you about white man's religion. Well, actually, about Christianity. Don't know much about being a Jew," Crawfish said, drawing on his cigar and then tapping it to remove the ash. "Newton's whispering that I shouldn't, at least not right now. He says it would sound so rigid—and contrived—compared to that beautiful thought, and you might get the wrong idea. I think he's right. I'll just have to think more on it before explaining. He says the time would be better spent working on your verbs."

They began to exchange more about their different ways. Crawfish explained about white men coming to America from all over the world; Lockhart told of the great circle of Lakotas, of which the Oglalas were one small tribe. Crawfish spoke of great cities; Lockhart talked of packing up an entire village in minutes and moving to a new place, sometimes once every week during summer.

Crawfish explained the governmental structure of the United States and how special it was. Lockhart explained that it was every Oglala's choice to do whatever he or she pleased, to follow whomever he or she pleased. Crawfish observed that this was one of the problems white men had in trying to deal with Indians; it would be impossible to get every Indian to sign a treaty. Lockhart observed that no man should be allowed to take away another's rights without his consent.

Crawfish deliberated on the white man's need to clear away the land to build homes, roads, and bridges, to create boundaries, all driven by the desire to acquire wealth and live as well as one's ability would let him. Lockhart talked about animals as teachers, of plants as healers and of stones as providers of wisdom. Crawfish told about the railroad, steam engines, newspapers, the telegraph and the sewing machine, how factories made clothes, tools, utensils, and shoes. Lockhart explained that the buffalo gave the Oglalas everything they needed, from food and clothing to bedding, tools, and medicine. Crawfish talked about how white men could tell what they were worth by counting their money and property. The greatest white men were rich. Lockhart said owning things was important only so a red man could give more to others; the greatest Indians were the greatest givers.

They even talked about outhouses, but Lockhart was too shocked at the idea to listen for long. Lockhart finally told about the Oglala belief that the spirits of animals and people dwelled on the buttes to the far west. Human spirits usually stayed close to their loved ones for a while. After a year, they were fed for the last time by their living families and began traveling along *wanagi tacanku*, the Ghost Road. He told of the Shadow Ceremonies and that many spirits remained behind as shadows or came back as owls or other things. He told of Young Evening's Ghost Lodge built by his good friend, Touches-Horses.

"In the night sky, we see their campfires along the Ghost Road." Lockhart pointed upward as they sat around their gray campfire.

"White men call it the Milky Way."

"Milk…Way? *Wasicun* keep cows there?"

"No, it's just a name to describe a collection of stars and planets that sort of look like milk spread across the sky. The earth is a part of the Milky Way, Vin," Crawfish said.

Lockhart frowned in disbelief and blurted, "The old woman guards the Spirit Road and pushes the unworthy spirits back to earth. They stay here, do mean things. Holy men can see them."

"Like Stone-Dreamer?"

"Yes, he sees them, talks with them. He saw Young Evening and talked with her several times. Do *wasicun* see spirits?"

"Oh, I suppose some do. There's always somebody talking about seeing a ghost somewhere."

"White men believe in ghosts," Lockhart declared.

Crawfish decided not to pursue the subject further and changed the discussion to the unpleasant fact that most white men felt it was a noble act to kill an Indian, any Indian. The white man saw Indians as ignorant savages standing in the way of progress. The white people and the red people would never be able to live together. Lockhart must be ready for this kind of thinking when they went to Denver City, he explained.

"We are together. Friends. You and me."

"Yes, I wish it were that simple."

"We smoke cigars on it, and pray for this—for all white and red men."

"Couldn't hurt, I guess."

Chapter Seven

A week passed quickly. In addition to increasing his vocabulary, Lockhart was learning the alphabet, writing the letters on sheets of paper stored away for Crawfish's own writings. A stack of written—but unsent—letters stood forgotten in the corner. Each was addressed to his late wife. Initially, the ink and scroll pen were awkward for the young warrior. He refused to quit, and gradually his handwriting was quite legible, almost artlike in its form. Every night, after the formal lessons, Lockhart worked on reading one of Crawfish's books or magazines and practiced his handwriting by candlelight until he fell asleep.

Lockhart vowed to himself that he would succeed in this strange white man's world. He would be their equal in the things they valued; he, too, would have the house, carriage, and fine horses that his friend wished for. It was exciting to think about and spurred his learning even more—and his search for gold. Each night he watched Crawfish blow his nose twice in a handkerchief before going to sleep. The young warrior decided it was a *wasicun* ceremony.

After supper on their tenth day together, and after washing his clothes, Crawfish asked Lockhart to help carry the three pouches they had filled since the young warrior had joined him. At the base of one of the sagging willow trees, he removed three rocks and explained that work on the hiding place had been done only at night—just to be certain no one could see what he was doing. Of course, he knew nobody was around. Still, it seemed more secure that way.

Lifting away a hunk of cut sod to reveal ten filled pouches in a shallow hole, Crawfish said, "I figured it was the smart way to do it. That way no one could accidentally, or otherwise, see where I was keeping the stuff. You—and Newton—are the only ones that have seen it." Crawfish's face didn't twitch. Generally it didn't when he was talking about gold or working with Lockhart on his language skills.

"Thank you for your trust," Lockhart said, enunciating each word.

Crawfish smiled broadly and nodded. "That was well said, Vin. You are really coming along. Folks won't know you from a college-bred easterner by the time we go to Denver City." Even in the darkness, Crawfish could see Lockhart beam at the compliment.

"See, I had ten pouches when you came. Now there are three more. And we'll have that one we've started finished by the end of the week, for sure. One of them is yours, Vin," Crawfish said with great satisfaction in his face.

Lockhart placed a rock, then another, on top of the sod and Crawfish pushed it into place. The red-faced prospector nudged the first rock a little to the left, studied the new position, then pushed it again. As soon as the task was finished and Crawfish was satisfied with the overall appearance of the cache, they ambled back to the hut. A silver moon had taken control of the cool July night sky, but neither noticed; both were excited about their growing wealth.

"You remember me telling you about land titles and claim deeds, don't you?" Crawfish said as they entered the dark hut.

"Yes, white man's ways with Mother Earth strange. Put words on a paper, let one man own what *Wakantanka* has given all."

"Well, maybe so. But without doing it that way, a man wouldn't be able to build anything that would last. Think about your…ah, your real folks. Your mom and dad. They owned land and built a homestead on it. That was theirs, their home. Your home that you found. That's mighty special, Vin. It's a very different life than always roaming around—like your Indian friends. And I'm sorry to say this, but that's why they will eventually lose… everything. The white man won't let them roam around."

Lockhart didn't respond as Crawfish popped a match off the table and lit a small candle resting in a tin can, cut in half for the purpose. Fragile yellow light fought its way into the darkness and came to rest on the faces of both men.

"I keep the claim deed hidden in that magazine. There. That piece of paper gives me a legal right to mine this piece of land. It's been recorded in Denver City. That's the law, Vin," Crawfish said, holding the tin-can candle toward the stack of magazines and pointing toward a *Harper's* issue near the bottom.

Lockhart was still silent, staring at the magazines, and Crawfish wondered if his statement about the Indian losing everything had upset him. Finally the young warrior asked, "Why do you keep *valuable* paper there?" He emphasized the word "valuable." It was a word Crawfish had added to his lesson the night before.

"Excellent use of 'Valuable,' Vin. Excellent," Crawfish said, quite relieved that his friend's pensiveness was about this subject, not the other. "Well, I figured nobody would look for the deed there. Besides, I didn't want to keep all of my eggs in one basket."

"Eggs?"

"Yeah, that's an expression—not keeping all of your eggs in one basket," Crawfish said. "It means you don't put everything in the same place. You spread it around. You know, if you had all your eggs in one basket and dropped it, they might all break and you wouldn't have any. But if they're in two or three baskets, some would be safe. I figured if someone found the gold, they might not find the deed—or the other way around."

"Do not put eggs in one basket. You teach me much. Thank you."

Crawfish chuckled and said, "Here, hold this and I'll get the deed out for you to read."

With Lockhart holding the candle, Crawfish placed most of the magazines to one side and carefully withdrew a wrinkled sheet of paper from a graying *Harper's* magazine. He handed the deed to Lockhart, and the young warrior slowly began to read the legal description.

"The United States Territory of Colorado…"

" 'Hereby,' " Crawfish said to help him over an unfamiliar word. Lockhart looked at him, frowning.

"It means, ah—with these words."

"Should say that."

"Yeah, well, that legal language, Vin. It's always stilted. Makes lawyers feel more important, I guess."

"Who are these…lawyers?" Lockhart asked, completing the reading and handing the deed back to Crawfish.

"Who are…lawyers?"

"Good question—and one I can't answer fast. Let's just say, for now, they're smart white men with a lot of book savvy. In fact, I've been thinking it's time you learned something about white men besides reading and writing, Vin."

"I want learn to be a smart white man—like lawyers," Lockhart said.

"Well, you're going to need to know a little history, and certainly something about money. Ciphering is a must, too. You'll need to know the laws of the white man. And you need to know how to handle yourself with fisticuffs—and poker. What you say to that?"

"Yes, I want learn all about white man. Make me rich!"

"Won't hurt," Crawfish said with a glint in his eye as he picked up a deck of worn and dog-eared cards lying on his bed. "A man should definitely know how to handle himself in a game of cards. We'll start on poker tonight. All right?"

"Poker?"

"Yeah, you're going to like it."

"Good. Will you teach me white man nose ceremony first?"

"White man what?"

Lockhart pointed to his nose and repeated his request: "Will you teach me white man nose ceremony?"

"I'm sorry, Vin, I don't know what you're talking about."

Lockhart frowned and said, "Before you sleep each night, you make sound with nose. Hold sacred white little blanket. May be only white holy men can do."

Crawfish burst into uncontrolled laughter, tears ran down his cheeks, and his face turned even redder than usual. Each time he tried to say something, a giggle took him away again to hearty laughing. Lockhart started laughing too, just from watching his new friend. Finally Crawfish wore himself down enough to talk.

"Oh my, Betsy-comes-a-milking! Vin, that's no holy ceremony, believe me. I just blow my nose each night.

Done it for years. Clears me out and, I guess, helps me sleep. Nothing to it, I'm afraid, just a silly habit."

"No ceremony?"

"No ceremony."

"Me make nose sound?"

"If you want to."

"May be not."

Crawfish chuckled again and began teaching Lockhart the ways of poker over a wavering candle. He spread a deck of cards across the floor of the hut and talked about their differences.

"This is an ace."

"Ace. Look like shovel."

"Yeah, the ace of spades does. The ace is the most powerful card in the deck."

"A-i-i-i-e-e."

"There are four aces. See?"

Lockhart shouted, "Four? You not tell me this Oglala game! White man sees four as sacred number?"

"Well, not really. It just works out that way in cards. There are four suits. Four different kinds of families."

Lockhart nodded his head and said, "*Wasicun* see four is sacred. I knew it."

Lockhart smiled, started to say something, but decided against it and continued: "See how they are alike. These are all clubs. These are all spades…"

By the end of the evening, they were more or less playing five-card-stud poker. Lockhart liked the game but hadn't yet learned to keep from expressing glee at a good hand. Crawfish had to keep reminding him that it was important not to let an opponent read his face. He said, "You've got to be stone-faced—like an Indian." Both men roared in laughter at the phrase. They played for small pebbles, but Crawfish explained that the game was played for money; Lockhart wanted to do so, but Crawfish refused. The prospector told Lockhart about houses in town that offered places to play different card games and sell whiskey.

Lockhart indicated that he knew what whiskey was and didn't like the taste. Crawfish acknowledged that was a wise decision but went on to say that he had been considering buying, or opening, a saloon. He also told of places that offered women for a price. Lockhart thought he was talking about a marriage process, and the prospector finally gave up explaining the concept of prostitution.

Yawning and stretching, the prospector quit for the night, blew his nose twice, and quickly went to sleep. Lockhart continued working with the cards, carefully placing them into mock hands and evaluating their relative strengths. Then he decided his leggings needed to look more like a white man's trousers, and he worked to turn them into a rough pair of pants without the breechclout or the open groin area. He used cutout portions of the breechclout to give him the material needed to complete the pants.

He had a shirt—besides his father's—to wear, instead of his buckskin warshirt. They had found the other shirt beside an old campfire downriver four days before. The dirty, striped, collarless shirt fit him. A single sock, a small sack of coffee, one can of peaches, and a coffeepot with the bottom burned out were the only other items they found. They had laughed about the coffeepot and wondered how it happened. Crawfish had washed the shirt that night, but Lockhart rarely wore either of his shirts, preferring to work with his chest and arms bare. On a cold morning, he wore the frock coat until the day warmed up. His warshirt was already folded and put away with his few other things. It was deep into the night before he was finished. Morning came far too soon for the young warrior, but Crawfish let him sleep in when he prepared breakfast.

"Come and get it, you poker-playing bum!" Crawfish shouted good-naturedly.

Lockhart sat up in his buffalo robe in the hut and grinned sheepishly at the skinny prospector squatted over the campfire. Next to where the young warrior lay was the scattered deck of cards. Quickly, he pushed them into a neat pile and placed it on the table beside Crawfish's cot. In seconds he was dressed in his newly revised buckskin pants and his striped shirt. Next came the wide-brimmed hat and frock coat, followed by his shoving his revolver into his wide studded belt. The weight of the weapon felt good. His mouth turned into a thin strip when he remembered that he hadn't cleaned any of the weapons last night as Crawfish insisted he should.

"Hey, come on! It's getting cold!"

"I'm coming. I'm coming. Keep your shirt on," Lockhart answered. The rhythm of his words was a match for Crawfish's voice inflection, only lower. The prospector smiled at the glib response.

"Hey, I like your pants! Real good job," Crawfish exclaimed. "You're looking more like a white man every day. Except for that earring. Don't know any white men who wear earrings—except pirates."

Lockhart grinned at the compliment and touched his ear where the small red pebble hung from its leather loop. It was the one Oglala thing he hadn't been able to put away.

"Newton wants to know if you have any buccaneers in your family," Crawfish joked, chuckling.

"Buccaneers?"

"They're outlaws who sail on big boats and rob other ships."

"Newton thinks my people steal?"

"No, no. Never mind. It was a joke."

"I not get joke."

"I know, Vin. Come on and eat," Crawfish said, grabbing the coffeepot from the edge of the fire with a gloved hand.

Like a thunderbolt on a dear day, a fierce whinny from Lockhart's black horse suddenly slashed into their morning. Lockhart spun around, pulling his pistol as he turned, and ran toward the horses. Crawfish dropped the coffeepot, spilling hot liquid onto his pants and the cooking coals. He cursed, scrambled to his feet, and scurried for the rifles.

In six strides Lockhart was through the thin row of trees and into the picket area where his two horses and Crawfish's mule were tied. His eyes caught a golden mountain lion. The magnificent beast was crouched on the crown of a huge boulder, which anchored the rock-strewn ridge and cut off the camp from view to all but the closest rider. The cougar was snarling his anger at having his silent advance discovered too early by the black horse. Now he was trying to decide whether or not to attack at all. Lockhart's bay was frantically pulling against the rope that held it to this place, and the mule was kicking wildly into the air.

Magnificently, the wide-chested black stood with ears laid back, pawing his right hoof against the ground, daring the big cat to come closer. Lockhart stopped and stood quietly in the shadows of the tree line. His mouth was a thin line of concern, but he eased the pistol in his hand to his side.

"Goddamn, a cougar!" Crawfish exclaimed as he came alongside Lockhart. As he spoke, the red-faced prospector raised his rifle to shoot. Lockhart pushed the gun barrel toward the ground. The explosion rattled through the thin mountain air and ricocheted off a flat rock ten yards to the right of the picket line. The mountain lion disappeared with the sound.

"What the hell are you doing?" Crawfish yelled, and levered the gun to shoot again. "That big son of a bitch was after your horses and my mule!"

Quietly, Lockhart said, "No, Crawfish. I will take care of this. The panther is here because of me."

Without waiting for Crawfish to respond, Lockhart walked to the empty boulder. Crawfish stood, completely puzzled as his young friend called out in Lakotan.

"My spirit helper, hear me. This is Panther-Strikes. My spirit helper, hear me. This is Panther-Strikes. You have been faithful to me and I will remember you always. Please know I join the *wasicun* and will not need you. It is not their way. Go and help others."

Lockhart went immediately to his black, which was still agitated. The young warrior's soft words and hands slowly quieted the great horse. Crawfish joined him, his face filled with a question. Lockhart didn't wait for it to find words in his friend's mouth.

"Oglala warrior has spirit helper to watch over him on war trail, help him with hunt. Spirit helper come to him in vision. A time when he is shown his path for life."

"Did you have a vision like that?"

"Yes."

"Hogwash 'n' belly beans, that is something! Tell me about it," Crawfish said excitedly, then quickly added, "Please."

Lockhart hesitated and said, "My spirit helper was panther. Panther is strong. Swift. Silent. Think smart in fight. My name, when I with Oglalas, was Panther-Strikes. Now I am Vin Lockhart—and I am a *wasicun* and a prospector!" His smile was wide.

"So you think that catamount was around here, watching over you?"

"It is his duty. But he is also the great cat. I think he was telling me that our horses should be kept closer."

"I see," Crawfish said. "Man, you boys sure do have a lot of things talking to you."

"What?"

"Never mind. Let's move these rascals closer and eat before it burns up," Crawfish said. "I've already spilled half the coffee."

"I see your pants received some."

"Yeah, holy wishwash, I got a little excited when all the commotion broke out."

After moving the animals to the camp side of the trees, they finally sat down to breakfast, but it was mostly blackened and Crawfish cursed his leaving the food on the fire. Lockhart shrugged his shoulders and ate at the corners of a blackened piece of venison while Crawfish made another pot of coffee. Before leaving for the claim, Lockhart returned to the boulder where the panther had been and left a small beaded bag containing the reminder-medicine of his vision and his spirit helper. It had been put away with his other few Oglala things. Beside the bag he placed a mound of crushed cigar tobacco, wrapped in cloth cut from the tail of the shirt he had found, as an offering of thanks.

Returning to camp, Lockhart avoided Crawfish's eyes. He said nothing but was clearly eager to get his mind off the morning. Crawfish honored the unspoken request by foregoing his usual tool-gathering procedure and just grabbed the things needed. They took the horses and mule with them, tying them to tired willows close to the river and letting them graze. Immediately Lockhart began dumping shovel after shovel of river rock and sand into the sluice, like a man fanning a six-gun.

"Whoa! Whoa!" Crawfish shouted, half laughing. "Remember, the river's a lady, treat her gentle. We don't want the gold to sink deeper."

Lockhart stopped in mid-shovel, his eyes glazed—a man elsewhere and fighting to get back. Crawfish broke the spell by lifting a small, flat rock containing a tiny fossil from the dark mud spread on the sluice.

"Look at this, Vin. A fossil."

"Fos-sil?"

"Fascinating, isn't it? To think that a little crab, or whatever this was, lived centuries ago," Crawfish said, running his fingers lightly over the indented silhouette in the light-colored rock. "Sand filled in around this little fellow and, somehow, the whole thing turned to stone. Maybe the pressure of the glaciers made it happen, who knows?"

He handed the stone to Lockhart, but the young warrior looked as if Crawfish had thrown it at his face.

"Stone not sing to white man, does it?" Lockhart asked, his face blank and his eyes cold. He made no attempt to take the flat rock from Crawfish.

Returning it to the ground, Crawfish said quietly, "No, I guess not."

Lockhart pursed his lips and turned his head to allow the words to settle in his mind. "Do white sons hear stones, ride with spirits?"

"No." Crawfish stared at the stone, then at Lockhart, for once empty of words.

"Stone-Dreamer not my father."

"Sounds like he loved you like he was."

"I white man. I not hear stones sing."

Without another word, Lockhart walked toward the river and began shoveling. To make up for their slow start, they worked until nightfall at the river. Crawfish was surprised at the size of the nuggets they were finding deep in the sediment along this stretch of the river. By day's end, Lockhart was smiling again and they had found half a pouch of gold. Back at the camp, Crawfish decided it was time to keep his promise and began teaching the young man how to box. It would also force his friend's mind onto something, instead of the past. Lockhart had never seen anyone fight this way. His friends liked to wrestle, but no warrior ever hit the other with a folded hand.

Crawfish started the training session with an explanation: "I may not look like it now, but back at Yale, I was the best in my weight class at boxing. I think you should know how to box. It's what I would teach my son—if I had one."

"What is 'Yale'?"

"Ah, Yale is a university, a place where men go to learn. To really learn. Only a few get to go there each year."

"Yale. Can I go there? I was chosen for sun dance. High honor."

"I know it is, Vin, but Yale is a long way away from here," Crawfish said, pursed his lips, and went a different direction with his description. "Yale is right here. It is the learning you are doing. When we are finished, you can say you went to Yale."

"I went to Yale. Vin Lockhart went to Yale."

Crawfish chuckled, and Lockhart said it again. Soon both were laughing heartily. Lockhart didn't understand why his friend was so jovial, but he couldn't resist joining in.

"Double your hands into a fist. Yeah, that's it. Now raise them like this," Crawfish said. While the young man watched, Crawfish threw punches into the air and bobbed his head as if to duck an imaginary opponent.

Lockhart asked, "Is this white man ceremony?"

"Well, some might say so," Crawfish replied. "It's a way of fighting. Not with guns or knives—or any other weapon. Just a man against a man."

"Count coup?"

"I suppose so, if you knock your opponent out."

"Vin Lockhart count many coups."

"I know you have. And if you learn this, you will be able to count many more. On men who are bigger than you. And stronger. Now, watch me and do what I do." Crawfish threw a punch into the air and Lockhart did likewise, then another. It was quickly evident that the young man didn't get the significance of the actions.

"Newton, I don't know any other way to do this—do

you?" Crawfish said, turning his face away and frowning. "Yeah, I didn't think so. Well, I'll tell him what I'm going to do." He turned back to Lockhart and said, "Vin, I'm going to hit you with my fist. To show you what I mean. I am not angry with you. This is to teach you about boxing. Understand?"

Lockhart nodded, and Crawfish landed a solid blow to his stomach. The young man bent over, grabbed for the pain, and fought to find air that had left so violently. Crawfish put his arm around him and said, "Breathe easy, now. Easy. I'm sorry. I'm so sorry. I didn't mean to hurt you. I was trying to show you what it means to box."

Finally Lockhart stood up straight, shook his head, and said, "Crawfish show me how to...box. I understand. Do more."

As the last word spat from his mouth, Lockhart swung at Crawfish with a vicious roundhouse blow that the skinny prospector easily ducked, stepping inside of the movement and driving a tight jab to Lockhart's chin. From the ground, Lockhart rubbed his chin and eyed his smaller mentor warily. Bouncing to his feet, Lockhart raised his fists as he had been shown and began to circle Crawfish intently, but staying out of range.

"Do you see how I used your own force to my advantage?" Crawfish asked, amused by the younger man's posturing. "You must swing with your arms in tight. Drive from here, not here. Much more power this way. Quicker, too." He motioned how the blows should be delivered. "Keep your chin down. Push it against your chest. Yeah, like that. That'll make it harder for anyone to hit."

"Hard for Lockhart to keep there."

"You'll get used to it." Crawfish finished his statement with a lightning jolt to Lockhart's stomach, followed by an uppercut toward his chin. This time, however, Lockhart stopped the blow with his left forearm and delivered a powerful jab to Crawfish's nose. The blow stunned him and he staggered backward.

"Good. Excellent," he said, shaking his head to clear it. "I think that's enough for the day. We'd better get at your reading lessons."

"Vin Lockhart would rather box."

"I can see that," Crawfish said. "Find me something to stop this bleeding." He pinched his nostrils to hold back the flow of blood while Lockhart sought a rag.

Chapter Eight

The summer passed swiftly and the river continued to make them rich. Sounds of drilling floated frequently into their ears as their lonely gold camp became an island of isolation within a sea of big-company silver mining. Yet only an occasional mule-drawn wagon was ever seen.

The friendship of the two very different men became strong. Lockhart's grasp of the white man's world expanded while their cache of gold grew. Crawfish broadened Lockhart's studies to include history, geography, manners, law, and even a little about Christianity. Boxing was soon dropped from the educational regimen, because the young warrior quickly became too good with his fists for the prospector to handle. Playing cards, however, was another matter, and Crawfish took great pride in his consistent winning.

Lockhart's skill at hunting kept them nourished with fresh meat, and the prospector seemed equally gifted at finding wild edible roots and plants, even an occasional wild-goose egg, to spice up their meals. Their combined bread supply of sourdough flour and cornmeal was long gone, as were the beans. Lockhart didn't miss the beans. Nor had he adopted his friend's penchant for washing his clothes so often, even though he had only two shirts.

The Moon of Yellow Leaves returned, bringing the flirtation of snow and pangs of emptiness to Lockhart when he realized the significance of the season. It also brought discussion about heading for town, at least for the winter. Both men were becoming eager to leave the lonely station. Lockhart wanted to try out his *wasicun* ways in the white man's big village, and Crawfish wanted to cash in their river wealth and look for a saloon to buy.

Finally, one crisp autumn evening, Crawfish gave Lockhart an assignment to write his thoughts about the mountains. Lockhart balked at first, saying he wasn't ready to do such an important thing, but the prospector insisted. Crawfish left to do his daily washing. Two hours later, Lockhart put down the crinkled sheet of paper and read. The words were his, written with the pen and ink Crawfish had given him months before when he began learning to write:

"A holy man tell me stones sing to the few men who know how to listen. I want to hear but I cannot. Stones do not sing to me. I look up at the mountain and know only it has been singing since the earth was a young child. I see the eagle, the bear, and the sheep. They hear the great song of the mountain and it gives them life. I must learn to hear it sing."

A grin crossed his face and connected with the prospector, who returned it with a lopsided grin of his own.

"Well done, Vin! Well done. That's a lot more than writing—that's poetry, my friend. The Oglalas have beautiful beliefs. Out here, I can understand why they feel as they do. City people can't understand. They just can't,"

Crawfish praised. "Now you can write love letters to a pretty girl."

Crawfish caught himself with the realization that his last words would hurt, hut Lockhart was too thrilled with his just-completed page to relate the compliment to his dead wife. The young warrior hit his lower lip to hold in the excitement welling within him and read the passage again out loud. He could read and write! All thanks to this ruddy-faced man with the wispy heard and the strange ways.

"By golly, let's celebrate with a cigar, Vin. We've got a few left. What do you say?" Crawfish said. "You can read, write, and talk better than most anyone I know. Bless my soul if they won't think you're an honest-to-tootin' easterner when we get to Denver City."

"Thanks to you, Crawfish, my good friend. I get the cigars."

After lighting his cigar, Lockhart once again blew smoke to the four directions, then the sky and the earth and the spotted eagle. Crawfish had watched his young friend perform this ceremony every time they shared a cigar, and repeated it himself now as a way of honoring Lockhart's past life.

"You know, we must have nearly eight thousand dollars scraped out of this pretty little river," Crawfish said between puffs of white smoke that curled toward the open door. "Plus the two thousand I had when you came."

"Yes, and two thousand is mine."

"Right. See, Newton, what did I tell you? He's as quick as a big-city bookkeeper. What? No, you don't even like cigars. Vin knows you are proud of him. You don't have to get sick to prove it. Yes, he has learned fast. Of course he can read a contract. Well, you tell him about the earring. I think it's just fine. Well, you can bring it up when we go to town. Yeah."

Lockhart smiled at the teasing; the earring was his last

link to Stone-Dreamer, and somehow he couldn't bring himself to take it off.

"Say, I almost forgot," Crawfish said, "I saw fresh mountain lion tracks coming back from the river."

"The panther has returned?"

"Looks that way. We'll keep our stock close, maybe he'll stay away from the man-smell," Crawfish said. "Besides, there's plenty of game around. That bunch of bighorn sheep are getting to be regulars around the claim."

Lockhart frowned, and Crawfish realized he had missed the significance of the tracks altogether. The red-faced prospector rubbed his eyes and stretched to rid his body of the autumn chill and tried to focus on his young partner's concern.

"Well, of course, I forgot," Crawfish said, returning the frown. "The panther is your spirit helper. Do you think he's still looking for you?"

"I think maybe so."

Crawfish thought for a moment and said, "I wouldn't be in such a big hurry to send him away. A man never knows when he will need some good luck."

"White men don't believe in spirit helpers. You said so yourself."

"Well, not exactly. But lots of them sure believe in angels, and some pray to saints. That's pretty close, don't you think? White folks don't know everything, Vin. They could learn a lot from your Oglala friends. Maybe we don't have spirit helpers beause we don't believe in them. Maybe it's as simple as that."

Lockhart shook his head and puffed vigorously on his cigar. "I am a white man. I am not a fool. The mountain cat looks for food, not me," he said, waving his arms to signify the mountain range.

Crawfish started to comment, but Lockhart wasn't interested in further discussion. The young warrior went directly to the hut, returned with the Tennyson book of poems, and walked toward the southern opening of their camp. As Crawfish watched, Lockhart began reading "Charge of the Light Brigade" aloud. He shouted the words, and they banged against the mountains and returned in wounded echoes:

> " 'Half a league, half a league, half a league onward, all in the valley of Death rode the six hundred. 'Forward, the Light Brigade! Charge for the guns!' he said; into the valley of Death rode the six hundred.
> 'Forward the Light Brigade! Was there a man…' "

Crawfish smiled, realizing his friend was trying to let the panther know that he had become a white man and no longer needed the spirit helper or believed in its power. After finishing the poem, Lockhart removed the pebble earring and threw it toward the farthest ridge. He turned and began walking back to camp. Then he stopped.

Had he heard a tiny cry when he threw it?

"How foolish to be tied to such nonsense," he muttered. "I am a white man!" His shoulders rose and fell. He sighed and walked back in the direction of his throw. A few minutes later, he found the small stone resting inside a clump of buffalo grass and returned it to his ear. He may not be an Oglala anymore, but it was not right to throw away something Stone-Dreamer had given him. He rationalized to himself that it would be the same as discarding his real father's hat and frock coat, or the wedding-day photograph. The pebble earring was the only thing left that had been his adopted father's. He told himself that believing there was any power within the small stone had nothing whatsoever to do with keeping it.

Crawfish dropped his attention to the graying fire so his friend wouldn't think he had been watching. As he walked toward his mentor, Lockhart asked loudly, “Crawfish, when do you think we’ll go to town?”

“I think we’ll go next week,” Crawfish said, after pursing his lips and swallowing any thoughts of discussing the panther matter further. “Got to. We’re almost out of cigars and coffee. Flour’s gone, so are the beans. Not so you’d care about that!”

Lockhart chuckled and said, “I look forward to going to Denver City. I want to see the horse carriages you keep talking about.”

“Good enough- We’ll take the gold, sell it, and enjoy ourselves for a while. You need to see all of the sights. There are lots of ways to spend gold, my young friend! Clothes. Whiskey. Gambling. Fancy houses. Books, too. We’ve earned it.” Crawfish waved his arms to reinforce his enthusiasm.

“Winter here will be hard. Snow comes fast, I think. Heavy snow.”

“Yeah, I’m too old for that. Too old,” Crawfish said, shaking his head. “Who knows, I might even sell this claim and buy a fine saloon. You know, serve good whiskey. Not that rotgut stuff. Run honest tables. A real handsome place.”

Lockhart stared into the fire, then quickly turned his eyes toward the darkness. Crawfish saw his friend’s warrior discipline in this sudden movement; staring into a fire made a man blind to the darkness if he had to turn and fight. A warrior never really relaxed nor should he. The old prospector smiled and continued on the subject that had been on his mind for some time.

“What should I name my saloon? Gotta be a real good name. Not some number,” Crawfish said, a wide furrow across his red and balding forehead.

“Name of your saloon?”

“Yeah, you know—like the ‘Silver Queen’ or ‘Gold Strike.’ Maybe I should call it ‘Crawfish’s Place.’ Naw, that doesn't sound right. It's got to sound special."

"Are you going to buy a saloon, Crawfish—and not come back here?"

"Don't know. Maybe. I do know we'll have plenty of money to do whatever. Once we check in, though, they'll be swarming all over this area like bees around honey. It'll be easy to sell this claim, that's for sure. But it won't be worth a damn in another year—unless you're into digging mines."

Lockhart watched his friend's face twitch on the left side. He hadn't seen it do that in several weeks. Lockhart still wondered if the white man's God had something to do with it. Crawfish looked sad. The prospector with the beet-red face and the scrawny beard pointed at the mountain and said with melancholy lacing his words, "Yessir, that lady is going to be cut into every which way. She's holding gold and silver in her belly. Lots of it, I'll bet. We've just been taking what she didn't want. We've been polite. The others won't. They won't care."

Lockhart nodded and felt sad too. This lonely camp had become his home, and now he sensed it would be ending and he would be unconnected again. He fought back stray thoughts of Young Evening and living with the Oglalas.

"All right. First things first, though, Vin," Crawfish said with a gusto, breaking into his own reverie as well as Lockhart's. "We need some meat for a few more days. Think you can hit one of those rascally mountain sheep bouncing around above us the last few days?"

"Yes. I'll leave before dawn. We'll have fresh meat for breakfast."

"Betsy-bell-and-locomotion, that sounds good to me," Crawfish responded with excitement.

Realizing that the prospector's colorful phrases didn't mean anything had been another milestone for Lockhart. They always hit him first like he was hearing a strange language. Crawfish didn't curse, however. Lockhart had said "Goddammit!" once when a shovel had slipped out of his hands, and the prospector had advised him that polite people didn't use such a phrase and explained why. An explanation of Christianity had followed. Lockhart hadn't used the curse since. He decided, though, that Crawfish got away with the same idea with some of his colorful expressions. He wondered if the white man's God caught the real meaning of those expressions too. Crawfish had told him the Oglala's *Wakantaka* and the white man's God were the same, hut Lockhart wasn't certain his friend was right about that. Maybe they were just brothers. He had wondered, too, if the "talking-wire trees" he had seen across the prairie were tributes to the Son of God dying on a tree, but Crawfish had assured him they weren't.

Soon Crawfish was snoring loudly and Lockhart was left alone with his piece of writing and the last of his cigar. He reread what he had written, redotting an i for accuracy, and blew out the stubby candle nestled in a flat dish beside him. Carefully he folded the paper, placed it in his shirt pocket, and took his cigar stub outside. A string of cigar butts lay in a straight row, a foot from the hut. Crawfish had insisted they be placed there. He added his to Crawfish's and returned. Sleep didn't come easily as his mind painted all sorts of rich pictures of Denver City.

Early dawn was pulling yellow and orange streaks across the uneven rocks where Vin Lockhart lay with his rifle and a canteen. He had been there for three hours. The morning was chilled and laced with frost. His black frock coat was not any too warm. Sleep had eluded him most of the night, so he finally got dressed and left for his planned hunting position in the dark. Twenty-five yards above him was a sturdy rock shelf where the sheep had been coming recently. From where he lay he could see the mountain in three directions. Their hut below was the size of a small rock.

While he waited, Lockhart pulled the page of writing

from his coat pocket and reread it, then quietly recited lines of Tennyson's "Charge of the Light Brigade" as best he could remember, to pass the time. Crawfish told him few *wasicun* used such phrases in their conversations, but he was still eager to show off what he knew. Denver City! Wouldn't that be something to see! Each day Crawfish had talked more and more about buying a home and buying a saloon or a gambling house. Lockhart was certain the prospector did, indeed, intend to sell his stake.

He sensed movement and soon saw the glistening black horns of a mountain sheep. Now two animals appeared, strutting toward the front of the rock shelf to view the coming dawn for themselves. He raised his rifle to his shoulder, levered it, and aimed.

"Vin! Help! Vi—!" A cry from the camp screeched across the empty morning. It was Crawfish from the camp! Lockhart stood and stared, causing the sheep to bolt. What had happened?

"Crawfish! Are you all right?" he screamed, and the only sound was the echo of his words. Frost smoke from his mouth emphasized their futility. Something terrible must be wrong!

He bounded down the side of the mountain, jumping from boulders to rock clusters to narrow outcropping? of grass. It seemed as if he was twice as far from the camp as he was. Two shots rang out from the camp and he yelled that he was coming. His boot landed on a smooth, round rock and he lost his balance, spinning helplessly to the ground. Pain jolted through him from his ankle to his head. His elbow was scratched and bloody, too, but it was his twisted ankle that was pounding. He stood slowly, trying to regain his breath and his balance. After retrieving his rifle, he put pressure on the injured foot and winced from the responding pain.

But he had no choice and gritted his teeth to shut it out. Every other step down the foothill was a new moment of agony as the twisted ankle reacted to his weight. Finally he sat on his rump and slid down a steep slope, holding his arms away from him to provide balance with his rifle in his right hand. As he reached the riverbank, a shot whistled a yard from his left leg; another whispered death near his ear.

From the far side of the camp, five mounted riders blistered their horses into a gallop. Lockhart kneeled and emptied his rifle at them. The middle shadow straightened and slumped against his horse's neck. The last shadow grabbed for his shoulder. Limping badly, Lockhart hurled himself across the river where it was shallow and up the bank to the hut.

Crawfish lay on the ground, five feet from their graying campMre. He was bloody and beaten. His face was crimson; two bullet holes oozed dark blood from his chest and shoulder. Lockhart's mind ruptured into a seesaw convulsion as the dead body of his friend became that of Young Evening. He yelled, and the sound was that of a wild animal. Turning away from Crawfish, he retched violently before he could do anything else.

A frantic review of the camp told him the story: Bandits had descended upon the lone prospector and tortured him, then shot and left him for dead. His eyes went to the hidden cache of gold and knew the prospector had finally given in. The rocks and sod were thrown aside, leaving an empty hole. The hut was ripped apart and its contents splashed across the camp. From the looks of the scattered magazines, they had also found the claim deed.

His own buffalo robe was thrown close to the campfire. One corner smoldered from the remaining heat in the ashes. He pulled the robe away and stomped it out. Had they been watching them for a long time? Had they waited until he left so they could attack his friend when Crawfish was alone? That thought burned hard in his pounding chest. He knelt beside Crawfish and held the back of the prospector's head with his hand. Blood quickly covered his fingers and ran down his arm. One eye was swollen shut and his eyeglasses were smashed, but Crawfish recognized his young friend and tried to smile.

Crawfish grabbed Lockhart's arm, squeezed it as hard as his fading strength would allow, and whispered, "V-V-Vin, I—I—I couldn't hold out. I—I—I'm s-s-sorry."

"That doesn't matter now. You rest."

"Y-y-yes, it does. You h-h-have to get our gold back. Go after them-m-m..." Lockhart put his ear to Crawfish's mouth. His friend had fainted, but he was still alive!

Quickly, he cleaned Crawfish's face and the bullet wounds with fresh water and a shirt that lay on the ground. Recalling how Stone-Dreamer had treated his wounds, Lockhart ran for moss growing under the trees. He packed chunks of it over the oozing holes in Crawfish's body and wrapped them in place with strips of the same shirt. Then he covered Crawfish with blankets and his buffalo robe.

He was torn between staying with Crawfish and going after the bandits. Crawfish's last wish, before passing out, was for Lockhart to go after them. Should he stay with his friend? If he did, there was little chance of getting their gold or the deed back. From Crawfish's description of the selling process, Lockhart figured the gang would quickly sell the gold and refile the deed at the bank. If he had any chance at all, it was to go now and get the marshal to arrest them. He must go. He must. In town, he could also find a *wasicun* doctor to come and heal his friend. If he got back in time.

Frantically, Lockhart built up the fire so it would provide warmth—and keep away curious animals, at least for a while. He pulled the stone earring from his ear and kneeled beside him. He placed it in his friend's unmoving hand and closed the fist around the small pebble.

With a quivering voice he said, "*Wasicun* God, I do not

know the right way to ask you. I have not met you as I should, but hear me, please!" He paused and began to recite: "God is great, God is good. Him we thank for daily food. By his hand, we are fed. By his love, we are led. Amen."

He stopped, bit his upper lip, and continued in Lakotan, "*Wakantanka unsimala ye*—Great spirit, pity me... hear the unworthy Panther-Strikes. Hear the unworthy Vin Lockhart. In a sacred manner, I send a voice to you."

He choked on the last words, touched his friend's face, and looked up at the gray sky. "Hear me, one of you great spirits. Give Crawfish the strength of the s*icun* in this stone and let him stay in this world. Do not judge him by my thoughts about the *tunkan*, Eyes-of-the-Wind. Do not keep your power from him. If that is not to be, let his spirit walk easy toward the spirit world, give him books and cigars—and let him find Almina. Let not my words offend you, *Wasicun* God. Amen."

He stood, stared down at his own shadow, and added, "Newton, look after your friend while I am gone."

Crawfish's sawed-off shotgun in its quiver-holster lay on the ground beside a turned-over chair. He walked over and slid its sling over his shoulder. He couldn't remember saddling his black mustang, but he was soon galloping toward Denver City. Crawfish and the camp itself were soon out of sight. It was easy to track the running hoofprints in the soft sand adjacent to the winding river. The riders were definitely headed for Denver City as he expected.

One of the bandits' horses had a distinctive swirl in the corner of its front iron shoe. Another horse had a deep crack in its back one. He would know the horses if he saw them again. He was sure the first rider was mounted on a gray horse. His black laid back its ears and tore into the trail, taking on the force of his rider. Horse and man roared as one past armies of machinery, miners, and mills spread across the foothills and up into the lower mountain range. Lockhart's mind flashed from Crawfish's bloody face to Young Evening's to the photograph of his mother and father and back again in a frenzied mental whirl that wouldn't stop.

After a mile he discovered an armed man lying alongside the trail. The man's horse was nowhere in sight. It had to be one of the thieves he had wounded. Lockhart stopped his horse and dismounted. Holding the reins of the eager animal, he kicked the body to make sure the man was dead. The kick was harder than it needed to be, but there was satisfaction in it. Certain the man was dead, he yanked the two pistols from the bandit's holsters and methodically pulled out a fistful of cartridges from the bullet belt loops. He shoved both guns and ammunition into his coat pockets and rode on.

Lockhart rode into the treeless guts of Denver City, almost without seeing the bursting settlement. The wonderful anticipation he had been nurturing was gone with the blackness of his friend's torture and shooting. Crawfish had taught him that white men lived by written laws and in every town there were men selected to administer those laws: a marshal and a judge. His first need would be the marshal. Where would he find such a peace officer? This lawman would certainly want to assist him in bringing these bandits to justice—and see that they did not profit by selling the gold or filing the stolen deed as their own.

He slowed his horse to a walk down what must be the main street of town, losing the tracks he had followed among the blistered marks in the dirt street. He would . find them again, he was certain of that. There was no doubt that the bandits were in Denver City. He would find them with the help of this officer of the law and bring them to justice. Inside, he was already fighting the urge to go after them himself, but he knew Crawfish would want their punishment to come from the white man's law.

His eyes swallowed the sights that he had heard about

in lengthy and colorful descriptions from Crawfish—and discarded them as unimportant now. He stroked the long-legged black's neck to calm the animal as he searched a long row of tents and huts at the edge of town. These temporary structures disappeared into more permanent houses and buildings of wood, stone, and brick as he entered the heart of the settlement. A modest Cherry Creek ran alongside the settlement, usually a model of gentility. When its banks overflowed, though, the whole town usually suffered.

He was oblivious to the rattle of high-walled freighter wagons moving across unyielding ground. The steady ping of a blacksmith's hammering came at him from somewhere down the street. The jingle of carriage bridles. The whistling and snorting of agitated horses. The raw bite of mule skinners cursing the day with the help of strong whiskey. A tin-panny piano brought a strange ringing to his ears.

For the first time in his life, he saw women in dresses of light and bright colors. It had been a year since he had even seen a woman at all, but his eyes burned for something else. Where would he find the marshal in this agitated place? Instead he passed a general supply store, a women's dry goods and clothing store, a gunsmith store, a loan agent's office, a livery, a meat market, an advocate's office, a hotel, and many saloons and gambling places. But nothing so far that indicated he would find a *wasicun* peace officer there.

Keeping his black to the middle of the street, he stared into doorways and windows, glanced at people passing, looked for anything that would guide him to the place of law enforcement he sought. Everything was so different from anything he had ever seen, even from what he had imagined from Crawfish's stories. An unending swirl of shapes, sounds, and color challenged his courage and invited him to turn around and run from this strange place.

He clinched his teeth to drive away the tremor of fear.

Over a windowed office was a sign reading "Clark Gruber & Co.," and there was another sign on top of the building reading "Bank & Mint." That was one of the gold assay offices Crawfish had told him they could take their gold to exchange it for *wasicun* money. He slowed the black to a stop and peered inside. No one was in the dark office or waiting outside. Evidently it was too early in the day. Maybe the bandits had to wait. Somewhere.

Moving on, he passed a two-story building and a woman with heavy makeup and a low-cut dress leaned out of the window to greet him warmly.

He yelled back, "Where is the marshal's office?"

She responded by smiling and pulling away the top of her low-cut blouse to make certain he didn't miss her barely covered breasts.

"Do you know where the marshal is?" he asked again.

She huffed, pointed down the street, and yelled, "Come back and see me."

He waved his thanks and rode on. She seemed very friendly, he thought. Maybe he had judged this village of white men wrongjy. He continued his search for a marshal's office with renewed intensity. Passing the Black Ace Saloon, Lockhart noticed a sweaty gray horse among the horses tied to the hitching rack. He dismounted and went to the sorrel next to the gray. He grasped its left back leg and lifted the hoof. Nothing. He repeated the process with the right back leg. There! The deep crack in the horseshoe he'd seen on the trail.

Easing the leg back in place, he pushed between the sorrel and the wet bay to its right. A swirl in the corner of the bay's front iron shoe told him what he wanted to know. The bandits were in the saloon. No gold was on their saddles, so it was with them. A fist of thought hit his mind. It was *his* gold—as well as Crawfish's. *They* had taken away the future of both of them. They had taken away Crawfish's wonderful saloon—and glorious carriage! They had taken away *his* opportunity to step into the white man's world with a certain authority.

His bloody revenge upon the Shoshonis returned to his mind. He saw again his unstoppable destruction of those who had taken away the most important part of his life. *They* had done it again! Instantly, his body swarmed with hot anger. No! No one was going to take this gold from him without a battle. No one was going to kill his friend without a war. No one was going to laugh at him without first knowing his wrath.

To his far left, on the planked sidewalk, two men exchanged pleasantries. Neither paid attention to the black-coated stranger tying up his horse. One was a small shopkeeper with a long white apron worn over a neatly pressed shirt, a fresh paper collar, and a simple black tie. Thick white hair appeared to have lost a tussle with the wind. The other man was much taller and broader in the shoulders, a handsome gentleman fully aware of his appearance. His three-piece suit was well-tailored and new. His full beard was nicely manicured, and a fine cigar decorated his mouth. Glimpses of a silver-plated Colt in a shoulder holster flashed under his coat as he gestured grandly. The smaller man's part of the conversation consisted mainly of head nodding.

Lockhart sensed the presence of the big man behind him, just exiting the Black Ace saloon. He heard a chuckle from inside, followed by a whispered command to shut up.

Chapter Nine

"Hey, what are you doing messing with our hosses!" growled a huge stranger as he strode confidently toward Lockhart.

The big-bellied man was wearing a pair of belted guns. Faded suspenders struggled to hold up his filthy trousers. A wide-brimmed hat was pushed back enough to reveal where the sun hadn't been in a long time on his forehead. A flushed face, under a thick mustache and heavy eyebrows, was set off by a sprawling nose that had been broken more than once. He was assured of his strength, buoyed by his friends' hearty encouragement and their morning drinking. Proof of their success—three saddlebags filled with pouches of gold—lay under the table as they drank to celebrate their new riches. A folded placer claim was in his pocket.

Without turning around, Lockhart said, "I was looking for the gold you stole from my friend."

Inside he was cold and ready. The huge bandit didn't

hear Lockhart's whispered request to his spirit helper. It was a reflex, even though he had made it quite clear to the panther that he wasn't needed anymore. That thought trailed the request before Lockhart's mind became cold.

"Are you callin' me a thief?" the big man ordered, putting his left hand on Lockhart's shoulder. His scarred-knuckle right fist was cocked.

He expected Lockhart to turn around slowly, intimidated by his sheer presence and wanting to talk away the insult. A thundering smash to the young man's face would initiate a swift, one-sided pummeling. That would put a quick end to this pesky witness who had trailed them from the gold camp they had discovered. The bandit gang had seen him ride in, watching from the saloon. Their objective was to kill him or leave him badly maimed in what looked like a private fight. A claim the young man had tried to rob the big man would be vigorously supported by the rest of the gang.

They didn't fear the marshal, but they didn't want this prospector running around town, making accusations, when they went to change the placer deed and cash in the gold. Only this black-coated stranger didn't look like a prospector. Even the huge man admitted that to himself just before he left the saloon. He looked like one of them. No matter, the black-coated stranger would die or be crippled for life. Four other men had met a similar fate from the huge man's fists and bear hugs: Two were dead; one was paralyzed; the other was in a Kansas hospital and might never leave there.

As Lockhart turned, the heavily muscled bandit launched his sucker punch. But Lockhart's counterattack was so swift that the two townsmen watching couldn't decide later if he threw one, two, or even three punches. Lockhart deflected the incoming blow with his left arm, ducked under the kareening off-target swing, and delivered a searing jab to the man's ample belly.

Air screamed from the huge man's mouth and the bandit doubled over to keep the sudden agony from destroying him. Lockhart stepped closer and viciously drove his knee into the big man's groin. Nauseating pain froze the outlaw's entire body. Lockhart drew the pistol from his belt at the same time and jabbed its barrel into the man's half-open mouth. The entire reaction was a blur. The big man's eyes widened as the cock of the hammer registered over the agony consuming him.

Lockhart looked into his pained face and said quietly, "You have one thin chance to live. Show me where the gold is you stole from Crawfish—and the deed. Take me there right now. You will walk in front of me. If your friends do something I don't like, you die before anything else happens."

The taller man cocked his head at hearing "Crawfish" and glanced at his shorter associate. Both men had stopped talking and now watched with fearful curiosity. Neither wanted to resume their conversation, or end it and leave. The taller man was observing Lockhart intently, as if trying to decide whether he knew him or not. The black-coated stranger's manner of speech was not that of a ruffian, more like a college professor's.

Swallowing hard to alleviate the remaining pain and holding himself with both hands, the huge man nodded his agreement and Lockhart pulled the pistol barrel from his slobbering mouth. As he did, the thief swung a thunderous haymaker, lunging toward Lockhart from his bent-over position. Lockhart sidestepped the blow and cracked his gun barrel alongside the man's head. The big man crumpled to the ground with his fists locked in place for fighting.

"Look out!" screamed the small shopkeeper as he dove to the sidewalk. The warning came out of his mouth before he had even thought about it.

His well-dressed companion hesitated before flattening

himself against the planks next to his quicker friend. In the alley, to their immediate right, was a slump-shouldered shadow with slitted red eyes. The rifle in this second bandit's hands bellowed and clipped the top of Lockhart's shoulder as he swung to face the warning. Lockhart's hand flinched in sharp reaction to the blow and his pistol clanked against the sidewalk. The gunman anxiously tried to cock the rifle again, his bloodshot eyes jumping from the lever mechanism to Lockhart and back again.

Forgetting the sting of the rifle bullet and the wetness spreading along his shoulder, Lockhart shoved both hands into his coat pockets, grabbed and cocked the revolvers resting there, and fired both through his coat. The two guns roared twice, smashing lead into the man's face and neck and ripping holes of smoke in his long coat. A gurgle followed a half-cry and the second thief fell to the sidewalk, curled up like a baby. He whimpered and was still.

"Hey, there's a gunfight at the Black Ace!" rang out the announcement from down the street. Somewhere a woman screamed and people were running. Lying prone and tense on the sidewalk, the well-dressed gentleman rolled his shoulder forward to make certain his shoulder-holstered Colt wasn't visible. He didn't want Lockhart to see it and mistake him for an enemy. He seemed uncertain about what to do next and mouthed "Should we get out of here?" to the white-haired shopkeeper. The smaller man cautioned against any sudden movement. His eyes stayed on Lockhart; his small fists tightened like he was rooting for him.

Two tendrils of smoke wandered upward from Lockhart's frock coat as he pulled the pistols from their pockets. Behind him came a soft shuffle, and he spun to meet it. Coming around the other side of the saloon building were two armed men, the remaining gang members. His movement surprised them. They had expected him to be looking the other way. Their plan was to catch Lockhart in a cross fire if their big friend didn't stop him. It would be easy to claim he had tried to steal their gold. No one would care about a stranger dying. But their shots were hurried, too hurried, the result of confident men who expected others to handle the situation and suddenly realized their plan wasn't working.

Lockhart fired once before diving off the raised sidewalk and toward the line of tied horses. Two shots followed him. The first missed, but the second clipped the arm of the prone shopkeeper and he yelped. The taller man next to him looked like he was going to cry. Lockhart landed between his black horse and a frightened bay and was momentarily lost among a flurry of legs and hooves.

Three slugs blistered the dirt street between the sidewalk and the reining pole. A fourth burned the flank of the bay and the horse whinnied in pain and reared, snapping its reins. The crazed animal ran down the street, stirrups flopping like insufficient wings. The other agitated horses pulled at their leather restraints. All but the sweating gray and Lockhart's black separated themselves from the rack and galloped away.

A fifth shot burned Lockhart's hip as he crawled from the horses toward the street. From behind the marginal safety of the two horses, Lockhart twisted his body into position and fired back. The remaining bandits were mere dark shapes with orange flame spitting at him. Inside the saloon, men were huddled beneath tables or lay flat on the floor, hoping to avoid stray bullets. On the street, everything had become an oil painting of people frozen behind any convenient shelter to await the end of the unexplained violence disturbing their daily activity.

Without looking back at his tall friend, the little storekeeper crawled around the edge of the saloon building and disappeared down the alley, holding his bloody arm. His taller companion attempted the same movement but couldn't find the courage to move at all. His suit pants were soiled at his groin. A drunken miner wandered out of the' saloon and stood with a drink in his hands, like he was watching a show, oblivious of the actual danger. Sounds of someone praying, mixed with a few frightened gasps, rushed to fill the void of sound between shots.

Both bandits had ducked behind the other side of the building and were taking turns firing. Lockhart worked his way around the gray horse and back toward the raised sidewalk. Reaching the sidewalk, he crouched below it, snapped several shots at the hidden gunmen's position, and placed one pistol on the planked platform. He yanked loose his black mustang's reins with his free hand and flipped them toward the animal. Without looking, he fired again toward the bandits. A quick wave of his hand further encouraged the mustang to get away from the shooting. Only the gray horse remained, and it was rearing and kicking in a frantic desire to be somewhere else. Lockhart decided against trying to let it loose. That would take too much concentration—and time he couldn't spare.

A bullet spit a chunk of wood from the edge of the raised plank sidewalk, thudding inches from his taut face, and he ducked instinctively. But he had seen enough to know what he would do next. Each time one of the remaining bandits fired from behind the side of the building, he had to expose a part of his face and left shoulder. Lockhart yanked free the sawed-off shotgun from its shoulder quiver and pulled back the twin hammers. When a partial silhouette appeared again, he drove both loads of buckshot into the man's uncovered face and left side. A pistol sailed eerily into the haze.

Wildly, the wounded man pulled a second gun from his belt. Movement was slow and awkward. His shirt was half crimson, his face washed in blood. He stumbled to his left, strangely seeking safety in the middle of the open street. He fired once, the bullet flying two feet above Lockhart.

Hiding behind the building, the remaining partner yelled for his friend to return.

Lockhart dropped the shotgun, regrabbed his second pistol, and both guns thundered. The wounded bandit jerked strangely. Two black holes appeared over his left shirt pocket, about an inch apart. He tried to level his wobbling gun, but his shot drove a hole into the street at his feet. Finishing shots from Lockhart's pistols tore into the bandit's temple. He spun backward with the impact, firing another shot into the morning air. His body thudded against the ground's hardness and bounced like a dropped apple.

Without waiting, Lockhart hurdled onto the sidewalk, firing with both pistols, and rushed toward the alley where the remaining bandit was hiding. Lockhart's shots blistered the wood. Unseen by Lockhart, the last of the gang screamed out, "Don't shoot. Don't shoot. I surrender. The gold's right here. P-p-please...don't shoot-t-t. P-p-please."

"Come out—and give me a reason to kill you. Any reason," Lockhart barked. "You killed my friend."

The young warrior stood with both guns aimed at the corner of the building but couldn't remember how many shots he had fired. His guess was that the guns were empty. Without showing himself, the bandit tossed a pistol and a shotgun onto the sidewalk and yelled again, "I'm coming out—with my hands up. H-h-honest! Please don't shoot. I didn't kill your friend. It was Milton. In the street there. I-i-it wasn't me, I swear!"

Lockhart again tried to rethink the number of shots he had taken, hoping to come up with at least one bullet left. He was pretty sure there was none. But if he tried to reload, the bandit would take advantage and run or go for one of the downed weapons. Without hesitation, Lockhart ordered, "Come on out. If you do it right, I won't shoot."

"P-p-please! I'm bringing the gold. In both hands.

Please, don't shoot. I'm unarmed. I swear."

From around the corner, the petrified bandit slowly walked, holding two sets of heavy saddlebags. From under a high-crown hat, his hooded eyes would not meet Lockhart's glare. His chubby body was shaking under a long, dirt-streaked duster. The shoulder of his coat was painted with dried blood from being hit by Lockhart at the camp. He had a pudgy face, more like that of a child, but framed with unshaved stubble. His bullet belt carried two rows of ammunition—one for a pistol, the other for a rifle. Lockhart could see a sheathed knife hanging from the belt and an empty holster. The man's knees were muddy from kneeling in the alley. His thick fingers grasped the saddlebags as if letting them go would send him into eternity.

"Lay the gold down. Right in front of you. Keep your hands up and away from your coat. That's it. Now, take out that knife—and your other gun. Lay both beside the gold," Lockhart barked.

"I—I—I'm d-d-doin' it. This wasn't my idea, mister. Honest, it wasn't. I—I—I don't have another g-g-gun. R-r-really. See?" He dropped the knife, held up his coat, and slowly turned around so Lockhart could see his back clearly.

"Where is the deed?"

"Ah, I—I—I don't have it. I—I—I think Branson has it. Over there." The thief pointed at the downed fat man.

The acrid smell of gunsmoke, sweat, and fear lay about the tightened sidewalk, which seemed like a world unto itself. Townspeople were still crouched behind every possible hiding place, not yet believing the gunfight was over. Three men hurried out of the saloon and away, taking advantage of the silence. Standing against the wall, the drunken miner began to clap his hands. From behind him, Lockhart heard a commotion and turned to meet it. Marshal Eli Benson and two deputies were coming across the street, holding rifles.

Marshal Benson, a flat-faced man with a pale complexion, a shaggy mustache, and thick eyebrows, smiled triumphantly and said, "Hold it right there, gunslick. You're under arrest for the murder of these men."

Wisps of spidery smoke wandered away from the barrels of Lockhart's pistols, innocently drawing attention to them and where they were pointed—one at the surrendering bandit and the other at the marshal's chest.

"I am Vin Lockhart. I am a prospector. I come to get back the gold stolen from my friend, Desmond Crawford, and me—by these men. They beat and shot him. They gave no chance to my friend. They wanted me to have no chance. No, you will not arrest me, Marshal. I am not guilty of breaking any *wasicun*...any laws."

Lockhart's growling announcement carried the angry snarl of a cougar, His fiery eyes locked onto Benson's face and wouldn't let it go. For a moment, the bandit thought about taking advantage of this distraction and running. But he had seen the black-coated stranger stop his friends when they had all the advantage and knew he didn't have the nerve. Instead of fleeing, his hands went higher.

A murmur of support slithered through the gathering crowd and reached fulfillment in the fiery testimony of a cowboy in woolly chaps and a dirty linen duster. His right cheek bulged from a huge tobacco chaw.

"By God, those bastards had it coming!" the cowboy bellowed, and spat a long stream of brown for emphasis. "One ag'in four ain't murder, law dog, that's self-deefense. Never seed a better job o' it, neither. Like the feller said, you ain't got nuthin' to arrest 'im fer." Hands on his hips, he spat again, proud of the thickness of the spitum.

Marshal Eli Benson spun to frown at the response but caught the nodding heads and agreeing responses. He tried to look confident, but Lockhart's words—and the crowd's sympathetic reaction—assaulted his composure. He hadn't expected this stranger to do anything except drop his weapons. He hadn't expected the crowd to support an obvious pistol-fighter. The black-coated stranger before him was working for somebody, maybe somebody important. Nobody goes up against four men and wins—unless he's good and getting paid well.

Who was he working for? Didn't the man realize his deputies would kill him if he shot at the marshal? Was he crazy—or just certain his own boss would get him out of jail? How badly was he wounded? Would he dare shoot a lawman in front of witnesses? Questions shot through Benson's mind faster than a fanned revolver.

"There was no murder committed here, Marshal Benson, only the exceptional defense of one man against many adversaries."

The confident statement came from the tall gentleman who had been talking with the little shopkeeper earlier. He stepped forward from the front edge of the crowd jamming around the sidewalk. His suit coat was off, carefully folded over his bent right arm and positioned in front of himself to hide the stain at his groin.

"Mr. Woodson? You saw this fight?" Benson's voice was immediately lit with surprise and pleasure.

Now he knew who this pistol-fighter was working for. It made sense. Ortho Woodson was one of the wealthiest men in town the owner of the O. A. Woodson Mining Company—and one of the more ruthless businessmen when it came to getting what he wanted.

"Yes, I did, Marshal. This man clearly did not start this trouble. Self-defense. Others will testify to the same conclusion, I'm sure."

"No need for that, Mr. Woodson, sir. Your word is good enough for me," Benson proclaimed quickly, trying to hide a smile that wanted to jump across his face. He motioned for his deputies to follow him back to their office, but the businessman wasn't finished.

"I suggest you and your deputies arrest this man for

attempted murder—and robbery—and any of the others that are still breathing. Move the bodies so we can go about our business."

Watching Woodson was the drunken miner leaning against the wall of the saloon. He burped, apologized to himself, and wobbled forward, deciding to add his testimony. The sidewalk proved to be an unsteady platform, so he retreated to the wall and kept his right arm against it. He burped again, grinned, and said nothing. Lockhart took advantage of the new situation to shove the pistol in his left hand back into his coat pocket and begin reloading the gun in his right hand.

After the first cartridge was in place, he looked up at the curious Marshal Benson and said, "Yes, my guns were empty. Of course, you would have protected me, wouldn't you, Marshal?"

Benson licked his mouth, pursed his lips, and said lamely, "Perhaps another time."

Lockhart placed the loaded gun in his other pocket and walked to the filled saddlebags on the sidewalk. He stood next to them, watching as one deputy led the last bandit away with the prodding of his rifle barrel. Lifting both heavy sets of saddlebags, strained with pouches of gold, Lockhart put both over his left shoulder and moved to the prone fat thief who had attacked him first. The huge man was moaning and only barely conscious. Shoving him over on his back with his boot, Lockhart immediately saw the folded claim deed deep in his shirt pocket. The fat man tried to raise his head, muttered something unintelligible, and fainted. Lockhart withdrew the paper and sensed someone stepping close to him. Raising up, Lockhart was face-to-face with Mr. Woodson.

"Good morning, Mr. Lockhart. Let me introduce myself. I am Ortho Woodson. I own the O. A. Woodson Silver Mining Company."

"Thank you, Ortho Woodson, for speaking for me. Do

I need to do anything more—about this? I am not certain of the way of the laws."

"No, no, it was self-defense—and that's that. Think nothing of my help. Riffraff like that needed removing. Probably the ones that have been attacking my wagons."

"My friend needs a doctor. I must go back fast. Where is a doctor?"

Woodson ignored the request and said, "Let me buy you a drink and let's talk. I could use a man like you. Make it worth your while."

Lockhart didn't respond to the offer, which only served to trigger more interest in Woodson. The tall businessman smiled and patted Lockhart's saddlebags.

"I can make this look like chicken feed," Woodson continued, patting the saddlebags and straightening his shoulders. "A man as good as you are with a gun could be very helpful to me—and my company."

"Thank you, Ortho Woodson," Lockhart responded. He hadn't broken the habit of saying a person's complete name when addressing them. "Right now I need a doctor for my friend. We can talk later, if you like. Where would I find a doctor?"

"Looks to me like you could use one yourself, Mr. Lockhart. You've lost a lot of blood. Doc Tragger's drugstore is right aross the street. See the sign? Well, wait a minute, he might not be in yet. I hear he had a late poker game last night."

"Thank you, Ortho Woodson," Lockhart said, and headed into the street without further conversation.

"After you get through doctoring, Lockhart, let's have that drink. I'll take real good care of you," Woodson said to the hurrying Lockhart. Woodson watched him for an instant, then turned around and headed for an attractive woman standing near the far alley.

Before reaching the far side of the street, Lockhart saw his black horse standing quietly beside some tied-up horses. The hitching rack was outside another saloon ten stores away from the drugstore. Lockhart shook his head to clear away the fogginess seeping from loss of blood and the drain of battle emotion. He had forgotten all about his own horse! How stupid, he thought. How did he expect to get back to Crawfish? He walked over to the animal, talking quietly. The horse whinnied a welcome, and Lockhart rubbed its nose as he took the leather. Quickly, he checked it over to make certain the mustang hadn't been hurt. Satisfied, he looped the reins around the tie rack and went back to a small storefront with a large sign above it reading "Drug Store."

Pushing his face against the window, he tried to see inside. No one appeared to be there, but the door was unlocked so he entered. Stepping inside and easing the door into place without a sound, Lockhart stood and gaped. A curious sunbeam entered as Lockhart did. It danced across the shadowy shelves lined with bottles, containers, and cans. It was a weird new world for him, filled with a mixture of odd aromas, muted colors, and strangely shaped containers. It surely was the kind of mysterious, moody place where a *wasicun wicasa wakan*, a white healer, would stay, he thought.

The small space was cramped with rows of patent medicines, pressed soaps, apothecary containers, cod liver oil bottles, and herbal concoctions. One side of the store featured glass showcases for jewelry and perfume and eyeglasses. In another corner were displays of cigars, tobacco sacks and tobacco plugs, men's hats, racks of bolted cloth, cooking pots, and men's and women's shoes. A pill press, a stone mortar and pestle, and a balance scale sitting on the main counter caught his momentary attention. Near it was an open wooden box filled with knives, saws, scalpels, pinchers, pins, and screws.

A human skull grinned at him from a top shelf, next to a large sealed jar filled with yellowish liquid and something that looked like a heart floating in it. A Bible lay next to the two gruesome displays. Inches away was a large piece of rose quartz, almost luminescent even in the gray room. "Aiiee," Lockhart muttered. This was a place Stone-Dreamer would like, he decided. He examined the assortment of patented medicines and pressed soaps, reading them aloud as best he could: " 'Dr. John Bull's Worm Destroyer,' 'Hamlin's Wizard Oil,' 'Ayer's Cathartic Pills,' 'Hostetter's Stomach Bitters,' 'Quinine Sulfer,' 'Cuticura Antipain Plasters,' 'Dr. Kilmer's Female Remedy,' 'Balm of Childhood,' 'Procter & Gamble Polo Soap'..."

A lanky man with a high pompadour—created by an ample dose of cinnamon oil—and a thin goatee stepped into the store through a back-room door. His buttoned gray vest didn't match navy trousers. He studied Lockhart and said, "Looks like you were a part of that gunfight across the street." He paused and added, "Looks like you won."

"I need a doctor to come with me. My friend is hurt bad. He is shot two times. Are you a doctor?"

"Yeah, I'm Dr. Tragger. So he was in that fight too, eh? Looks like you could use some patching yourself."

"No, my friend is sleeping in our camp less than... one meal ride from here."

"I see. Well, son, I do all of my surgery in this room back here. Take out bullets. Amputation. Whatever. You'll have to bring your friend in. I got no one to tend the store right now. The missus is down with, well, you know, female trouble."

Lockhart frowned. He was light-headed and struggled to find the right words. The *wasicun* medicine man probably needed coaxing. Sometimes Stone-Dreamer did.

"Crawfish cannot ride. He is shot. He is very weak. I pray he is still alive. I will pay in gold. I have already cleaned his wounds, put on moss and—"

"You did what?"

Lockhart was surprised at the reaction and explained again what he had done as Dr. Tragger walked briskly toward the far shelf.

"Oh, my God, man! You can't put crap like that on a wound. What were you thinking of?" Tragger exclaimed, and reached for an amber glass bottle. "Here, you need to buy this. It'll make him feel better until you can get him in here."

He handed Lockhart the container and went back for something else, totally involved in the process, and said, "And he'll need this. Hamlin's Blood Pills. Cures twenty-five diseases. At least. Worth every penny."

Lockhart didn't like this man. Even if this was some part of a *wasicun* healing ceremony, he was too exhausted to hide his disgust.

"No." Lockhart's declaration was a bullet to Tragger's back.

Without turning around, Dr. Tragger stopped with the tin container in his hand. He heard the bottle slam down on the counter.

"No need for this. A great holy man showed me the way to heal. You are wrong. You not know much, I think."

Tragger spun and blurted, "What? Sounds like some stupid redskin's idea of medicine to me. This is patented stuff, man. Sold all over the United States. Good Lord, I'll have you know I amputated over five hundred arms and legs during the War. I have a citation from General McClellan!"

But Lockhart was on the way out the door. The slamming cut off Tragger's last plea to at least buy a bottle of Hamlin's Wizard Oil. Outside, Lockhart muttered that he would care for Crawfish himself. He would call upon *Wakantanka*—and the *wasicun* God to help him. Both would get it done. He was unaware of the people watching him as he rode out of town.

Chapter Ten

On a bright spring day over three years later, Vin Lockhart paused to light a long cigar, bringing a snapped match to his chiseled face and cupping the flame with both hands. The action gave him the opportunity to view busy Larimer Street without appearing to do so. An old habit of someone used to trouble. Under his tailored broadcloth suitcoat, an ivory-handled, short-barreled Smith & Wesson in a shoulder holster gave him a comfort only a man of the gun understood.

Denver City, with all its rich and raw, glorious and gutty ways, filled his senses. The town was swaggering with people, mostly men, on their way to buy and sell. News on the street was that the Union Pacific was finally coming. For him the big news was that he—and Crawfish—had just completed the purchase of the Black Horse Hotel. It was their fourth enterprise since the eccentric prospector recovered from his wounds and sold the placer claim. The first was the purchase of the Silver Queen saloon and gambling house; the second was the purchase of speculative land to the south. Both ventures had done well. Last week they had also purchased two buildings on main street for a third of their value; the seller had serious debt problems.

Lockhart's eyes drifted easily to the surrounding buildings of flatboard and stone flirting with nearby multigabled mansions. At the town's edges, the last vestiges of an earlier boomtown settlement remained in the form of dirty tents, rude huts, and hewed-pine logged cabins. In many ways, the town's evolvement matched his own: from savage Oglala warrior to scrappy prospector to polished businessman. Crawfish's teaching had taken him a long way, and he had repaid it amply by saving his friend's life and his gold—and helping him turn it into more.

A well-dressed rider astride a barrel-chested gray horse trotted past him, and his mind followed with the image of his former Oglala brother-in-law, Touches-Horses, and his special way with horses. It would have been an animal worthy of his attention, he thought. Then he realized that no memory of his Oglala days had reached him in a long time. Behind him a sudden movement caught his preoccupied mind, and Lockhart spun to meet it. His right hand flashed toward the shoulder holster as a small ball bounced against his well-polished boot. Chuckling at his overreaction, he squatted to retrieve it.

"Thanks, mister," a blond boy hollered, took the ball from Lockhart, and ran back to his two friends in the alley behind him. Lockhart shook his head and muttered to himself, "You're a jumpy man, Vin Lockhart."

Time had gone fast since he had tended to Crawfish until he was strong enough to ride into town, and then only barely ahead of a bad snowstorm. They had come laden with bags of gold and their gear packed on two horses and a mule. It had been nearly six years since he lived with the Oglala Sioux and was honored with three split and marked eagle coup feathers. More than five since his beautiful Young Evening had been taken from him so savagely, driving him into a black depression. Finally he had managed to seal off all memories of the Oglalas, even his days with Young Evening. Discarding all of his Oglala things had been the final step in separating himself from his past. He had even buried the "Panther" pebble earring at their abandoned gold camp. Cutting his long brown hair followed. To white men, it only meant he was trying to look civilized. To his Oglala friends, it was the destruction of something holy, reserved only to show great mourning.

A thin whisper of white smoke curled around his dark gray hat with the flat beaver brim, edged in matching silk, and danced away into the midday air as he contemplated what had just passed through his mind. Why was he reminded of those bittersweet days right now? He had found a new life in this prosperous, silver-mad settlement, become successful and respected.

"Are you all right, mister?"

Lockhart realized the boys had stopped their playing to watch him. The blond boy had retraced his steps and was standing ten feet away, concerned but wary. Lockhart shook away the wisps of those haunting memories and saw the worried young face staring at him.

"Why, why, that's mighty nice of you, son. Yes, I'm just fine. I was thinking about—the days when I used to play ball like you're doing."

"Would ya like to join us? We could use another player. Billy has to do some chorsin' for his paw. You know, his paw owns that store over there." The boy's face was bright with enthusiasm and pride.

Lockhart couldn't hold back a wide grin. Here he was, first swaggering in self-pride about his hotel purchase and then wallowing in self-pity—and the boy was offering him the highest honor he could bestow, being invited to join them in the game.

"That's mighty nice of you, lad. What's your name?"

"Abraham…Abraham Kincaid, sir."

"Well, Abraham Kincaid, I wish I could—but I've got some chores I've got to do myself."

The boy looked genuinely disappointed. Lockhart reached into his pocket, retrieved a coin, and held it toward the boy. "Tell you what, you know those sticks of candy—in that big jar—at Bacon's General Store?"

"I sure do!"

"Well, you and your friends take this and get one each—on me."

"Gee, thanks, mister." The boy grabbed the money and spun back toward his friends, then stopped and looked back. "Oh…I didn't ask your name, sir."

Lockhart smiled. "I'm Vin Lockhart."

"Thanks, Vin—Mister Lockhart!"

"Thank you, Abraham—," Lockhart caught himself before he said the boy's last name. He had finally broken the habit of repeating a person's complete name.

The boy's eyes caught a glimpse of the ivory handle. He frowned as if trying to decide something and finally said, "My paw don't carry a gun. He says they're bad and only bad men carry them. Is that true?"

"Well, Abraham, I'm sure your father knows what he's talking about. You listen to him."

"But you're not a bad man, are you?"

"My business sometimes puts me where there are bad men."

"Oh." The answer seemed to satisfy the boy, but only momentarily. "Have you ever killed anybody?"

"That's a mighty personal question, Abraham. I don't go around shooting people."

Abraham thought for a moment, nodded his head in agreement. Before he could rejoin his friends, Lockhart said, "Now, let me ask you a question, Abraham. How come you fellas aren't in school?"

Instantly a grin cut the boy's face in two, and he said, "Miss Henderson done got sick today, so they called it off."

It was Lockhart's turn to nod in agreement. He watched the boy run to his friends and exuberantly tell of their newfound wealth. They ran together down the street, waving back at him. Lockhart waved and smiled. This was a day to share his happiness, he thought. It had to be one of the happiest moments of his life. He had just left their hotel's general office, where they had finalized the purchase. Crawfish was inside reviewing renovation plans.

Satisfied that his Indian village memory was nothing more than his mind beginning to relax after hard negotiations, he took another puff, letting the second string of smoke chase the first. He would join Crawfish later and talk with the current hotel manager; they had decided to retain C. W. Damian in his position. Lockhart liked Damian's friendly manner with the hotel's customers and wanted to hear his thinking about their plans.

Lockhart himself was excited about it; they had been studying the Black Horse Hotel for three months without anyone knowing. He liked the rows of dormer windows along the front and the overhanging balcony inside. He envisioned an elegant place with grand furnishings, custom rugs, and a central stained glass window, like those he had read about in a magazine. Crawfish was keen about building an adjoining high-class gambling casino if they could buy the retail shop next door.

"Good day to you, Mister Lockhart."

Lockhart recognized the voice before he registered the greeter's wrinkled face. "Well, how are you, Judge McKinsey? Is the day to your liking?"

"Ah, yes, a fine day. A fine day for our great city."

Judge McKinsey's breath sparkled with liquor already. Lockhart held a poker marker from the judge, but he and Crawfish had decided to let it go. They might need a favor someday.

"Say, Vin, I almost forgot. I need to gp by your place, got a small debt to settle, you know," Judge McKinsey said, his expression attempting to be one of casual concern.

"Well, that's nice of you to remind me, Judge. Let's just call us even. Having you as a friend is payment enough. In fact, the next time you're in the Silver Queen, the first round is on me. I'll tell the bartender first thing when I get there."

"Mighty generous of you, Vin. I appreciate it. I surely do."

Judge McKinsey strutted past, happy with the encounter, and Lockhart walked on in the other direction. After a few steps, Lockhart paused again and pulled a heavy gold watch, dangling from a chain, from his vest pocket. Snapping open the lid, he checked the time. If he was lucky, Mattie Bacon would be able to break away from her work at Bacon's General Store long enough to walk with him awhile, before he went to the Silver Queen as he had promised Crawfish. That idea severed any lingering concern over the sudden recall of his life with the Oglalas. He had been working too hard, he told himself, and not getting enough sleep.

Maybe she would join him for dinner and the theater tonight to celebrate the new purchase. Mattie's father wouldn't like the idea, but he wasn't keen about Lockhart being around his daughter anyway. There was nothing Lockhart could do about it but let time soften the situation.

A Concord stagecoach rumbled past him and he waved at Old Ernie, handling the four-horse team.

"Hello, Ernie, how's it going!" Lockhart shouted.

The tobacco-chewing driver spat a brown string of tobacco juice that curved when it hit the wind. He eyed the spit warily, making sure its direction was toward the wheels, before waving brusquely.

"Hellfire, Mr. Lockhart, it's all hoss crap 'n' miners! Ain't that the devil?"

Lockhart grinned and shouted, "Come in for a drink when you get back. I'm buying."

Ernie waved his appreciation and snapped the reins. His stagecoach was followed by a second coach, but Lockhart didn't recognize the driver. Both coaches were filled with hungover miners headed back to the big silver mines in nearby Oro City. Six heavily armed outriders accompanied the coaches; they would be carrying silver ore on the return trip.

An Irish miner hollered at Lockhart, "Hey, Mr. Lockhart, me darlin,' comin' back I'll be—when I gots some pay. Keep the sweet cards warm fer mese'f."

"I will keep some good Irish whiskey handy too! The first round's on me!"

A loud hurrah from the crowded miners followed the rattling stagecoaches down the street. Lockhart walked on. He enjoyed giving favors like that to ordinary men. It surprised him when the realization crossed his mind that an Oglala warrior was measured by his generosity. He laughed off the remembrance. The sun felt good on his shoulders. Casual conversation, creaking saddles, whinnying horses, and cursing freighters came at him like a strange, but reassuring, orchestration. Glistening carriages contrasted with heavy wagons loaded with commerce and solitary horsemen headed for the surrounding prairie or into the breathtaking mountains for another glimpse at glory.

"Good day to you, Mrs. Bradley," he said, touching his hand to his hat as he passed the smiling matron on the planked sidewalk.

The older woman touched her upbraided hair in response to the attention and shifted her body into bolder motion as she strolled past, wanting desperately to glance back to see if he was noticing. Her curiosity wouldn't let go, and eventually she turned to see the striking businessman stopped at the doorway to Bacon's General Store. Hitching her shoulders to recover from the imagined slight, she went on, muttering to herself.

Self-consciously, Lockhart glanced down at his dark suit, brushed away an invisible piece of dust, tossed away the cigar, and removed his hat before entering Bacon's. He saw her instantly. Mattie Bacon was rearranging a table of folded cloth of different shapes and colors. Her back was to him and the doorway. By the looks of her movement, she was daydreaming more than working. Her full name was Mattilda Anne, but even her father called her Mattie.

"I'm interested in a bolt of red cloth for a fair lady," Lockhart boomed, his tanned face breaking into a wide smile.

Mattie Bacon turned to the sound, her dress chasing the motion. Her eyes caressed his. Coyly, she asked, "Who would that be?"

"Oh, I don't think you would know her."

He stepped closer to her, ignoring the man and woman who walked past him on the way out of the store. Mattie was warm-faced with sparkling blue eyes that always gave away her emotions. Her smile was soft music. Cinnamon hair was rolled into a fashionable bun and her firm figure was advanced by a simple gray dress, accented with a white collar and cuffs.

"She's quite lovely, likes violets—ah, spring rains—and a bay horse with—"

"Does she like music?" Mattie interrupted.

"Oh, yes. She has a fine singing voice, too. I've heard her sing in church."

Mattie started to spring toward him and hug the confident man in the doorway, but her sense of decorum stopped the action before it was more than a stutter step.

"When's the last time you were in church, Vin Lockhart?" she teased.

"Oh, let's see," he mused with an exaggerated rubbing of his chin, "probably, well, the last time you sang—a solo."

"That was last spring."

"Oh, was it, now? I can see it like it was yesterday."

"But I forgive you for not going more often. And don't give me that line about preferring to be alone in the mountains instead. That sounds like a good excuse to go fishing tome."

"I see, well, do you forgive me enough to take a short walk and see the day?" he said, tilting his head as he asked. "I have some good news to share."

His dark hair was still full, covering his ears; his face was lean, with high cheekbones and a nose that hinted of being broken once. He was medium-sized, and the strength of his arms and chest was hidden by the tailored clothes. His face was angular, cut from tanned stone. His smile matched the devilishness in his blue eyes. Four women customers turned toward him with appreciative smiles and hopeful eyes, but he was watching only Mattie Bacon. She glanced around at the customers spread throughout the store, and then her eyes sought her father. He was tending to a fourth customer, who was paying for her purchases.

"I'll be out for a minute, Dad," she said without pausing for approval.

The balding Albert Bacon looked up, saw Lockhart, grinned with half of his thin mouth, and returned to his task. His forehead expressed the worry that his mouth didn't. Lockhart wasn't the right choice for his daughter.

Oh, there was certainly nothing wrong with owning a

saloon, especially not a fine one like the Silver Queen. And there was little doubt that he was a young man of means, and according to some, a man with a considerable future. But hints of a violent past, rumors of a gunfighter reputation, were enough to worry any responsible father. Her daughter, on the other hand, wasn't interested in "the idle gossip of boring storekeepers and old women." Albert Bacon shook away his frown and focused on his customer; his only child was as headstrong as her late mother had been.

As Lockhart and Mattie turned to leave, he saw the faces of Abraham and his friends behind a corner, they were waiting patiently for someone to notice them. He was surprised to see them here, figuring they would have come to the store immediately after they left.

"Wait a minute, Miss Bacon," Lockhart said. "I think you have some important customers to wait on first."

"Important? Who?" she asked with a trace of annoyance, but her eyes quickly traced Lockhart's own. "Oh, those boys? They come in and out of here all the time. When school's out. Say, they should be—"

"Teacher's sick," Lockhart said, and she wondered why he would know.

Albert Bacon looked up from figuring a bill and said sternly, "Those boys are probably waiting for me to turn my back so they can steal something. You go on now 'n' get!"

"Just a minute, Mr. Bacon. Those boys are friends of mine—and I happen to know they came in to make a purchase."

Mattie was surprised by Lockhart's statement. It was more than an offer of information. His voice was polite, but a good listener could hear the iron rattling in his words.

Bacon didn't catch the undercurrent and answered sharply, "With what?"

"They have money."

"Well, that'll be the first time. They're just street—"

"They earned it—from me. They came to buy candy sucks."

Bacon glanced warily toward Lockhart. This time he heard something he hadn't caught before: Lockhart cared about these no-account boys. It always made Bacon nervous when things didn't go the way he thought they should, or people didn't stay within the labels he affixed to them. His gaze carefully avoided Lockhart's eyes and came to rest on his daughter.

"Mattie, will you take care of these lads, please, dear? I'm helping Mrs. Collins." He smiled at the stern-faced woman, whose glare was a more immediate problem, and resumed adding up her purchases without looking further at the boys, his daughter, or Lockhart.

Mattie walked over to the three boys and warmly sought their requests. Moments later they ran past Lockhart, waving prized candy sticks and shouting, "Thanks, Mister Lockhart!"

"You're welcome."

Abraham paused at the doorway, cocked his head to the side, and said, "Is that your wife?"

"No, Abraham, she's a friend, like you."

"I like her. I think she should be your wife."

"Hey, you get along now!" Lockhart said, and grinned.

Abraham laughed and ran out the door.

"What's that all about?" Mattie asked as she walked beside him.

"I ran into them earlier this morning. They invited me to play and I couldn't, so I gave them money for candy for being nice enough to ask."

"You're a strange one, Vin Lockhart. Would you have really played with them?"

"Sure. Why not"

Smiling, Mattie took his arm, and they strolled down

the planked sidewalk. After a few steps in silence, Lockhart said, "Might be some rain coming in from the mountains tonight. Had a feeling all morning that something's heading this way."

"You sound like an old man," she teased. "Or a farmer. How are you going to keep up with those boys feeling that way?"

"Sometimes I feel like the first," Lockhart said with a soft smile.

She smiled back and searched his face for a return of the feelings she had for him. He was kind to her, polite and surprisingly gentle, but hard to read sometimes. As with many men in town, his past went unspoken. She longed to ask him but knew it would be impolite; asking a man about his background just wasn't done in the West. His manner of speaking was always fascinating to her. It was an educated style of expression, yet there was a sense of simpleness that she couldn't put her finger on. When he was ready he would tell her, she told herself. She had been drawn to him the first time they met, when he came into her father's store to purchase a hat.

That was a month ago, and he had barely spoken to her that morning. But he came back the next day and the next, each time with the pretense of buying something else. He had asked her to dinner on his third trip in as many days. Her father had agreed to the courting only after realizing she intended to do so, with or without his approval.

"Good to see you, Vin," said a tall gentleman, ambling along with a silver-tipped cane.

"And you, Ortho."

Mattie was silently impressed. Ortho Woodson was one of the most influential businessmen in town, owning a large silver mine as well as other businesses. Several other people passed them and greeted the couple; she could walk like this forever, she thought. Finally, he shared the news about the purchase of the hotel and the plans for its renovation into a grand place.

"Oh, Vin, that's wonderful! I can't wait to tell Dad. He's such a—"

"Your father is a fine man, and he worries that his only daughter may be mixed up with a..."

"A scoundrel who will steal his daughter's heart away?" she teased.

"Well, I think he should rightfully be worried about me."

"And why is that, pray tell?"

"Because you might break my heart."

"Oh, Vin."

They walked on, arm in arm, without talking, and crossed the dirt-clodded street. First they coyly dodged an ornate carriage with bells on the halters of twin sorrel horses, laughing as they maneuvered around it. At mid-street, they sidestepped a rumbling Russell, Majors & Waddell freighter, which was lunging back and forth with an overload of camp supplies.

"Watch whar yur a-goin', dammit!" barked the driver as he snapped the lines and thundered past.

"And a good day to you, too, sir!" Lockhart waved in mock friendliness. Mattie imitated the greeting and giggled.

Her father had warned her about Vin Lockhart. He told her the stories of his being a pistol-fighter and how he had come to town and bested four men who sought him. She had heard the same tale, only it was six men. Mattie understood her father well, and men like him—but not those like Vin Lockhart. She knew some men feared him, and her eyes drifted to the slight bulge beneath his coat. He always carried a gun, but she had never seen it in his hand. A lot of men carried guns but not those like her father. He didn't even own one. She decided it was the nature of Lockhart's business that dictated carrying a weapon, but she wished he didn't anyway.

Yet the moment she thought she understood him, he would do something completely unlike her easy image of him. When they were on a picnic together last week, he had been captivated by a small red bird singing in a nearby tree. Around children he was gentle, caring, and always had time for them, like the boys at the store. And he was well-known for his generosity to older men and women who needed help. She was captivated by his silent strength but never certain what he would do next or why, or even how he really felt most of the time. She shivered and wasn't sure if the electricity throbbing was uncertainty—or desire.

Just before they reached Bacon's General Store, a small meadowlark fluttered onto a torn branch of a scraggjy oak tree in the alley. The wild tree's trunk bent outward to avoid a collision with the buildings. Without realizing it, Lockhart stopped in the middle of their stroll and stared at the tiny yellow-and-black creature as it began to warble a thin song.

"*Jialepa*," he whispered, Lakotan for "meadowlark." Mattie watched him curiously, glanced toward the bird, smiled, and then looked back to Lockhart. He didn't notice. He continued in the words of his adopted father, "Do you have a message from *Okaga*, the South Wind? Or have you come from Stone-Dreamer to tell me a story of the stones singing?"

"I wish you'd look at me that way."

The words came like a gunshot across his hypnotized mind. He jumped slightly as they registered and looked around to see her smiling at him

"Why, ah, yes. They are magnificent little things, aren't they?" He recovered and smiled thinly. "The Oglala… Indians…believe the meadowlark can speak their language and brings messages from the South Wind."

"Oh, that's very pretty. Do they think horses can speak

Irish too?" she cracked, expecting his usual easy laughter. Instead, there was only a soft smile.

"Where did you learn that—about the meadowlark, I mean?" she asked.

After hesitating, he told her some guy in the saloon had told him. Why does this wisp of yesterday have to bother me now, he thought, and gritted his teeth to deny its return.

"How about dinner and the theater tonight?" he asked unexpectedly, forcing his mind to change directions. "We'll celebrate the new hotel."

"That sounds wonderful," she purred, stepping closer to him. Her breasts brushed against his arm. "Everyone coming into the store talks about the play. It's *Hamlet*, you know."

"My carriage will be at your house at six-thirty."

"Make it seven. I'll need to fix Dad his supper first."

"Seven it is," he said, and kissed her on the cheek.

She returned the kiss on his mouth. Kissing was another *wasicun* thing he had enjoyed learning.

Chapter Eleven

" 'He was a man, take him for all in all, I shall not look upon his like again.' "

The emaciated actor, clad in a theatrically bright costume, delivered the lines in a loud, methodical voice. A heavy sword at his waist bothered him as he moved about the crowded stage; its sheathed blade clanged against props and slapped against the legs of other actors. Each time, chuckles followed from the men in the audience.

Mattie Bacon and Vin Lockhart sat on the third row, next to the aisle, in the full Opera House. Lockhart tried to imagine the actor as a fighter in spite of his physical appearance. He well knew some men looked dangerous and weren't; some didn't and were; and some did look dangerous and definitely were. He had seen all kinds. Judging a man effectively had a lot to do with staying alive. Still, he couldn't hold back a grin at the man's obvious discomfort with the weapon.

Mattie was radiant in a dark-green dress with puffed

sleeves and a lacy white bodice. Emerald earrings from the Orient, a recent present from Lockhart, enhanced her serene face. Every time Lockhart glanced over at her, she was looking at him. Each time he smiled warmly and touched her hands resting in her lap. Each time her own smile embraced his face.

A black pin-striped suit with a matching vest, accented with a light blue silk cravat and held in place with a small silver stud, set off Lockhart's rugged face and frame. Mattie was disappointed to see that his shoulder holster remained but said nothing about it. Sometime she would, though, she thought. It just wasn't necessary in town. Mostly, though, she wondered how many women envied her place beside him this evening, and she smiled again—to herself.

" 'There is nothing either good or bad, but thinking makes it so,' " another actor shouted, his face contorted to reach the last row. Lockhart wasn't certain he agreed with that assessment, but he let it pass through his mind unchallenged. He would discuss the concept tomorrow with Crawfish.

As he watched the actors prance about the raised and draped stage, a vivid remembrance took over his mind, more protracted than his brief return to the Oglala camp this morning. His mind brought him again to a time the Oglala said was gone from his walk-around life and residing in his soul life.

Memories of their joyful camp poured through his imagination as if someone were working a pump handle—memories long locked away by anger, anguish, and alcohol. Instead of painted backdrops and gesturing actors, he saw the happy encampment with painted tipis placed in a sacred circle to hold in the power of the universe. Buffalo hides were stretched and drying in the warm sun. Dogs barked at imaginary problems. Women were preparing quillwork on new warshirts, cooking in darkened kettles, and chatting quietly with one another. Warriors were riding their ponies in races against each other, telling stories of war triumphs and working on arrows and knives.

The Oglala camp was alongside a talking stream, perfect for swimming, bathing, and fishing. Horses were hobbled and grazing. Contented men and women were laughing, talking, working, enjoying their special circle of life. Old friends that he hadn't seen in six years were moving about the camp. He could see honor giveaways, events of great excitement, where warriors gave away their most prized possessions to mark their generosity and increase their standing among the tribe.

Instead of the actor in blue tights, Lockhart could see his former stepfather, Stone-Dreamer, just as though the two of them were walking together. The holy man was wearing a full-length white elkskin cape over his customary white buckskin shirt and leggings. As a headdress, he wore his favorite winter wolfs head with owl and eagle feathers dangling from the side. He was speaking in an unknown language, holding fire in his bare hands. Hanging from long shoulder straps was the familiar large white pouch containing many sacred stones.

Lockhart saw his good friend—and former brother-in-law—Touches-Horses, quietly training a magnificent paint horse. He could turn a mustang into a superb mount like no one else. Touches-Horses and the animal became truly one—and never with the heavy-handed style of breaking a horse like most horsemen, red or white.

Clap! Clap! Clap! Clap! "Oh, wasn't that grand!"

Lockhart's mind snapped back to the theater. The cast was lined across the stage, bowing grandly and inhaling the praise of an appreciative audience. His body was damp with sweat his face moist his mind fighting to regain reality. Why had this Oglala scene come over him? He hadn't thought about them for a long time. He had rid his mind of that madness. Why did he recall living with them this morning? Was he just worn out from trying to buy the hotel? Why had he been pulled back now? He must not let that happen again; it was too horrible to return to those thoughts.

"Are you all right, Vin, darling?" Mattie asked, placing her hand on his arm.

He inhaled the room's activity, letting it give him balance, and said, "Oh, yes, quite. A little warm in here, isn't it?"

"Oh, I thought it was just right."

"I guess that's what comes from being next to you."

Concentrating on her allowed him to close off those memories once more. He hoped it was only a silly click of the mind that wouldn't occur again. Even his dreams had long been cleansed of those days—of Young Evening's awful death; of his savage revenge; of his adopted father's disappointment over his lack of a stone-vision; and of the stories of grandfathers riding at his side. Mattie lowered her eyes for an instant and sought his again. The softness in his words she read as fondness for her, not the weakness of returning from a place he had left behind forever.

They sat and talked, savoring each other's closeness, while the crowd milled its way out. Faces glowed from the golden rain of gaslamps stationed throughout the building. Several men greeted Lockhart as they escorted their wives out. Obligatory smiles from the women came to Mattie. The notorious madam, Christina Lore, winked at Lockhart as she passed. Mattie was incensed, but Lockhart dismissed it with a contagious grin and a shake of his head.

After the last patrons cleared the theater, Lockhart leaned over and kissed her. After several minutes lost within each other's mouths, they realized where they were, laughed, and left the hall. Outside, the twosome strolled alone, hand in hand, toward his carriage with the two black horses tied to a hitching rack. The surrounding street and sidewalks were empty, as if the theatergoers had never existed.

From the alley a growled command broke into their sweet interlude: "Give us your poke, fancy man—and maybe we'll let you go on. Your fine lady friend'll want to stay with us for a while, won't ya, honey."

Laughter followed the threat, like a coyote yapping at a straying companion. Lockhart turned slowly to face two men, one lanky and slump-shouldered and the other quite short and wild-eyed. Both held revolvers. Moonlight ricocheted from the barrels. The taller man held a double-action Deane and Adams .44 pistol, and the shorter thief brandished a cocked Colt revolver. Discolored and broken teeth made the contemptuous smile of the taller man even more sinister in the night's shadows.

The shorter man laughed again and asked of his partner, "Can I shoot 'im now, Luke? Huh? Huh, can I, huh? That gal's a plum, shore 'nuff. You kin have the money if' n I kin go first."

"Naw. You kin jes' wait, Aaron. No need to make more noise than we hafta," Luke, the taller thief, said as he pulled a large knife from his belt with his left hand. The ugly blade glittered in the pale light.

"Oh, Vin!" Mattie cried out, and grabbed Lockhart's arm.

Lockhart patted Mattie's grasping hand and stepped between her and the two holdup men. He whispered, "Stay behind me. Don't move."

With his best disarming smile, Lockhart said, "No need for guns—or knives, gentlemen. We're just peaceful folks enjoying the theater."

As he spoke, he reached into his coat pocket as if to retrieve his wallet. His eyes dropped to the ground in apparent submission.

"See, Aaron, that thar be a ri't smart feller," Luke said, glancing at his shorter accomplice. "This nice fella's gonna give us his money real easy-like. No fuss. Why, I don't believe he'd mind if'n we had ourselves a closer look at his fine-lookin' lady, neither."

"Well, after I shoot the yella bastird, I aims to find out jes' what she's got under that purty dress. I figger she's in need of a real man. That all right with you, Luke, huh?"

"Long as ya give me all the money. I'll take seconds."

"Yeah, all righty, then!" Aaron agreed, laughing hysterically.

Lockhart's wallet spurted out of his hand and fell to the sidewalk.

"Oh, I'm sorry," he said as he leaned to pick it up.

"Hey, you're as clumsy as you are yella," Aaron snapped.

Both thieves followed Lockhart's movement toward the wallet. An ivory-handled Smith & Wesson appeared in the blur of Lockhart's hand and roared orange flame three times into the night. The first and third slugs slammed into the smaller bandit and he flew backward. Aaron's gun exploded and the bullet nipped at Lockhart's left coat sleeve and disappeared into the night. The smaller thief's gun then took on a life of its own as it left his hand and flew into the air. Lockhart's second bullet caught the taller thief in the stomach. Luke dropped his gun and knife, grabbed his midsection with both hands, and squealed.

"Y-y-ya done kilt A-A-Aaron an' ya gut-shot me, ya bastard!" screamed Luke, bending over to stop the pain. He looked at his right hand and it was bright red.

"Your friend's weapon was cocked; yours would take longer to fire," Lockhart said methodically. "You were the lucky one, I guess."

He looked back to see how Mattie was doing, and the man used the distraction to regather his courage and pulled a hideaway gun from his belt with his bloody right hand. Whether a planned feint or only an instinctive reaction, Lockhart swung around and laid the pistol in his fist against the man's skull, spinning his face sideways. Blood splattered on Lockhart's coat and shirt and laid a thin streak of red dots across his nose. In the tattered moonlight, he looked again like a warrior painted for war.

The thief collapsed at the saloonkeeper's feet like a dropped blanket. Lockhart stared down at the battered man and at the blood drops across his chest. He felt the warm spots on his face, tasted them on his lips, and tried to wipe them clear with his hand. Behind him a wild cry exploded from Mattie.

"It's over," he said, and took Mattie in his arms. Her wailing was a drum to the uncontrollable heaving of her entire body.

"Oh, Vin, I was so scared," she whispered. Layers of tears stained her pale face. "Y-y-you shot a man. Is he d-d-dead?"

"I'm afraid so."

"I-i-is this man dead too?"

"Don't know. But he's hurt bad."

"Oh my God, Vin! How can this be?" she said loudly into the night air, and pulled away from him. "Did you have to k-k-kill them?"

"They didn't leave me much room, Mattie. Two men. Two guns. That isn't exactly Sunday school."

He moved to comfort her again, and she cried out, "Leave me alone, you…you—murderer!"

From the theater came sounds of running. Soon three men exited the building: a bald-headed man with a shotgun, a stocky man in an ill-fitting suit brandishing a long-barreled pistol, and a third with an unsheathed sword. Lockhart recognized the latter as the actor having the problem with the weapon on stage. They paused outside the theater before the bald-headed man pointed toward Lockhart and Mattie. In seconds, the stocky man and the actor were examining the downed thieves while the bald-headed man introduced himself.

Holding out his hand, he said solemnly, "I'm Russell Jerguson, the manager here. Are you folks all right?"

"We're not hurt, thank you, Mr. Jerguson. I'm Vin Lockhart," Lockhart replied, shaking the extended hand firmly, "and this is Miss Bacon."

"Vin Lockhart? Damn, looks like they picked the wrong man to mess with. Pardon my language, miss."

The other two men left their examinations and rushed over.

"Both are dead, Jerguson," the stocky one said. "Bet they're the same two that robbed the Newtons two weeks ago."

"Yeah, probably," Jerguson replied, pursing his lips in evaluation and examining Lockhart carefully. "Well, I appreciate what you've done, Mr. Lockhart. We can't have our customers attacked when they leave. That's why I hired Phelps here—to keep things safe."

The stocky Phelps defended himself quickly: "I thought everyone had gone. I was checking the alley out back. Thought I heard something."

"Yeah, while my customers were being set upon out front."

"But—but, I didn't know…"

. "It doesn't matter now. Mr. Lockhart did your job for you."

Lockhart responded only by handing a handkerchief to Mattie. Her crying had waned. Only an occasional deep inhalation could be heard, as she tried to regain the air her horror had caused her to lose earlier.

The actor swelled his chest and introduced himself, expecting praise: "Sir, I am Thomas R. Harris…"

"Yes, I know who you are, Harris. Miss Bacon and I enjoyed your performance tonight," Lockhart said, resisting the temptation to mention the clanging sword.

"I can't wait to tell my friends in the troupe about this. They will be jealous to hear they missed a true Western gunfight!" the actor continued. "What an honor to meet a real gunfighter, sir."

"Afraid you've got that all wrong, Thomas. I'm just a businessman protecting himself. Most any man in Denver City would've done the same."

Jerguson gave a knowing look to Phelps but said nothing. Lockhart introduced the recomposed Mattie to the three theater men. She responded meekly to their courtesies. The actor leaned over and picked up a small, triangle-shaped stone from among some pebbles near the dead thieves. Blood stained its snow-white surface. He turned it over in his hand like he'd found a chunk of gold.

"Going to keep this for a souvenir. A real gunfight!" he babbled. Lockhart glanced at the stone in Harris's hand. From deep within his yesterdays came Stone-Healer's advice: "Angry Dog, if a stone looks like it wants to talk to you, pick it up and take it with you. Give it a chance to give you power from the unseen world."

The actor was uncomfortably aware of Lockhart's stare and nervously held out the stone in his open palm. "Ah, would you like this…M-M-Mister Lockhart? I don't need it, really."

Lockhart blinked away the memory and shook his head. "No. You keep the *tunkan*—the stone."

"You folks go on ahead now. We'll take care of this mess," Jerguson urged.

"Thank you. I appreciate that. Good night," Lockhart said, and directed Mattie toward the carriage and stopped. Turning back toward them, he said, "Tell Marshal Benson I'll be in to see him in the morning."

"As you wish, Mr. Lockhart," answered Jerguson. "But that's not necessary. I'll fill out the report. It was clearly self-defense."

Thomas R. Harris watched the couple, his mouth open

and his expression like that of a little boy seeing his hero for the first time. He squeezed the white stone in his fist and said, "Can you believe that?"

"Yeah, Vin Lockhart is a bad man to mess with," Jerguson said. "Just wish I'd gotten to see it."

As Lockhart helped Mattie into the carriage, she asked, "Are you g-g-going to leave those d-d-dead men there, Vin?"

"Jerguson and his men will handle it. I'll drop by the marshal's office in the morning. To make it official. It was self-defense. There won't be anything to it."

"Just like that?"

"What do you mean?"

"You killed two men. Doesn't it bother you?" she asked. Her forehead furrowed in concern; her eyes were wide and near tears again.

Lockhart tilted his head slightly to the side, then clucked the two black horses into moving before responding. Finally, he spoke without looking at her: "No, Mattie, it doesn't. They intended to kill me—and do with you what they wanted. They got what they deserved."

"Is that why they called you a gunfighter?" Her words were as sharp as the thief's blade.

"Mattie, I'm a man who was protecting the woman he cares for. I carry a gun. Most men I know do that. Men like your father don't, and that's fine. Apparently, he has never been attacked like that."

"Don't bring my father into this! He could never kill anyone!"

"I hope he never has to make that decision."

"Oh, you don't understand," she snapped. "You liked killing those men. It was easy. They didn't have a chance."

"No, it's you that doesn't understand, Mattie. You don't understand what it's like to push away fear long enough to keep yourself alive. To take a chance so that you might see another sunrise. I could be the one lying there and you could be in that alley—with your clothes torn off and…No, you are the one that doesn't understand, Mattie."

She was silent for minutes. Lockhart concentrated on handling the team as they worked through the quiet streets to her father's modest home near Cherry Creek. As soon as the carriage pulled in front, Mattie was out and walking toward the house before Lockhart could wrap the reins around the setting whip. Realizing she didn't want him close, Lockhart watched her enter the house without a word, snapped the lines, and left.

At the stable, he turned the animals over to the half-breed stable boy, gave him two bits, and walked into the night air. The Denver House, where he stayed, was a block away. The walk would feel good. Mattie's reaction hurt worse than a bullet. But the salon owner should have expected it, he told himself. Where had she ever been around violence? There was no way a woman of her refinement could see herself with the likes of a Vin Lockhart. He had been foolish to think so. It was better this way; he wasn't meant to have another wife after Young Evening.

Glancing in the direction of the boardinghouse, Lockhart couldn't believe his eyes. Coming toward him was Stone-Dreamer himself! The shaman was dressed in his usual white buckskins and carrying that large white pouch slung over his shoulder on long straps. Lockhart would have known him anywhere.

"How you doin', Mistuh Lockhart?"

Lockhart blinked. The tentative greeting came from a bearded miner a few steps away, not Stone-Dreamer. Across his shoulders, a rope held a tightly rolled gray blanket that swung at his side. How could he have mistaken this man for the old holy man? The question shot through him. With a string of puzzled glances, the miner altered his direction enough to ease past without causing Lockhart to move, expecting little response to his salutation from the successful businessman.

"Sevens and eights," Lockhart replied with enthusiasm born of relief. He stopped and offered his hand, which surprised the miner, who shook it eagerly. The miner growled a chuckle and responded, "Yessir, Mistuh Lockhart, but it'd better be eights over—an' know'd who yur a-playin'."

Lockhart grinned at the soundness of the advice and felt foolish at thinking Stone-Dreamer would be walking down the streets of Denver City. White people were scared witless about Indians, whether it was reasonable or not. A volunteer posse had been organized to chase a band of scalp-hunting Utes just last month. No Indian in his right mind would stroll through town, night or day. Of course, shadows at this time of night could easily cause visual distortions, especially after such a traumatic evening, he told himself as he continued walking. He glanced back at the miner who was ambling briskly in the other direction, seemingly buoyed by Lockhart's friendliness.

Lockhart shook his head in disbelief at the swing of the day. First, their business holdings were enlarged with the hotel's purchase—then he had locked-away memories yanked out of his soul. Worse, the woman he cared for had made it quite clear she didn't want anything to do with him. All of her interest in him had evaporated—as his unwanted reputation with a gun was enhanced. No wonder he was seeing things like Indians, he thought to himself and lit a cigar.

Vin Lockhart rose early the next morning. He hadn't rested well, consumed by Mattie's rejection. Finally he had accepted his earlier claim that she simply wasn't the woman for him and had slept for two hours before finally rising. A dream of her face twisted in hate had jolted him awake. It was time to concentrate on business and forget Mattie Bacon, he decided. He didn't need the distraction.

There were other women around if he wanted one. The hell with her, he said aloud as he dressed.

Going over the hotel plans again, while everything was quiet, would ease his troubled mind. He skipped the breakfast served at the boardinghouse, and the attentiveness from the owner, Mrs. Arbuckle, that went with it. Instead he headed directly for the Silver Queen, but changed his mind and walked over to Crawfish's house, which was only three blocks out of the way. Crawfish would know how to guide him concerning Mattie—and he did want to talk with him about the hotel.

It was quiet on the secluded residential street as Lockhart walked across the grass to the front door. The gabled house was too big for one man, he thought, but Crawfish had purchased it the same day he had purchased a silver-accented carriage. Lockhart had surprised him with a matching pair of fine black carriage horses as a gift. He knocked and waited, but there was no answer. So he knocked again. Still no sound from inside. Impatient, he jumped over a stand of chokecherry shrubs and peered through the front window.

Inside he could see Crawfish sitting at a table, drinking coffee and reading the newspaper and deep in concentration. Lockhart returned to the dark oak door, found it unlocked, and eased it open. Closing the heavy door behind him, he walked silently toward his friend.

"Morning, Crawfish, how are you doing?"

The older man jumped at the sound, looked up, and smiled.

"Oh, my goodness, Vin, you nearly scared me out of my shoes! Such a quiet man. Like an Indian you are," he said, and laughed at his own joke.

"Well, I didn't want to disturb a man when he's working.

Lockhart walked to the table and held out his hand. The eccentric prospector stood and shook it warmly. He steadied himself with a cane now and dressed well, but he looked the same as ever: red-faced with a beard that sprawled away from his head like it was fleeing.

"Well, you look mighty poorly for a fella who just bought a grand hotel. Did you celebrate too much last night? How about some coffee?"

"Sure. If you have sugar," Lockhart responded.

Crawfish took a white cup and saucer from a nearby walnut cabinet, filled it, and handed the hot brew to Lockhart. He pointed in the direction of the sugar bowl.

Crawfish slapped the back of his left hand against the newspaper in his right and said, "There's more news about trouble with Indians north and west of here. In the territories. This story says the railroad wants all the buffalo killed so the Indians'll starve and have to give themselves up. Can you imagine your old friends cooped up on some pathetic reservation?"

Lockhart nodded but said nothing as he poured a second spoonful of sugar into his coffee cup.

Not getting the reaction he had expected, Crawfish changed the subject: "Been thinking we should buy that clothing shop next to the hotel. We could knock it down and that would give us the room to add on a grand gambling area—instead of trying to cram it into the lobby. What do you think?"

"I think you've already made up your mind," Lockhart said. "Who owns the place?" He was certain his old friend had already investigated.

"Now what makes you think I've done any checking?" Crawfish asked. The left side of his face twitched slightly. "Can you believe that, Newton? After all we've been through together. Yeah, I know. I'll tell him. Judge McKinsey owns it. Or, rather, the bank does. He's heavily in debt."

"Just saw his honor not long ago. Told him his marker was canceled. Why don't you go see him about a deal?"

"You don't think it's too soon?" Crawfish asked.

"No. It makes sense. But I want to make sure those ladies running that shop get resettled in a good place."

"What about letting them use one of those three buildings we bought last month? Wouldn't one of them fit them well?" Crawfish asked with a twinkle in his eye.

"Just what I was thinking."

"Want to go with me?"

"No, I've got to see Marshal Benson."

Crawfish eyed his young partner for a minute, broke out in cackling laughter, then realized Lockhart was serious and asked, "What for?"

"Two rummies tried to rob me—and Mattie Bacon—when we left the theater last night."

"They say timing is everything," Crawfish said without a grin. "Guess those fellows should've waited for someone else."

"We were last to come out."

"Is that why you've got a case of the long face?"

Lockhart rolled his tongue along his lower lip and said hesitantly, "I—I don't think we'll be going out anymore."

"Why not?"

"She didn't take well to my…killing them."

"Were they carrying?"

"Yeah, both had guns. One had a knife, too. They were going to kill me, then they'd…well, you know."

Crawfish rubbed his unshaved chin and said, "I see. She'd rather you were dead and she was raped. Women."

"Maybe so. It doesn't matter."

"Well, I know saloons and gambling halls and hotels, not women," Crawfish continued. "Never saw one yet that fired where she said she was aiming. Part of the breed, I guess. My advice is you'd better leave her alone for a piece. Won't do any good charging in there this morning."

"I didn't plan on it," Lockhart said, and took a swallow of his coffee.

"That wasn't the look I saw in your eyes," Crawfish observed. "Now take the missus, God bless her soul. She was a handsome filly back when we started courting. Oh, man, I tell you, she could stop a man's heart with just a look. And smart? Almina Johnson, she was then. Wish you had known her, Vin. You two would have gotten along real fine, I know it."

"I wish that too," Lockhart said. He had heard this story several times, but there wasn't any use in mentioning that fact. Crawfish loved to tell about his courtship and, in particular, their first carriage ride.

Quickly changing the subject, Lockhart asked, "Crawfish, have you ever...ah, seen something...that wasn't really there? Like a mirage or something?"

The older man wrinkled his forehead. His eyes sparkled with mischief, and he asked, "Are you asking me about Newton?"

"Oh no. I'm talking about thinking you really saw something, or someone, and nothing was there."

"Heck, that's easy to do. Happens to me all the time. But usually after I've had some of our whiskey."

Lockhart forced a laugh and said, "Well, I'd better be going."

"All right. Give my best to Marshal Benson. You'll be lucky if he's there at this hour. I'll catch up with you later at the Queen."

Swallowing the rest of his coffee in one gulp, Lockhart stood and headed toward the door.

"Remember what I said about that girl," Crawfish hollered after him.

Chapter Twelve

Two hours later Vin Lockhart was reviewing the Silver Queen accounting ledger in the back office, but his mind was on Mattie Bacon. His brief meeting with Marshal Benson had gone well; the lawman liked keeping on the good side of saloon owners. But the saloon owner hadn't accomplished much since coming to the saloon, only a decision to send over a case of the Silver Queen's best whiskey to the theater manager as a thank-you for last night. His mind wouldn't let him forget the look on Mattie Bacon's face when she called him a murderer.

Lockhart's cramped office was dominated by a large, rolltop desk, where he sat. The desk itself was empty except for a small stack of papers; six decks of cards were shoved into the cubbyholes, where he also kept the ledger and a book of Tennyson's poems—an edition of his own—that he liked to read when he had the time. Both men now used the same desk because Crawfish rarely came to the saloon anymore.

A drained beer stein was perched on the top frame of the desk, its position for at least a month. Lockhart's coat and hat were tossed across the only other chair. The rest of the room's decorating consisted of an unopened case of whiskey and a silver frame holding a ripped oil painting of three horses. A loaded Winchester leaned in the far corner. The solitary closet door was slightly ajar, revealing several suits and shirts hanging inside.

Knock! Knock!

Without waiting for response, his head faro dealer, J. R. Parks, slammed into the room. He cleared his throat, pushed his ever-present silk top hat back on his head, and rattled, "T-t-there's f-f-four wild Indians just walked in, Vin. I mean wild. Paint 'n' feathers. T-t-they asked to see 'Veen Lock-Hard.' Don't that beat all? They aren't doing anything wrong, I guess. I mean, hell, it's a damn wonder they haven't been killed already. Should I go get the marshal?"

Lockhart stared at the intruding man as if he didn't comprehend the message and Parks said it again, ending with the same question.

This time Lockhart responded, "No, I'll take care of it."

Lockhart's words were delivered as he left his chair, grabbed his coat, and went to the closed door. Opening the door only enough to see through a crack, he studied the main room as he put on his coat. At this time of day, the saloon was sparsely attended. One bartender and one hostess were on duty. A regular foursome was playing small-stakes poker at their traditional table. Another table was filled with businessmen. The bar itself had eight patrons; five were miners. Only one of the pool tables was in use—and by regulars.

Lockhart's mouth was a slit of tension. Four Oglala warriors were standing with their backs to each other. Their tight circle gave them a view of the entire room and appeared like a final stance of defiance. In front of each warrior's moccasined feet was a small bundle of tobacco, surrounded by a freshly cut cedar wreath, accented with sage and sweetgrass.

Lockhart knew them. Thunder Lance, Sings-With-Stones, Bear-Heart, and Spotted Horse were warriors of respect from his old village. Bear-Heart had been one of his "second fathers." Each had represented the tribe—as he once had—in the sacred *Wi wanyang wacipi*, the sun dance. He was certain none of them had been in a white man's big city before—or even near one. They gazed in wonderment at the the rainbow of colors and shapes they could not comprehend. None had probably been inside a building, Lockhart figured. Much less seen a gas lamp, a mirror, a piano—or a woman in a shimmering dress. Truly this must appear to be a place worthy of *Wanagi Yanka.* Lockhart blinked and shook his head to make certain this wasn't another hallucination. It wasn't. Parks watched him, fascinated; this man he knew as fearless and unflappable even in the worst bar fight was pale and trembling slightly.

"Vin, what's the matter? Are you all right?" Parks asked.

"Yeah, I guess so. My past just rode in."

"What?"

Lockhart took a deep breath and entered the main room. No one noticed him. All eyes were on the Indians and their attention was on the room itself. The warriors were dressed in their finest leggings, long breechclouts, warshirts, and beaded mocassins. Apparel worn only for the most important of occasions. Their silky black hair was unbraided and freshly combed. Topknots were standing straight up. Their smooth coppery faces were stained with paint. Each wore a single eagle feather attached midway down a long scalp lock in addition to special wind feathers. None were armed, not even carrying a knife.

Lockhart sensed the ways of Stone-Dreamer in this sudden appearance. He realized each warrior was dressed to represent one of the four winds, wearing its sacred color and a symbol of its winged messenger. That would have been the holy man's doing; he had rehearsed them in a special ceremony. Lockhart knew that no one in the saloon had any idea about the significance of their attire or the reason for their being here. Parks was right in being surprised they hadn't been shot at already.

Their quiet, solemn manner had a lot to do with their safety so far as every man in the place watched them suspiciously. Two miners had drawn pistols and held them on their laps. A townsman held a Scofield revolver at his side. Behind the bar, Billy the bartender slowly laid down a towel and glass he was drying. He reached under the counter, withdrew a double-barreled shotgun and held it just out of the line of sight.

Representing *Eya*, the West Wind, the cheerful Spotted Horse was wearing a multistrand necklace of black beads that completely covered his neck and the upper portion of his chest. The right half of his face was painted black to represent the West Wind, with a lightning bolt of the same color on his left cheek to show that *Eya* brought the Thunderbeings. In his hair were tied two swallowtail feathers, messenger of the West Wind, with its scissor-cut ends also representing lightning. In the warrior's hand was a medicine bag of spotted horsehide, his own spirit helper recognition. Lockhart remembered Spotted Horse as a man without fear in battle, quick to laugh and make jokes.

Bear-Heart, leader of Lockhart's last hunt with the tribe, wore a dyed-red warshirt, decorated with reddish scalp locks, porcupine quillwork, and beaded strips. The powerfully framed warrior represented *Yata*, the North Wind. His entire face was painted red for the Wind's color. In the warrior's hair hung the wing of a magpie, *Yata's* messenger. His right hand held an offering stick, decorated with vermillion paint and matching quill and beadwork. Over the same arm he carried a folded red blanket. Around his thick neck hung the massive necklace of bear claws Lockhart remembered, symbol of the warrior's own spirit helper.

The fierce-tempered, but usually sullen, warrior pointed to the gas lamp chandelier anchored in the ceiling. Glass baubles shimmered a serenade of the flickering lights. When the dancing lights reached Bear-Heart's leggings, he jumped back to keep them from touching him. Lockhart read his lips as Bear-Heart solemnly pronounced "*Wanagi Yanka*" to his three comrades. At that moment, Lockhart noticed the warrior's wrists and smiled. Tin cans opened on both ends were proudly worn as cuffs; the paper labels still remained. It looked like both were for canned peaches. Lockhart wondered where he had found them.

Sings-With-Stones, the gentlest of the four as Lockhart recalled, turned to see the chandelier, got a glimpse of himself in the long mirror behind the bar, and whispered something Lockhart couldn't make out. Sings-With-Stones was a warrior whom the *inyan* had talked to. He had received a stone-vision and become *wakanlica*, connected to the spirits through the stones. Lockhart had been envious and had ignored the warrior as much as possible. Sings-With-Stones had been contemplating becoming a shaman when Lockhart left.

The slightly built Oglala warrior, with the finely featured face, was portraying *Yanpa*, the East Wind. Vertical stripes of yellow banded his entire face; his boned breastplate was dotted with yellow beads and ochre-painted shells. A stuffed dead crow with outstretched wings, the third wind's messenger, was perched at the side of his head. Dangling from his ear by a buckskin strip was a small, wrapped stone. In both hands were reverently carried a beaded quill pipebag, carrying a sacred pipe, *can-nunpa wakan.*

Thunder Lance would have stood out among most of his fellow tribesmen, standing well over six feet tall. He, too, had been on Lockhart's last hunt with the tribe. He was dressed in a white buckskin warshirt and leggings. His cheeks glistening with two white circles, the warrior was a dominating sight, serving as *Okaga*, the South Wind. Lockhart guessed Thunder Lance was the group's leader and not Bear-Heart. Strong reminders of Thunder Lance's own medicine helper were carried in a small, beaded pouch tied to a thong around his neck. A meadowlark wing, *Okaga's* messenger, was laced to the beginning of his scalp lock.

Covering Thunder Lance's left arm was his personal medicine shield of thick buffalo hide, supported by a long belt over his shoulder. The shield was uncased, indicating a need for its protection. Across the stretched skin were stained shapes known only to him. Seven old scalp locks were tied across the lower edge, equal distances from each other, forming a half-circle. In his right hand was something wrapped in soft white elkskin.

Thunder Lance motioned toward one of the silver-gowned waitresses across the room, observing to the other warriors that she must be related to *Wohpe.* This was the woman, in Oglala legend, the North Wind and his younger brother, the South Wind, fought over when the world was formed. Her mouth opened in sheer panic at being singled out and the blond waitress stepped backward to get away from the misunderstood attention. She stumbled against an empty chair, spilling the drinks on her tray. The collision heightened the tension in the room. Someone was mumbling a prayer. Someone else was cursing.

"That thar's Crazy Horse. I'd know'd that man-killer anywheres," came a muffled declaration, followed by "An' you kin bet that tall 'n' is his runnin' mate, Red Cloud."

"Put that damn shotgun away, Billy. The rest of you, put your guns away. They didn't come here to hurt anybody. Can't you see they're not armed?" Lockhart commanded. Both his words and the tone of his voice harvested the attention of everyone in the saloon, including the four warriors.

A huge miner was the first to respond and growled, "Wal, I'll be goddamned. Mistuh Lockhart dun loves hisse'f some Injuns."

If the caustic remark was meant to draw Lockhart's ire, it failed. He was focused on the four long-ago friends staring at him as if seeing a ghost. Sings-With-Stones visibly trembled.

"Hau! Veen Lock-Hard! *Wanagi Yanka!*" Thunder Lance saw him first and hailed their old friend with all the courage he could muster.

"*Tanyan yahi yelo,*" came a bold welcome from the fearless Spotted Horse. Only the edge of the words gave away his fear.

In turn, the other two warriors excitedly made sign and uttered quickened phrases of hallowed greetings reserved for the spirits.

Lockhart smiled as he advanced and spoke fluently in their language, "*Hau!* My good friends—Thunder Lance, the great leader of warriors...Sings-With-Stones, who is favored by the *inyan*...Bear-Heart, he of the grizzly's power and strength, who taught me to be a warrior... and Spotted Horse, whose cheer matches his great courage! So long it has been since we have smoked together. You have come a long way—but I wonder the meaning of your journey."

Lockhart was amazed his old friends had found him at all. Excitedly, the warriors told him directions came from Stone-Dreamer himself. They said the old holy man had undertaken the *Hanblake Oloan*, the special prayer for advance knowledge. He had performed a red blanket, cutting one hundred small pieces of his own skin from his arms and giving them to *Wakantanka.* The four warriors had assisted him. They were obviously frightened by the undertaking and avoided looking directly at him or meeting his eyes.

Thunder Lance explained their mission in a thin, nasal voice: "Stone-Dreamer sent us to ask for the help of his son and to whom the stones have sung—and he who rides with spirits." His voice trailed off in direct contrast to the importance of the words.

As if to explain the holy man's request, Thunder Lance held out the elkskin-wrapped object with both hands, extending them to allow Lockhart to see it more clearly, and said, "First, *Wanagi Yanka*, Veen Lock-Hard, we bring you a sacred memory."

He pulled back the hide with nervous fingers. The unfolding produced a choker necklace of whitest elkbone and darkest blue stones. Lockhart gasped. Young Evening had given it to him on their wedding day. He had left the choker on her ghost bundle on the morning he rode away from the village. He couldn't find any words to say and stared at the choker without attempting to take it from Thunder Lance.

Parks silently entered the room and stood beside the bar, watching as fascinated as everyone else. The entire saloon was motionless and tense. Only an occasional cough broke the silence, and one drunken miner who repeatedly jabbered, "Why is them redskins in hyar?"

The tall warrior nodded reverently as he held the necklace toward Lockhart. Stunned, he finally took the necklace and his eyes briefly met Thunder Lance's and saw yesterday there, along with awe and sadness. As soon as he accepted the choker, Bear-Heart withdrew a small piece of red trade cloth from a pouch at his belt and handed it to Lockhart with deliberate ceremony. The cloth was wrapped loosely around a single piece of sage.

The others grunted approval, but he didn't understand at first. Then it came to him. This was a piece of the burial cloth wrapped around Young Evening's body. Proudly, Bear-Heart pointed to a place on the cloth where the tears of Touches-Horses had been absorbed. Lockhart could not see any discoloration but mumbled his understanding.

In a soft voice, Sings-With-Stones reminded Lockhart that his former brother-in-law had constructed a Ghost-Keeping Lodge for Young Evening to hold her body in state prior to burial and to assist her spirit in its walk to the other world. All the Shadow Ceremonies had been successfully conducted under the direction of Stone-Dreamer.

"One piece of this cloth has been buried in a place known only to Stone-Dreamer," the gentle warrior continued with rehearsed thoroughness. "Another piece was dedicated to the sacred buffalo. The other pieces, all but this one, were given to all tribesmen who kept a Ghost-Keeping Lodge of their own. It is yours to keep holy, Veen Lock-Hard. We were told Young Evening's spirit is passing through here on her way to the world of our grandfathers. We know you will want to honor her with these things."

Sings-With-Stones paused and glanced at Thunder Lance, who nodded approval. The gentle warrior's shoulders rose and fell in grave anticipation of his next duty.

"From Stone-Dreamer himself comes four *tunkan*, four sacred stones," Sings-With-Stones said. "They were presented to the council when Rides-With-Spirits walked the spirit trail. I bring four kola. A black-stone friend, a red-stone friend, a yellow-stone friend, and a white-stone friend. Stone-Dreamer thought the spirits that ride with you would be pleased if you had these *tunkan* instead of him."

Lockhart stared at the small stones as Sings-With-Stones took them one at a time from a beautifully beaded bag and placed them on the sage in front of him. Lockhart fought back the anger spiraling within him. He did not believe in rocks and spirits anymore. That was for ignorant savages, not a successful *wasicun* businessman. Without waiting for any response, the four warriors completed their assignment of delivering the request from Stone-Dreamer.

Touches-Horses—Lockhart's former brother-in-law—had been captured by white men and forced to train horses for them. He was being held at a horse ranch in the *wasicun* valley of Laramie City in the Dakota Territory. The white men were using his power over horses to train them for the long knives at Fort Laramie. Touches-Horses and another warrior had visited friends now living around the fort. A powerful white rancher saw Touches-Horses's mount and wanted it for himself. Touches-Horses would not trade the fine paint mustang, as it was his favorite. The white rancher was told by Touches-Horses's friends of his special way with horses; they didn't realize the consequences of such foolish talk. It is the result of living with the *wasicun*, Bear-Heart commented. Thunder Lance scowled at him. The white rancher's men had kidnapped Touches-Horses and taken the gentle Oglala warrior away in a *wasicun* wagon. Touches-Horses's friends are now shamed their talk caused this.

Initially, three scouts were sent to find him, riding out in different directions. Two returned with no news. The third, Blue Otter, found him but was himself captured by the white rancher's men. He escaped with Touches-Horses's help and made it back, just barely, to the tribe. Not much else was learned, as the warrior died of his wounds before he could tell more.

Bear-Heart observed with a warrior's viewpoint, "Blue Otter's medicine failed him. Sometimes the otter likes to play instead of work."

Sings-With-Stones gave the big-chested warrior a look

of disappointment at his words. Bear-Heart shrugged his shoulders. Continuing the report, Thunder Lance said there was much talk of a war party to bring him back, but Black Fire, Stone-Dreamer, and other Big Bellies and Shirt-Wearers counseled against this.

Thunder Lance sadly explained what happened next: "Instead of a war party, five warriors went in peace to trade for Touches-Horses. Take many presents." He paused, sighed, and said, "They were killed on the white man's tree of rope. Their names are now not spoken, ever again. They ride in our hearts."

Across the room, J. R. Parks stood with his mouth wide open, completely taken by the scene of his boss conversing with these wild creatures, savages he had only heard about. Billy poured himself a drink and downed it in one swallow.

Thunder Lance glanced at his warrior friends and continued with his report: "Many great warriors have asked permission to go and free him. Stone-Dreamer asks that we do not. He says our medicine will be weak if we try. He fears the white eyes are too many. He sees the battles ahead between our peoples and fears what might be. The four of us ask to go, but Stone-Dreamer believes only one can free him. Stone-Dreamer asks his only son—Veen Lock-Hard—to return and bring Touches-Horses back."

When the message was finished, all four warriors faced the floor in silence. Lockhart realized it took considerable bravery for them to ride in and confront him; he was of another world, the spirit world. They did not expect to return home from this journey. His respect for their courage grew greater but it also heightened his anger over the foolishness of their trip. He was a white man now, not an Indian.

Lockhart tried to hide the irritation he felt about their uninvited intrusion into his life. After all, he had left the tribe to rid himself of the past, of the ache of losing Young

Evening, of their foolish attempt to make him into some kind of a ghost or one protected by them. Didn't they understand he wanted to forget ever being with them? Wasn't it enough that his heart was black until just recently? Why did they have to come now? How dare they interrupt his new life? Didn't they realize what an important man he had become in Denver City? Didn't it ever occur to them that he might have plans demanding his attention?

What a foolish notion to come to Denver City! He had a life with absolutely no connection with them anymore. He had friends who simply wouldn't understand this part of his past. Besides, he didn't have the time to go running off to find a savage who would be dead whenever this Laramie rancher decided he wasn't worth keeping around. Why wasn't Touches-Horses more careful? Why did he go to the fort, anyway? How stupid can someone get! Was this why he had those strange recollections yesterday? Did Stone-Dreamer have something to do with it? How could that possibly be? He was a successful Denver City businessman, not some savage believing in an old man's magical phrases, sleight-of-hand tricks, or a bunch of dumb rocks.

He was a *wasicun.* A very happy *wasicun!* Recovering from the shock of their appearance—and his frustration at the naiveté of their request, Lockhart asked, "Are you hungry?" in the Lakotan tongue. He was rusty, but the words came without much thought. He could at least see they returned with plenty of food.

"Not so. Want only to return to our village," Thunder Lance answered. "Quick. If it is *Wanagi Yanka's* will. This is an honored place for spirits, not warriors. But we come to you with our hearts ready. *Hokay hey*, it is a good day to die."

Gesturing first toward the chandelier, Thunder Lance pointed to the big mirror and, lastly, to the excited barmaid's glittery dresses. She smiled seductively, thinking he was probably referring to her as Lockhart's woman, or at least to how attractive she was. Their desire to leave was easy to understand, Lockhart thought. He glanced around. Every customer was watching the encounter with liquored interest—some with anger, some with fear, some with a lust to kill.

"Got yurnse'f some redskins to do yur dirty work now, eh, Mistuh Lockhart?"

Lockhart turned slowly to face a big-shouldered man, apparently unarmed, with a dirty face. Dark hair, which hadn't seen soap and water for a long time, was stuffed under a brand-new derby hat. The sour man was standing with his hands on his hips. His miner friends were egging him on, but trying to do it without Lockhart noticing.

"We'uns in this h'yar town don't like havin' no redskins around—an' no redskin lovers neither," he continued with a contemptuous smile.

"Go on home, friend. You've got better things to do with your day than try to provoke me."

Lockhart turned back to the four Indians and asked them in Lakotan where they were camping, and Thunder Lance replied in detail. For their own safety, they needed to get out of here, he thought. He told them to return to their camp and wait for him there. He would come as soon as he could. Lockhart wanted to say he wouldn't be going back with them but couldn't bring himself to do it. Not right now. It would be too much for them. They might think the spirits were offended and out to get them.

With relief in their eyes, the warriors left the saloon. Behind them in the open floor remained the circle of tobacco bundles, cedar branches, sage, and sweetgrass. And the four colored stones. Thunder Lance was the last to leave. As he stepped to the doorway, the tall warrior turned back toward Lockhart and saluted him with "*Hau*! Veen Lock-Hard! Thunder Lance believes in *Wanagi Yanka's* strength! It shall be so."

Lockhart grimaced and waved goodbye, remembered the necklace and torn piece of cloth in his hands, and shoved them hurriedly into his coat pockets.

"Whatcha gonna do 'bout me, Mistuh Lockhart? Gonna shoot down an unarmed man? Huh? See, I ain't got none o' them big six-shooters, like you're a-wearin' so fancy-like," sparked the big man, standing six feet four inches, his forearms bristling with hard-work muscle. A wicked snear accentuated his challenge. "How about it, Mistuh Lockhart—fists. You 'n' me. Toe to toe. Like men."

Everything about the miner said he was a brawler. Big arms. Heavy chest. Whitened scars lined his knuckles. Broken nose and bloated ears. A long scar on his cheek was likely from a knife fight, Lockhart thought. He figured the man was a bully confident of his ability to whip him. Other customers were gathering behind the big man, as close as they dared to.

"That's the way, Judd. Tell 'im what fer." "Yeah, Judd, he's a-scar't o' you, look at 'im." "Let's see how tough you are, Lockhart—without that six-shooter." "Don't let that damn miner bother you, kick him out of here." "Throw the fool out, Lockhart." "Coldcock that drunken fool." Encouragement and taunts stroked the room, made worse by the relief everyone felt from the Indians leaving.

Why fight this man? Lockhart knew he couldn't afford being laid up from a beating. Or worse, what if the brawler knocked him out and snapped his neck or broke his back? Lockhart had seen such physical destruction before. It took only seconds for a person who knew how. There was no reason to risk a beating, and that was what he must assume would happen. The miner was at least forty pounds heavier than he was, but weight wasn't that much of a factor if a man could compensate with speed and skill. Thanks to Crawfish's careful training, Lockhart had surprised a number of bigger men who had miscalculated their physical abilities relative to his. But this wasn't the time to prove one's superiority in fisticuffs.

"Come on, Mistuh Lockhart, are ya feared o' me? Hell, I jest a poor miner. Take away that big gun an' you're nuthin' but a scared rabbit."

Lockhart said nothing as he returned to the far edge of the bar and ordered a whiskey from Billy. Standing at the end of the bar, the frightened barmaid wanted to say something warm and caring to him, but dared not. She wanted to yell out, asking what the Indians wanted with her boss, but now wasn't the time. What kind of civilized man knew and liked red savages?

Handing a half-filled glass to Lockhart, Billy nervously whispered, "Be careful, boss. That's Judd. He wins all the miner fights. Been bragging about whipping you to his friends there."

"Whar ya headin', Mistuh Lockhart? Gonna hide behin't that fine bosom of that ripe store gal over thar?" Judd continued, waving his huge hand in the direction of the barmaid. "A man sure could enjoy hisse'f a-showin' her what fer. How 'bout that, saloon boy? Bet them tits'd look real good in my hands. She looks nice 'n' juicy to me. What that gal needs is a real man. I'd ram 'er 'til she screamed for mercy."

The savage laughter that followed settled over Lockhart as he tightened his fist around the glass. His eyes darkened as they rose to meet Billy's. He whispered, "No, boss. It's all right." J. R. Parks moved toward the barmaid with the intent of having her go into the back office.

"Let it go, Vin. She's not worth it," came Park's retort. "That kinda talk happens all the time in this business—and you know it."

The barmaid frowned and looked back at Lockhart. Without paying attention to her or anyone else, he took off his coat and neatly laid it across the bar, alongside the gifts from the Oglalas. His shoulder holster and gun followed, with the big miner watching in silence, a cruel grin on his face.

"Oh, we gonna see how tough this h'yar saloon boy is—without no iron to back him up. I'm gonna break your back, Mistuh Lockhart. An' then I'm gonna piss all over you."

Chapter Thirteen

Lockhart didn't hear the last part of the sentence as the big miner rushed at him, throwing a freight-train haymaker with his powerful right fist. A left-handed, downward-sweeping blow followed. Both missed their target as Lockhart stepped catlike inside Judd's outstretched arms and slammed an uppercut to the miner's thick chin. The jolting thud stopped Judd's vicious attempt to get Lockhart in a bear hug after his first swings missed.

"Get him, Judd! Tear his head off!" screamed a bearded miner. At the card table, the heavyset player said quietly, "I'll take Lockhart for twenty." The other three players rushed to accept the bet.

Lockhart's short left jab was a blink behind the first blow, smashing into Judd's blubbering lips and yellowed teeth. Shaking his head to clear away the impact, the miner put the back of his hand to his bleeding gums. An instant later, he threw a devastating right cross that glanced off Lockhart's cheek, stunning him even though it wasn't a direct hit. But he was alert enough to duck the trailing left hook launched in a lumbering, thunderous style.

His head clearing, Lockhart returned to the attack with precision jabs to Judd's ample belly. Like most big men, the miner had always gotten by on his sheer size, his God-given strength, and his opponent's self-inflicted fear. He had never run into a smaller man whose fighting skills were well-honed and whose inner fierceness was more deeply rooted than his own. Warily, the big miner circled Lockhart and threw a battering right into his midsection. The miner's friends yelled their encouragement and several other patrons did too.

"Come on, Judd, ya got his ass now!" "Take him, Lockhart. Stomp that sonuvabitch miner into the ground!" "The widow-maker, Judd! Throw the widow-maker!" "Lead with your left, your left, Judd."

Gasping for air that wouldn't come fast enough, Lockhart swung wildly at the big man and missed completely. Judd's big right fist slammed again into Lockhart's ribs. A sickening pain seared through his body all the way to his groin. As the miner grabbed for him, Lockhart regained his poise and hammered a wicked left into Judd's face, jolting him backward. Judd's fingers held on to Lockhart's shirt, ripping it open as the huge miner lost his balance.

Lockhart knew he must finish this fight quickly or let the bigger man's sheer size advantage slowly overtake him. He punched with both hands at Judd's belly, like a gunfighter fanning a pistol—a devastating hammering at the man's internal structure. Sidestepping the staggering miner, Lockhart fired a popping left that split Judd's cheek, spewing blood on both of them. The miner's friends were stunned, not believing that the man they thought was invincible was being torn apart.

Lockhart's right uppercut snapped the man's head back like a lid flying open from a cracker barrel. As Judd fell to his knees, Lockhart grabbed the miner's greasy black hair with his left hand. Holding Judd's dulled face, Lockhart delivered a right-handed explosion that crunched the bones in his already flattened nose. Unconscious, the bloody miner collapsed headfirst onto the saloon floor. Lockhart was completely unaware of the unbreathing silence in the room.

Pale and panicked, Billy finally found the nerve to speak: "A-a-h-h, M-M-Mr. Lockhart, w-w-would you l-l-like another whiskey, sir? That one g-g-got spilled." He held out an overly filled glass, excess whiskey spilling onto his quivering hands.

Lockhart made no attempt to take the glass. J. R. Parks walked around the bar, took the drink, and quietly held it as Lockhart worked to regain his breath and return his mind and body to a nonaggressive state. Sweat bubbled and streaked over his face and body. His shirt hung off his shoulders and sagged around his arms. All three of his employees—Parks, Billy, and the barmaid—were fascinated by two sets of scars on his bare chest, strange-looking marks that stood out from the dark hair and tanned skin, scars that appeared to have been carefully placed there for some unexplained reason. Lockhart stared at his bleeding hands for a moment, unaware of anyone around him or that the saloon was returning to normal.

Someone slapped Lockhart on the back and congratulated him, then another and another. He barely heard Parks ask in a hushed tone, "Are you all right, boss? Here's something to settle you down."

Looking around, Lockhart saw Young Evening in the doorway. The black hole in his mind that held her memory back had broken open once more. He blinked and the image was gone, leaving only the door.

Before he could answer himself, a raspy challenge came from the doorway: "Mister, I do hope you are planning to use that gun to clean out your nose holes. If I thought otherwise, this sawed-off shotgun would make a right nasty hole in your yellow belly."

The voice was unmistakable to Lockhart. Crawfish. Swallowing his courage, a blond-bearded miner with a drawn pistol hurriedly attempted to replace it in his belt. His urgency made him miss and the gun clattered on the floor. Forgetting Parks's offered drink, Lockhart straightened his shoulders, slipped his shoulder holster into place, and sauntered over to the panicked miner.

"That your gun on the floor?" Lockhart said, his eyes tearing into the man's bearded face.

"Ah, wal, er…ah, yessir, it is." The miner gulped.

Lockhart leaned over, picked up the weapon, and shoved it, handle first, into the miner's stomach. The miner grabbed it with both hands, as the thrust drove liquored breath from his lungs.

"Easy, Vin. Easy," came Crawfish's calming advice. He leaned on the cane in his left hand and, with his right hand, casually held the sawed-off shotgun at his side.

Lockhart snarled at the miner, "Here. You wanted to shoot me. Do it. Now. Come on, you sleazy son of a bitch. It's a good day to die. Can you pull the hammer and fire—before I clear mine? Come on, let's find out. My hands are stiff already. Come on. Let's see how good you are when a man's staring at you."

Lockhart's face was hard; his eyes tore through the man's face. The miner's body was shaking so much, he could barely control it. His eyes fled to the corner of the saloon. Lockhart slapped him hard across the mouth and a line of blood followed down the man's chin.

"Come on! Pull back the hammer. That's what you wanted, wasn't it? What's stopping you now?" Lockhart started to slap him again, but this time the miner's eyes pleaded for mercy as he dropped the gun. It clanked loudly on the floor.

Lockhart looked around at the miner's friends. His unspoken challenge was not met. Only the shortest of the three miners wanted to say something, but the tall, skinny miner to his left jabbed him in the stomach with a sharp elbow. A one-eyed miner, on his other side, told him to shut up.

"Boys, have a drink on the. house, then get out of here. Take your two friends with you. The gunslinger here—and what's his name, yeah, Judd," Lockhart said. "If they're smart, they won't be seen in Denver City again. Tell them that if you care about them. Because I don't—and I won't be as understanding next time. I've got lots of friends to watch my back, so if one of your buddies is found in an alley, he'll never leave it. Understand? Good."

With only a slight hesitation, the three remaining miners nodded nervously at Lockhart, turned quickly away, and faced Billy behind the bar. Eager to get their free drinks, they ignored the wounded miner on the floor and the shaken, gun-toting miner behind them. Parks looked at Lockhart's untouched whiskey in his hand and drained it with one gulp. He returned the empty glass to the bar with a thud and a cough.

"A round on the house, Billy," Crawfish announced loudly, bringing an end to the tension. He laid the sawed-off weapon on the closest table, patted Lockhart on the back, and limped over to the fallen gun. Using his cane for balance, he leaned over, picked it up, and shoved it into his belt.

"You'd better be soaking those hands in some hot salted water, son. You'll pay for it if you don't," he said, beginning to grin. "I thought I taught you better, letting that big thug catch you in the ribs like that."

Lockhart smiled thinly and put his arm around his partner's shoulder.

"I'll get the hot water," Parks said immediately, and hurried away.

Crawfish flopped the miner's pistol on the bar and tried to get the attention of Billy, who was swamped with requests for free drinks. Exasperated at Billy's inattentiveness to this end of the bar, Crawfish turned back to Lockhart and said, "Heard you had some visitors. I figured it was some of your old friends, from the description. I came as fast as I could, brought the ol' thunderbuss along for good measure."

"I saw that. You even scared *me* with it."

Crawfish chuckled and glanced back at the weapon lying on the empty tabletop.

Lockhart continued, "Yeah, it was some old friends of mine. You just missed them. Where'd you hear about it?"

"I was headed for the Judge's, to discuss, well, you know. All of a sudden, some guy comes running past me, screaming about red savages being in the Silver Queen. It's obvious they didn't drop in for Sunday supper, Vin. What did they want?" Crawfish's forehead was furrowed in genuine concern.

"An…old friend, Touches-Horses, has been captured. Somebody around Fort Laramie's got him. A white rancher."

"Touches-Horses? Isn't that your brother-in-law?"

"Was."

"Doesn't that beat all. What in tarnation an' Betsy for?"

"Training horses. Touches-Horses was magic with a horse, I told you that. Remember? I've never seen anyone better. Sounds like the ranch is supplying horses to the army. Makes sense, they get a top trainer—for free."

Parks brought the pan of hot water and left to help Billy with the demand for the offered free drinks. Lockhart barely noticed him. From her position next to a table, the barmaid came forward and took Lockhart's hands. Gently she guided them to the pan and looked into his face, hoping for a smile. Lockhart was oblivous to her; the red-faced prospector wasn't.

"Thank you, Missy. That's right helpful."

Lockhart blinked his eyes and saw the yellow-haired woman for the first time and said, "Thank you, Allison. I'm sorry for being so rude."

"Think nothing of it, Mister Lockhart. You were magnificent. I've never had any man fight for me before." She fluttered her eyes and unashamedly asked, "How can I repay you?" Her fingers touched his arm and her eyes dropped to the scars on his uncovered chest and back to his face.

"You don't owe me a thing. No one talks to our people like that and gets away with it," Lockhart said, and concentrated on the heat filling his battered fists.

He'd almost forgotten what a fight did to a man's knuckles. There was a part of him that admitted enjoying it. Combat had released the anger he felt from being asked to return to the Oglalas. How dare they ask this of him? The tall miner and his one-eyed companion stutter-stepped toward the unconscious Judd. Grabbing the fallen miner's feet, they began to drag him across the saloon floor. Smears of blood trailed his exit. The shortest miner said something to the gun-toting miner. They looked at the pistol on the bar and left it there as they walked out, staring straight ahead.

"How you think they got him?" Crawfish asked, and vigorously waved both hands over his head at J. R. Parks to get his attention. Allison, the barmaid, leaned her elbow on the bar, not wanting to leave in case Lockhart might look at her again.

Lockhart was clearly annoyed at his partner's interest and grumbled, "Oh, he was stupid enough to visit some Indians living near the fort."

"Why was that stupid?"

"Come on, Crawfish. It was bound to happen. Taking good horses where there are a lot of white men? That's foolish as hell. He should've known better."

"Are you going back?"

"Of course not. I left them a long time ago. I've got no intention of going back for anything. Can't believe Stone-Dreamer would be so foolish to have them come here to ask me—and so careless with their lives. It's a damn wonder they weren't shot just riding down the street!"

"I don't reckon Stone-Dreamer sees it that way. As I recall, you told me Touches-Horses's mother has already lost a husband and a daughter. Now she's dealing with losing a son on top of all that. Damn, man, I've seen white folks go plumb crazy after just one of those blows."

"I know that."

"Well, she's come to him, pleading for his great wisdom, his great power, to help," Crawfish continued, glancing at Allison occasionally as if to wonder why she wasn't somewhere else and, in what passed for a whisper, said, "Now your father has nowhere else to go. Nowhere."

"Dammit, Crawfish! He's the one who started the whole spirit thing in the first place."

"He wouldn't be the first parent who measured his kid high."

"Oh, come on, now."

"That's what it looked like to me. Wish I had a father who thought I was great," Crawfish continued, glancing again at Allison, who smiled.

"Besides that, I can't just pull up and go riding off—and quit calling him my father. We've got a new hotel to plan—and a saloon to run," Lockhart said, removing his hands from the pan in response and splashing water on himself, Crawfish, and Allison.

"I'll take care of things until you get back."

"Don't be silly. I'm not going anywhere."

Allison looked at the front of her dress, dripping with

water, and saw that her nipples were accented by the wetness. She immediately looked at Lockhart to see if he had noticed. He hadn't. Her face showed the disappointment.

"Allison, can you give me a hand?" Billy yelled at her.

She shook her head positively and stomped away with neither Lockhart nor Crawfish paying any attention to her.

Crawfish looked down at the wet splotch on his freshly ironed pants and spoke without emotion: "How can you refuse? That's family, Vin. You know I don't have any. Wish I did. Folks that carried my stick high, no matter what. That would be something to grab ahold of and never let go."

"Crawfish, they aren't my family. My family is dead. What connection I had to these Indians is long gone. I'm a Denver City businessman. A good one. Everything I want is here."

"Are you telling me Stone-Dreamer doesn't think of you as his son? Look at me and say that. You're talking to Crawfish now," Crawfish said with a bite to his words Lockhart hadn't heard very often.

The older man cocked his head sideways and said, "Yes, I know, Newton, I know Vin is successful—and busy. No, I have no idea how Stone-Dreamer knew where he was, but he's a man of visions. He's connected to the spirits. No, I wasn't being sarcastic. I think he is. Yes, I know it's Vin's decision, not mine. What would you do if it were you, Newton, hmm? You always side with Vin."

He waved again at Billy, and this time the bartender saw him and quickly handed Crawfish a full bottle of whiskey and two glasses. Behind them, through the saloon door, came City Marshal Joe Benson. His dark suit and vest were accented with a gunbelt across his paunch. In his hands was a double-barreled shotgun. With a thin voice working hard to sound authoritative and confident,

Marshal Benson bellowed, “Show me where those Indian savages are and I’ll put an end to this menace.”

Crawfish took a long swallow from the bottle, laughed, and answered, “You’re a mite late, law dawg. But those savages weren’t redskins. They were miners. An’ I do believe they’ve slunk off to their respective rocks.”

“There’s no problem, Benson. You can go on with whatever it is you do.” Lockhart looked up at the lawman casually, then returned his gaze to his soaking hands.

Marshal Benson inhaled to maximize his chest and countered, “Lockhart, this town cannot, and will not, have wild red savages walking its streets. My reports were they were in full paint and feathers—and armed to the teeth. You’re under arrest for bringing red Indians inside the city limits.”

Lockhart glanced at Crawfish and withdrew his hands from the pan. From behind the bar Allison handed him a towel and a whiskey to a happy cowboy at the same time. She was trying to stay as close to Lockhart as possible. Her eyes lingered to let him know she would like to show her appreciation. As he dried his hands, Lockhart said, “Benson, I don’t know where you heard that crap. Those Indians were on a religious mission. See that circle of cedar boughs. That was a tribute to the town. They came in peace without any weapons. They left the same way some time ago. I guess your reports didn’t tell you that. I’m sure you’ve got something better to do, Benson. Good day.”

“I’m not finished with you, Lockhart” Benson alerted, pointing the shotgun in his direction. “Why did they want to honor the town? How come they came here, instead of my office—or the mayor’s?”

“I didn’t ask. They didn’t say.”

Chuckles sprinkled through the saloon as the customers drank and watched the shotgun-toting lawman with amused interest. Lockhart’s expression was grim; he massaged his hands to work through the bruising. Marshal Benson's eyebrows twitched in anticipation of his next pronouncement.

"You're still under arrest, Lockhart. There are two men outside who are pressing charges of assault and attempted murder," Benson barked.

Crawfish growled to Lockhart in a stage whisper, intended for the lawman to hear, "Now, boy, don't you go busting through your temper again. This poor man has just been badly misinformed. Give him another chance to make it right, will you?"

"Benson, walk around the saloon and find out what happened for yourself and then go away. You're not arresting me today, or any day. Billy, give Benson a drink. Allison, go and pat the nice man on the head."

To keep from toughing, Crawfish took a long pull from the whiskey bottle. His eyes caught Allison biting her lip to keep from giggling, and he lost it. Turning his head away, Crawfish spewed whiskey from his mouth in a long guffaw. The saloon erupted in laughter.

With great indignation, J. R. Parks declared over the noise, "Marshal, you've got it all backwards. Those two tried to kill Mr. Lockhart. Arrest *them* for attempted murder. I'll be glad to testify."

Allison crossed her arms and said defiantly, "He's right, Marshal. Ask anyone here. Mr. Lockhart defended my honor. It was wonderful to see. You should be ashamed of yourself for listening to riffraff." She glanced toward Lockhart to see his reaction and smiled as he nodded his appreciation.

Marshal Benson's mind quickly became aware of shouts of support for Lockhart and bold declarations of his innocence blossoming through the saloon.

From the farthest card table he heard someone growl, "Hell, let's run this silly excuse fer a lawman outta town."

Benson swallowed and knew he didn't have the nerve

to find out who had said it. Red-faced, he lowered the shotgun and hoped his voice wouldn't quiver with his announcement: "So it was self-defense. Again. I accept that, Lockhart. This time. But you watch your step. This town won't tolerate violence, and you keep showing up when there is some."

"Benson, what this town won't tolerate, for long, is a phony. I suggest *you* do the step watching. You're not good enough, even with that scattergun." Lockhart's hard retort cracked through the air like a ricocheting bullet.

"Are you saying you could draw that iron before I could fire?" Benson wished he hadn't made the rushed statement, but it was out of his mouth before he could stop it.

"No, I'm saying before you play, you'd better know the game. Look around."

Benson's eyes first caught Billy holding the bar towel in what seemed like an unusual position. A longer look discovered the twin barrels of a shotgun staring at him from underneath it. Next he noticed that Crawfish had his sawed-off shotgun cradled in crossed arms—its twin noses pointed at Benson's chest and his hand wrapped around the trigger guard. Benson's eyes flickered further and he saw the mild-mannered J. R. Parks, also behind the bar, holding a short-barreled Colt at his side. It, too, was cocked.

With a deep breath, Marshal Benson spun on his heels and left the saloon, walking slowly to maintain the perception of authority. Outside, customers in the saloon heard him advise someone on the street, "It's all safe now, folks. Nothing to worry about. I've taken care of the matter. There are no more red savages in town. You can go on about your business without worry."

Satisfied with the lawman's leaving, Crawfish surveyed Lockhart's torn shirt and said, "Vin, are you hungry? I am. How about I get us a table at Jacobson's. It'll be nice and quiet right about now. You wash up, find a fresh shirt, and join me. I can fill you in on the judge."

"I'd like that, Crawfish, as long as there's no more talk about Indians," Lockhart replied immediately.

"I promise."

"J. R., Allison, Billy, thanks for your help. Quite a day!" Lockhart complimented his key employees, shaking hands with Parks and Billy and smiling at Allison, who batted her eyelashes and feigned shyness.

Returning the pistol to his coat pocket, Parks said, "Everything will settle down quick. Free drinks have a way of doing that. Have a good supper. If those boys come back, I'll get you."

"They won't."

"How bad do you think the Indians will hurt business?" Parks asked, his small eyes squinting as if he were in bright sun.

Lockhart shook his head. "Hard to say. It'll be the talk of the town for a few days. Maybe we should leave that cedar and those stones where they are. Give everyone something to see."

"I like that idea. Makes us a real attraction."

"I'll be back in an hour. If you think another free round or two make sense, do it."

"Might at that. Figured I'd have some of the regulars sign a paper describing the fight first. Don't trust Benson."

"Good idea."

"Take your time. The crowd won't grow much for hours."

Lockhart headed for the back office and Allison followed him.

As he opened the door, she stepped close to him and said sweetly, "Can I come in and help you, boss?"

"That's mighty nice of you, Allison, but I can take care of it myself. Billy probably needs help, though."

Allison didn't know how to respond to Lockhart's simple declaration and huffed, "I don't understand. Aren't I good enough for you?"

For the first time Lockhart realized the extent of Allison's offer.

"Allison, you don't owe me anything," Lockhart answered quietly. "Our people shouldn't have to put up with that kind of talk. Especially not a beautiful lady like you."

"But I want you. I've wanted you for a long time," Allison purred, and stepped against his body, her breasts brushing against his chest. Her fingers finally touched those unusual scars. She looked into his eyes for the acceptance she sought. He gently lifted her hand away from his chest.

"I am flattered by your attention, Allison, and don't deserve it. You save it for the right man. Now, please excuse me. Crawfish will be waiting, and we've got business to attend to," he said, and moved into the opened doorway.

Allison hesitated again. She turned toward the bar and looked back at Lockhart with embarrassment in her eyes. She was red-faced, with tears filling her eyes, and words filled with hate spurted from her tight mouth: "I hope those Indians kill you."

She spun around again and stomped toward the far side of the saloon. Lockhart watched her and said, "They already have."

Chapter Fourteen

An orange moon was flirting with the mountains and any interested stars. Vin Lockhart was awake and had been for over an hour. In the darkness, the room crowded around him. He grabbed his pocket watch on the bedside table, held it closely in the dark, and saw it was 2:40. Fifteen minutes later than the last time he looked. Disgusted, he threw the watch in the direction of the far wall. It clanked against the plaster and fell to the floor.

Rubbing his hand across his mouth, he lay on his back, angry that sleep wouldn't return. Night sounds seemed louder than they should be through his boarding room window. An owl searched for small animals making a last mistake. Leaves sang their darkness songs. Tiny things whispered. Somewhere a drunk was delivering a speech, or thought he was. A carriage rattled along the street. Two horsemen came from the other direction. He could recite what was going on outside without looking. He wished he couldn't. After the saloon fight and supper with Crawfish, the rest of the day had been wasted in buying and taking food and supplies to the four Oglala warriors.

They were camped in a narrow draw separated from the trail by a wall of fir trees, aspen, and waving grass. He wouldn't have found them without good directions from Thunder Lance. It burned him that he had lost his nerve at the last minute and didn't tell them he wasn't going to look for Touches-Horses. Instead, he made an excuse about trying to get things arranged so that he could, emphasizing how difficult it was in terms he thought they might understand.

Now he told himself it was better this way. When he finally told them that he couldn't go, their report to Stone-Dreamer would be filled with expressions of how hard he tried. That he felt the need for an excuse angered him even more. In addition to his pocket watch, the bed table held the choker necklace, the torn piece of burial cloth and his pistol. He touched first the necklace. Young Evening had made it herself, keeping the gift a secret until their wedding night. The image was ever sweet to his mind.

But touching the cloth sprung memories of her death from their closed-off place in his soul. Until today the ache had been scarred over. It had been a long time since the agony of her death had shoved its way back into his thinking. Why must he return to that tortured blackness now? Dreams of Young Evening's death used to come so often that he didn't want to sleep. Usually he awoke with tears on his face, with traces of her last anguish chewing into his conscious mind.

His mind jumped to the Oglala messengers. Was the real problem that he was ashamed of them and their simple ways? Was that why he was so angry? Was he embarrassed because Bear-Heart wore tin cans? That Thunder Lance thought he was in some "spirit world" when he was only in a saloon? That they brought four rocks as if they were great jewels? Was he ashamed at the looks of scorn they got from his customers? These Indians didn't know anything about money, or owning property, or telegraphs, or reading, or mining, or playing poker, or dressing nice. Was he afraid someone might ask him about his past? Was that really the problem?

He told himself that he was no longer the wild savage who believed in talking rocks or helpful panthers; he was a successful businessman who understood there weren't any miracles, just hard work and some timely luck. And there definitely weren't any spirit helpers or singing rocks in the white man's world. Although he did prefer riding alone into the foothills outside of town on Sunday mornings, instead of attending the white man's church. He always felt renewed after such rides.

The God of the white man was *Wakantanka*, he had finally realized. He could be with God more easily out in the open sky than in a wooden building. But he wasn't Panther-Strikes anymore, and he certainly wasn't someone protected by ghosts. Why hadn't that strange tale died when he left their village? Why had it stayed alive all this time? Couldn't they see how silly the idea was? No wonder white people didn't want Indians around!

How could Stone-Dreamer—of all people—be so selfish, so presumptuous? How could he expect Lockhart to drop everything and return, just to find an Indian that once called himself his brother-in-law? Didn't the old man realize that people didn't make requests like that? Touches-Horses wasn't his brother-in-law anymore—and Stone-Dreamer wasn't his father. All that died with... her.

He shut his eyes and the room disappeared. A time locked away returned. Finally the man called *Wanagi Yanka*, Rides-with-Spirits, by his former Ogtala friends went to sleep again. A fitful sleep. Once he stirred awake, sensing something outside his room, but drifted off once more. Sometime during the night, a woman paused at his door, raised a hand to knock, thought better of it, and left.

For the next two days Lockhart didn't sleep well, trying to eliminate the pull within him to return. He avoided people as much as possible, particularly Crawfish, staying in his office or his room and responding to intrusions with little patience and less politeness. Only Crawfish had the nerve to frequently enter his self-imposed exile, but his friendly bravado was met with cold stares and one-word answers.

Early the third morning, he stared out the window. Instead of seeing a gentle sunrise, memories of Touches-Horses's friendship poured into his mind.

"Stone-Dreamer, you have no goddamn right to do this to me!" he yelled into the morning air. He ran over to the bed table, grabbed the choker and cloth piece, and hurled them out the window.

A drunken miner, leaning against the house below him, thought the curse and thrown items were aimed at him and raised his fist in defiance and stumbled down the street.

"That's it, that's enough. I'm telling those ungrateful fools today that I'm not going back with them. I've pussy-footed around this long enough," he declared, and slammed his fist against the wall and put the idea of going back out of his mind. Forever.

After dressing in his best business suit, fresh white shirt, and silk tie, Lockhart went immediately to the Silver Queen to celebrate his decision. He would enjoy a drink, then ride out to tell the warriors that he wouldn't be coming and they should leave. The saloon was empty except for three drunken miners and a cowboy with the hiccups. As he entered, Lockhart glanced at the disheveled circle of dried sage, cedar boughs, sweetgrass, small bundles of tobacco, and four rocks lying in the center of the hardwood floor. Crawfish had ordered it left alone. Some of the cedar boughs were pulled away from the original nesting and a few of the small bundles of tobacco lay outside the ring. Otherwise it was undisturbed.

A circle. The Oglala symbol to show man is related to all living things.

Lockhart muttered, "*Mitakuye oyasin.*" His eyes locked onto the three-day-old display and soon his mind followed. He remembered going to Stone-Dreamer after receiving his spirit-guide vision.

"Father, I have seen beyond. Will you now teach me the songs of the stones?"

"My son, I cannot teach you this. They are powerful songs."

"I know they are so, father. I know the *inyan* are the most ancient of people. I know they are very wise. I am ready to hear the songs of the stones."

"The stones will decide when you are ready, if ever. The songs of the stones come only to a few. The stones choose. Not the man."

"Like they have chosen you, my father?"

"Yes. But you should always listen for them. Their rhythm is in all men. It comes from deep within Mother Earth herself. The *inyan* moves always to the will of the invisible grandfathers. But most men are deaf to them. If you think they are beginning to speak to you, come and tell me about it right away."

Shaking away the memory, Lockhart walked over to the circle and kneeled down. "Which one of you wants to speak to me?" His challenging eyes went to each small rock. None made him want to pick it up. Without realizing, he began to mutter, "God is great, God is good. Him we thank for daily food. By his hand we are fed. By his love we are led. Amen."

There. That will help the stones realize he was a *wasicun*, not a stone-seeker. See. He talked to the *wasicun* God, not *Wakantanka.* And definitely not to spirit helpers or, most of all, to a bunch of rocks. Lockhart suddenly looked around to see if anyone was watching, embarrassed at his foolish actions. The cowboy with the hiccups smiled and raised his hands to indicate he couldn't stop.

Lockhart said, "Give that fellow a whiskey. Maybe it'll help."

The late-night bartender couldn't reach for a bottle quickly enough.

"Why, *hic*, thank you, *hic*, Mister *hic*, Lockhichart."

"And get those silly rocks and brush out of here when you get a chance, Albert. They make the place look messy."

"Sure, boss. Where do you want me to put them?"

"Doesn't matter. Throw them out the back," Lockhart growled. "And while you're pouring, give me three fingers too. And one for those boys back there. On me."

A strange sensation gurgled within him, like the feeling he got when he came back from his vision quest. He shook his head to clear it away and watched the brown liquid being poured into a scratched bar glass. A rush of warm air swirled around his ear, like someone breathing close to him, and he turned to see if anyone was there. No one was. What was that sweet smell? It must be the sage. No, not quite. It was musky. He hadn't smelled anything like that for a long time. Like walking at dusk—only there was the soft sweet fragrance of a woman. Young Evening! Was she here? Now? It must be the sweetgrass, he muttered. He tried to ignore it and downed the fiery whiskey, and ordered another.

The scent disappeared, but the turmoil within him wouldn't stop. He looked over at the stones and said, "Why can't one of you speak to me? Just one of you! Is she here? Tell me!"

Sweat broke along his forehead, and he knew he was going to vomit if he stayed. He spun around and left the bar without touching the second drink. The bartender watched his boss leave hurriedly and wondered if he had done something wrong. It was their best whiskey. The hiccuping cowboy asked if he could have the drink and the bartender shoved it toward him without looking.

Stone-Dreamer had no right to do this to his mind, Lockhart told himself as he pushed open the saloon doors to the street. He had made his decision—he was not going back. And that was that. No matter how much his stomach churned or his nose filled with sweet memory. Two incoming saloon patrons bumped into him as he swept through the doors. He backed up angrily at the intrusion. Both men apologized for what was not their fault.

The taller patron asked him with a laugh, "Any of those damn redskins still around?"

Lockhart stared at them before answering. Then he growled, "Yeah…me."

He couldn't believe what he had just said. He stomped away from the surprised men and went immediately to the ground in front of his lodging house window. He saw the choker and cloth still wadded together on the ground. Holding them in the open palms of his hands, Lockhart sang the Oglala warrior's call to battle: "*Hokay hey*! It is a good day to die! I am Oglala. Only the earth and sky live forever. It is a good day to die."

A thin memory reminded him that both he and Touches-Horses were proud members of the Kit Fox Society. After a deep breath, he murmured in a singsong voice: "I am a Fox…I am supposed to die…. If there is anything difficult/If there is anything dangerous/That is mine to do." He squeezed the choker and cloth in his fists and returned them to his pockets.

Two hours later he met with the warriors and told them to return to Black Fire's village. He would be going by himself, directly to Laramie City. They understood. Lockhart knew that his friends were anxious to be away from him anyway. It was not wise to tempt the spirits by being close to Rides-With-Spirits for too long. He knew it wasn't smart to tempt being anywhere near a white settlement. Not anymore.

Along with his other gifts, he returned the presentation stones, except for the white one. He told them he would return it when he brought Touches-Horses to the village. As a gift for Stone-Dreamer, he gave them a magical gold stone on a gold chain for Stone-Dreamer. It was alive, making a strange *tk-tk-tk* purring all the time, night and day. Inside its shell were strange signs and markings. Surely strong medicine from the spirit warrior to the holy man. He also gave each warrior a new rifle and a sack full of bullets, plus more supplies and four strong horses. They were moved by his generosity. He told them to advise Stone-Dreamer that he would bring Touches-Horses back to the village alive, or find where his body lay and begin the Shadow Ceremony—or die himself in trying to free him. The warriors looked at each other upon hearing the last promise.

Returning to town, he saw Mattie Bacon strolling along the sidewalk with her arm on her father's. He grimaced, but it was too late to turn around. She had seen him. Gritting his teeth, he legged his black horse into an easy lope past them. His eyes locked onto the distance. He had more important things to worry about than some spoiled young woman.

"Vin! Vin, please stop. I need to talk with you!" Mattie Bacon's voice cut through the morning air and reached him as he passed.

Everything in him wanted to stop and give her a piece of his mind, but it was better this way. Stopping would only create a scene and force her father to act brave or crawl—and he wasn't brave—so it was best to ride on. Mattie Bacon needed a townsman like her father. There were plenty around, he decided. He eased his horse down the street and turned off toward Crawfish's house. It was time to tell Crawfish of his plans.

His eccentric partner was well into his morning ritual of drinking coffee and reading the newspaper when Lockhart arrived. However, this time he heard Lockhart enter and greeted him warmly, in spite of his sour attitude the last two days.

"Well, good mornin', stranger," Crawfish hollered. "How are you doing today? Newton was worried about you."

"I'm going back, Crawfish," Lockhart blurted. "I've already told the warriors."

"Well, good."

"You don't look surprised."

"I am proud of you, Vin," Crawfish said, unable to contain a smile that kept widening as he spoke. "You're doing the right thing." He put down the newspaper to give his young partner his full attention as Lockhart walked to the table.

"Whatever, I'm doing it," Lockhart growled, but his grin gave away his real feelings.

"You want me to go with you?"

"That's good of you, old friend," Lockhart said, and placed his hand on Crawfish's shoulder. "But this is my problem."

"Think I couldn't handle it?"

"Of course not."

"Just remember there's a telegraph. How about some coffee?"

"No, thanks, I'm going to catch the noon stage."

"Hop-comes-the-bunny! Once you make up your mind, you don't leave much room for debate," Crawfish said, and laughed. "That sounds like the Vin Lockhart I used to know."

"The sooner I go, the sooner I get back."

"Sure. It will be good for you to get away."

They talked a few minutes about business details. Crawfish shared the news that the judge would sell them his building next to the hotel for no more than the mortgage balance. At Lockhart's insistence, Crawfish accepted a written note giving Lockhart's share of their business to him if the young warrior didn't return. Crawfish followed that with the presentation of his sawed-off shotgun in the special shoulder quiver. The shell loops were filled on the shoulder strap with new loads.

"Take this. I filled it last night. Had a feeling," Crawfish said, his eyes filling with tears.

"Well, thanks, Crawfish, but I hope to buy Touches-Horses from the bastards," Lockhart said.

"Maybe. Take it anyway, just to make an old fool feel useful. And this, too," Crawfish said, and opened his fist to reveal the small pebble earring Lockhart had buried at their gold camp.

"W-w-what's this? I buried—"

"Yeah, I know. I just couldn't leave it there somehow. Went back and dug it up. It saved my life, you know. It and you. Newton says so too. Been keeping this for… for the right moment."

Lockart grinned sheepishly and said, "All right. All right. I'll take it along—but I'm not going to wear the fool thing."

"Whatever you think is right, Vin," Crawfish said, and held out his hand. Lockhart took the pebble, stared at it, and shoved the Eyes-of-the-Wind *tunyan* into his pocket. They shook hands. Crawfish turned away and rubbed his eyes quickly.

"Ah, I'll have a talk with—ah, the Bacon girl while you're gone," Crawfish said, his voice cracking.

"Don't bother," Lockhart said, and told him about the recent encounter.

"Never can tell about women."

"She's no Almina," Lockhart said.

"Don't be so sure. Good luck, partner. I'll be thinking of you."

Back at his room, Lockhart packed hurriedly. A full money belt waited on his bed to wear, along with his shoulder-holstered Colt. Next to them were his rifle, the sawed-off shotgun, and packed saddlebags, set aside to take. Inside the saddlebags was the pebble earring Crawfish had given him. At first he was going to leave the choker necklace, burial cloth, and the white stone behind, but he changed his mind and packed them away too. There was no need to talk with Mrs. Arbuckle—his rent was paid for two months. Besides, Crawfish would enjoy chatting with her. He took three shirts from a dresser drawer and laid them on top of the other folded clothing in the leather valise.

Knock! Knock! He was irritated by the interruption, and his mind flitted along the possibilities and landed on Crawfish. There must be something his good friend had forgotten to tell him. He went to the door and swung it open. Mattie Bacon stood there. He thought she had never looked prettier, and he wanted to grab her and hold her. But his mind reminded him of reality. What now? he thought. Hasn't she made it clear enough that she doesn't want to be with me? Does she have to come to my room to rub it in further?

Her dark eyes caressed him before she spoke: "You're going away and you weren't going to say goodbye, were you?"

Lockhart didn't answer.

"May I come in, Vin? Please?"

Lockhart said coldly, "I've got to catch the noon stage. What can I do for you, Miss Bacon?"

Mattie winced and said, "I deserved worse than that."

"I think your feelings were clear—and that's fine. Now, if you will excuse me, I really need to finish packing."

"Just for a minute, please. I promise, then I'll leave."

He stepped aside and motioned for her to enter. She took two steps and spun to face him as he closed the door. Her face was taut and her eyes were nearing tears.

"I've been waiting for you. At Dad's store," she said hesitantly. "I kept hoping you'd come. I saw you pass... across the street. I saw you today. I had to come see you. I haven't been able to sleep since—since that night. I came here two nights ago and lost my nerve."

Her voice was agitated, and it was obvious she was uncomfortable being in a man's room. His heart was pounding with the nearness of her, but his mind kept preparing him for the fact that she was here to tell him off in no uncertain terms.

"I'm sorry. It wasn't exactly what I had planned," Lockhart said, his eyes avoiding hers. He was certain where the conversation was headed.

He would be polite, he had decided. At all costs, he would show her Vin Lockhart was, at least, a gentleman. Or should he tell her that another woman wanted him and make her jealous? How stupid, he thought. She wouldn't know Allison from a rock. Besides, the woman was a saloon girl who worked for him. Allison was probably drunk when she came on to him, he told himself. That was it. He wouldn't hold her actions against her and wouldn't say a thing about it, either.

"Vin, please forgive me. I—I—I was such a fool. Will you accept my apology—for acting so, so stupid? All you did was save my life."

Lockhart's mind wasn't prepared for the music his ears delivered. He stared at her as if deciphering each word in his soul. Mattie touched his hand, triggering a warm sensation that helped the message reach his brain.

"There's no need for that," he said, not quite believing he had heard her correctly. "I'm afraid you got a glimpse of what I'm like, Mattie. Your father was right."

"Last night, I told father about what happened. He was

silent for a moment and then started crying," she said, her eyes blurring with their own moisture.

Lockhart swallowed and ran his tongue along the inside edge of his upper lip. He didn't want to go back there.

"I told him I was all right and not to cry. I thought he was angry at you." She choked but went on, her eyes bright with tears welling in the corners. "Finally he told me...that he wouldn't have been able to save me, if it had been him. He said he would have given them his money and begged for them not to shoot him—and if they grabbed me..." She couldn't finish, and Lockhart gave her a handkerchief.

"That's the second one you've given me," she said, dabbing her eyes clear. "I'm going to keep them both, you know."

"I'd like that."

"Hold me, Vin," she said, opening her arms to him. "Please hold me. Please. It has been awful without you. I don't ever want to be away from you again. Ever. Tell me you feel the same way."

"No, Mattie. It's best to end it this way," Lockhart said, taking a step back, surprised at his own strength. "You've got your way of living—and I have mine. They are very different. Please, I would like you to leave now."

It was her turn to be silent. His emotions were crackling inside. All he could think of was bringing her close to him, but his Indian past was too much to ask her to accept.

"I—I—I want you, Vin," she looked up at him. Tears took over her face. "I can't live without you. I know that. It's terrible to love someone this much, but I do. Can't you forget what happened, please, and give me another chance?"

"You don't understand, Mattie. I'm not like the other men you've known. I'm, I'm—well, I'm an Indian. A wild Indian."

Mattie's eyes seized Lockhart's well-intentioned gaze.

With her voice flickering with emotion, she said, "I know all about it. That doesn't matter to me. The only thing that matters is being with you, all of the time."

"I figured you would've heard about the Indians in the saloon. That's not the..."

"Crawfish told me about your living with the Ogialas."

"Crawfish?"

"Yes, your dear sweet partner. I just left him at the store," she said, wiping a tear that had broken away from her eye. "When he told me you were leaving, I ran all the way here. I couldn't bear another day without you."

"But, Mattie..."

"He told me everything, Vin. I know about Touches-Horses, Stone-Dreamer—and Young Evening. I know of a great warrior named Panther-Strikes whose tribe thinks he is holy. I know where you are going and why. It only makes me love you more."

His hand touched her face. Slowly his fingers caressed her soft lips. She kissed them as they passed. His mouth followed his fingers, and her mouth opened to receive him. They kissed long and deep.

From their empassioned embrace, she pulled away and said, "Will you come back to me?"

"How could I not?" he said, holding her close to him with his right arm and running his fingers through her hair with his left.

"Please wear the stone earring Crawfish gave you," Mattie said, looking into his eyes. "I feel it will protect you and bring you back to me."

"So he told you about spirit stones, did he?" Lockhart asked, a sly grin running across his face.

"Yes. And he told me about a very special young warrior who learned how to read and write—and became very successful. He even told me about teaching you how to box." She paused and said quietly, "And about your real parents and what happened to them. I'm so sorry, Vin."

"Why, that old rascal! He must've raced over to your place right after I left. He shouldn't be telling wild stories like that. I'll have to have a chat with that old bird."

Her trembling ringers touched his hard face and slowly crossed his lips, repeating his earlier gesture. He drew her to him and they kissed again.

Lockhart's mouth retreated an inch from hers, and he whispered, "I'll wear that stone again if you'll keep the one Stone-Dreamer gave me."

Without waiting for her response, he went to his bag, took the small white stone from the drawer, and handed it to her.

"I will keep it with me every day until you return," she said, and stared at the small snow-white rock in her hand. She squeezed her hand over it and said, "Oh, Vin, my darling, please don't ever let me go."

"Mattie, everything in me wants you with me," Lockhart said. "And it has since the first time I saw you."

"Make love to me, Vin. Now. Before you go. I need a memory to hold me until you return."

She was surprised at her own directness. She had never done anything like this before. But there was no time to be coy. Her man was leaving soon. He was going into a dangerous situation and possibly might not return. She didn't let those thoughts linger. Her primary concern was to enjoy him. Her yearning was overwhelming. Her breasts ached. Her face was as hot as a July sunburn.

Mattie sensed his hesitation, so she walked to the door, locked it, and returned before he could say anything. With a wry smile, she set the stone on the bed and began unbuttoning his shirt. Her eyes sought his for permission only after the shirt was halfway opened. Pulling it apart, she began kissing his muscled, hairy chest. Her fingers traced the jagged scars from the long-ago sun dance ordeal. Lockhart stared downward and watched her performance before it registered in his swirling mind. His own breath was swift, in small hurried gasps.

"Mattie. Mattie! You can't do that…you…."

Gently, she touched his lips with her fingers to silence him and whispered, "The stage doesn't come for two hours."

He took her fingers in one hand, and with the other hand turned her face up toward his. He kissed her mouth; it was open and inviting. He kissed her closed eyelids and the soft nape of her neck, then went back to her eager mouth. The sweet smell of her, a gentle fragrance of cooking blended with the musky scent of her womanhood, engulfed first his nostrils, then his mind.

Chapter Fifteen

A dry wind moaned and cut across Vin Lockhart's face as he rode through the rolling hills southeast of Laramie City. Dawn eased across his left shoulder and he turned instinctively to watch the red and gold streaks come alive in the gray sky. It felt good to be riding on the land again and away from the tightness of the city, away from the restriction of his properties, away from the demands of securing wealth. His destination was the Bar 5 horse ranch.

Arriving in the Wyoming Territorial settlement yesterday, he had quickly learned this was the ranch that had Indian horse trainers. Only it was supposed to be a "secret," according to the talkative bartender. The chatty man had whispered that Virgil "Vinegar" Farrell was using wild Indians to train horses for the army. A whistle had followed his declaration and Lockhart had been appropriately shocked, agreeing that it was risky business. However, the bartender was more interested in telling

Lockhart about the mayor being upstairs with one of the saloon's ladies.

"If it's good horses you want, the best are definitely Vinegar's these days. They say he's got some Indians that can teach a horse to sing and dance," the bartender emphasized, nodding his head after the sentence as if passing judgment on it independently. "But I wouldn't waste my time trying to buy any from him. I hear tell he's got a fat contract with the army. You'd be better off buying from Axel Hoback, north of here. Or Luke Williams might have some."

Riding silently through the rolling land, Lockhart tried to keep his mind focused on the situation. He studied a band of fog as it drifted to the far hills connected to their distant mountain parents. A jackrabbit scurried in front of him, and he watched it run. He listened to the music of his rifle jiggling in the saddle sheath, his saddlebags bouncing against the black's flanks. Adding to the symphony were his horse's hooves rustling against dried grass, and the soft creaking of his sawed-off shotgun quiver tied to the pommel like a big saddle pistol.

Lockhart's mouth was already dry, and he drank from his canteen. It angered him that he felt the need for water so soon. As an Oglala warrior, he wouldn't have even thought about it. His thoughts weren't really on Touches-Horses or Vinegar Farrell. Instead, his thoughts wanted to fly back to Denver City and Mattie Bacon. He could hardly wait to return. Over and over, he had made love to her in his mind. She filled his thoughts as only one other person had. In many ways she reminded him of Young Evening. Not in looks, but the way she carried herself, the way she thought about things, the way she expressed herself. It was difficult not to daydream about spending his life with her. Their passion had caused him to miss the stagecoach.

Instead of waiting for another, he decided to ride his faithful black horse and trail a second horse, a dark sorrel, initially for supplies and eventually for Touches-Horses to ride. The pack animal had been left in the Laramie City livery while he made his initial scouting visit to the ranch. Today he wore a gray business suit and a wide-brimmed hat, instead of the range clothes he had been wearing from Denver City. Sweat was already touching his white shirt, but he thought the dressier appearance would be helpful and more deceptive.

But he was under no illusions about what he was riding into. In addition to the shotgun and rifle, he was wearing his shoulder-holstered Colt with a backup in his saddlebags, along with simple trail gear and a little food. His plan was straightforward enough. He would ask Vinegar Farrell about buying some horses and act interested in their training. He figured the approach would allow him to determine, for certain, that his former brother-in-law was actually there. It would also allow a firsthand look at what he would be up against when he returned to free him if that were the case.

After reviewing all the options he could think of, freeing Touches-Horses by returning at night was the one that made the most sense. Farrell was not going to be talked into letting Touches-Horses go. That would put a major crimp in his army arrangement, and confronting Farrell would make him alert to Lockhart's later moves. Offering a rich enough amount to buy his friend from Farrell was worth a try—and he was wearing a filled money belt for that purpose. But the feeling kept gnawing at him that Farrell would immediately be suspicious of his interest and reject whatever he offered.

Another realization had set in. If the bartender was accurate, and that was certainly questionable, there were several Indians being held. If true, his plan would require a major adjustment. All of them deserved freedom, and

Farrell certainly wouldn't release—or sell, for that matter—all of the Indians. So that meant a horse for each man. The bartender said three Indians once and then said twelve. So he must accomplish at least two things this morning: determine the exact number—and where they were being kept at night.

Should he try to bring the needed horses from town? Or should they take horses from the ranch itself? Green stock in the corrals would likely be too randy to ride or make too much noise in the process. He would make up his mind after seeing the place. His thoughts were gradually turning toward the yet unseen ranch. Over and over again he reminded himself that he could not react when he saw Touches-Horses. He absolutely couldn't. That would be a deadly mistake—for both of them. In his mind he rehearsed the possible scenarios when he might see Touches-Horses and how he should act.

At first Lockhart wondered if the army knew how their horses were being trained. And if they did, would they be indignant? He couldn't imagine men in their position allowing a man to enslave another; Crawfish had told him about the great war over who had the right to determine that. But he decided the army officers probably wouldn't care one way or the other. If they knew Vinegar Farrell was using Indians, the officers were likely told they were learning a trade so they could be successful in the white man's world. They probably thought it was one of those hare-brained ideas from an Indian agent. As long as they got good horses at the right price, it simply didn't matter. The thought was a sharp stick inside his mind.

At the bar a man in buckskins, standing next to Lockhart, had butted into the bartender's conversation and warned, "You'd best be careful with your windyin' about Vinegar Farrell. Ran into him 'n' his men a while back. He were sellin' whiskey 'n' shootin' irons to Injuns. Didn't seem to give a rat's ass who knew it, neither."

The bartender reacted defensively. His face went white. "I—I—I didn't say nothing wrong. This here stranger was just asking about where to buy good horses, that's all."

Ignoring the bartender, the buckskin-clad man had continued, "Seed Vinegar cut a man near in two with a shotgun at close range. Heard tell the feller bin a-windyin' to Indian agents 'bout Vinegar's carryin' on." That had dried up the bartender's help, but Lockhart had received directions to the Farrell ranch from a livery hand.

Vin Lockhart angled across a bald hill that looked like a giant grizzly's humped back. A gathering of lofty lodgepole pines had consented to some scraggly evergreen trees joining them along the trail. On both sides of the faint path were long ridges of rock that had escaped from the great peaks beyond. Ahead lay the farthest of the bare granite outcropping? that split into two huge shoulders to become a gateway to the open brown-grassy rolling hills ahead.

The heavy rocks brought the wise shaman, Stone-Dreamer, easily to his mind. He slid his hand into his coat pocket and felt for the stone pebble earring. Just touching it made him feel closer to his adopted father. If they were riding together now, the great shaman would be telling Lockhart to feel the spirit song coming from these *inyan*, the true grandfathers, the only life-forces to endure through the ages. *There*, he would say, *hear their singing? It is all around us. It is a song without beginning or end. It is a song of forever. I will sing the stone-songs and let them know we understand.*

The holy man would then begin singing some stone-song that only he knew. Lockhart gazed at the harsh rock ridges layered alongside the trail and above him. He smiled. He could see the conversation. It was like many they had, but that was years ago. Now Lockhart was a *wasicun*—and rocks were simply something to ride around or over. He pulled his hand from his pocket and patted the neck of his black horse.

A hawk flew overhead, searching for breakfast, he assumed. The sight brought him back to Stone-Dreamer and his time with the Oglalas. Maybe he was right; maybe there were spirits watching over him. There were places he had seen that looked and felt like they were doorways to the other world, whatever that was. Haunted places, men of the wilderness called them. Some didn't ever want to talk about what they saw; some talked of little else. He had talked with several in his saloon.

Lockhart had seen too many unusual situations, happenings no one could explain, to laugh at such talk. Or assume it was just whiskey talk. Who knew, for certain, what happened after death? Maybe Young Evening was waiting for him somewhere. Maybe it was somewhere close by. When he left the village years ago, he had seen her four different times, really seen her. Once by a waterfall with Crawfish. Once under a huge cottonwood. And twice early in the morning, just outside of the mining camp. On each occasion she had smiled and waved. Then she was gone. He hadn't seen her in Denver City. Ever.

Maybe she was beside him now. Spirits, both visible and invisible, were said to reside near kinsmen, sometimes. That's what old Stone-Dreamer had taught, anyway. When Lockhart asked Crawfish about the idea, the beet-faced prospector had just shrugged his shoulders and said he didn't know. Lockhart stared wistfully up at the sky growing more blue. Would Young Evening understand his new longing for Mattie? She had pushed aside the thick moss growing over his heart and made him whole again.

Like a thrown stone skipping across a pond, Lockhart's mind skipped to Stone-Dreamer, his Oglala stepfather. Oh, how he would like to see the great shaman again. To smoke a pipe and share the world from the old man's perspective. A mental cleansing came with just the remembrance. His mind strolled easily back to his happy Indian friends, to the fun days they had together. Most white people thought Indians were a stern lot, not given to laughter. But among their own, life was happy, joyous, even raucous. Laughing came easily and often, laced with practical jokes and enthusiatic storytelling.

The stillness of the day, mixed with his own loneliness, made him realize how much he missed their way of life and how much he missed their friendship. Funny, he had never been so content before in his whole life as he was there. Now that was closed. Forever. His Indian friends would never be able to accept him as an equal again. Stone-Dreamer had told him that, with heavy tears welling in his eyes. They could only see Lockhart as *wakan*, holy.

One long sad inhaling of the day's heat returned him to the danger yet to come. Would he die right here where no one knew him? Would he never see Mattie again? But would that bring him to Young Evening? Loneliness rode with him once more. He shoved his right hand into his coat pocket and touched the "panther" pebble earring, then the choker necklace from Young Evening. It was silly to be carrying them, but he had seen both when unpacking in the Laramie City hotel. He just couldn't leave them behind. It *was* silly, he admitted to himself, shaking his head and chuckling. Here he was the sophisticated white businessman, holding on to superstitions.

Ahead Lockhart could see the buildings that made up the Bar 5 operation: a clapboard house and a large barn of stone and timber, a bunkhouse with glassless windows covered with old newspapers, a small stone cooling house, an unpainted outhouse, and a toolshed. Four corrals were brimming with milling horses and covered half of the space between the main house and the bunkhouse. A fat creek slowly crossed the far side of the brush-cleared ranchyard, providing a pathway of tall green cattails and weary buffalo grass on both sides of the soft black bank. He squeezed the Oglala pieces and released them, withdrew his hand from his pocket, and touched the shortened stock of the shotgun resting alongside his knee.

The ranch had the look of a place not given much care. Vinegar Farrell hadn't built it, but neither the bartender nor the livery hand could remember who the first owner was or what had happened to him. It looked to Lockhart like all of the buildings needed repair. The bunkhouse roof had a definite hole, big enough to cause some serious wetness to its occupants come rain. The main house had once been painted white; now it was an uneven gray, with shaggy strips of paint hanging down the sides. Two windows still had glass panes; the rest were boarded over. Even the hard-stake corrals looked as if they been rawhided together once too often. As he rode through, he saw that the "5" was missing from the sign hanging under the lodgepole gateway. Men were moving purposefully around the corrals. A tall man was standing on the porch, watching him.

Vinegar Farrell couldn't remember exactly when he first saw the stranger riding toward the house. He was certain the rider wasn't in sight when he stepped out onto the wooden porch after breakfast. He remembered nudging the skinny, black-and-white dog from its nap and on to other activities so he could walk across the porch without interruption. It was a morning ritual.

Rolling his fourth cigarette of the morning, he paced off his edginess when the rider's appearance jarred his consciousness. Funny, Farrell thought, the stranger was obviously a white man—and from his dress, a townsman—but he rode like an Indian. Something about the way he dug in his heels and the way he swung his reins. Vinegar Farrell thought about going inside to get his coat; the rider might be an Indian agent or a federal man coming for an inspection of some kind. Who knew these days! He watched the black crows, on the only remaining piece of fence, look up as the rider passed. None flew away, eyeing him closely before going back to a survey of the land for their own breakfast.

Permanently burned by the sun and wind, Vinegar Farrell looked every inch a demanding boss. Tall and barrel chested, he was a man used to giving orders and having them obeyed without question. His nickname had come as a child and stuck, mainly because he was a sour man who could complain about a beautiful sunrise taking too long. His long frame was knotted with tension, but it always was, except when he drank.

Farrell's chiseled face was made even sharper by a thick mustache laced with gray. Light blue eyes took in everything and let nothing go. The dark circles under his eyes had little to do with his heavy drinking last night; they were a permanent part of his face, like the two-inch scar edging the right side of his mouth. Discolored pants were stuck deep into Farrell's high-topped boots, laced with spurs that hadn't come off since the day they went on. His gray flannel vest had its pockets jammed with makin's, a watch, and other items. Under the vest were suspenders and a collarless shirt that once had been white. A high-crowned hat, proud of many weather battles, sat low on his forehead. The only new thing he wore was a pair of store-bought, calf-leather gloves. He liked them and had eaten breakfast with them on.

Farrell's energy level was high. He never did like sleeping more than a handful of hours during the night. It seemed like a waste of time. The night always brought more worries, too. Probably a holdover from his earlier days leading a wild gang of outlaws in the territory. Training horses for the army—with almost free labor—was the most profitable thing he had ever done. By far. The army officers he worked with didn't care how he did it; they just wanted good horses. It sure beat getting chased and shot at by a posse of angry townsmen or persistent marshals.

A match snapped on the holstered pistol on his hip and its flame brought the cigarette to life. He inhaled deeply and watched the rider move across the broken ground, annoyed at the unwanted appearance and the worry such strangers always brought to his mind. The last stranger had been a well-intentioned Indian agent who heard about his captive Indian trainers and came to investigate. The agent's body was found not far from Fort Laramie itself, scalped, mutilated, and bristling with arrows. Indians were, of course, blamed. Farrell kept a collection of Indian weapons and arrows in his closet for such matters.

He walked to the porch railing and grabbed the top rail with both hands. His eyes studied the smooth line of his gloves over his fisted hands and smiled his approval. There was just something about a good pair of gloves. For one thing, a gun felt better in a man's hand. He spotted Hegan O'Brien, an Irishman with unruly hair and a toothy smile, coming from the outhouse. Farrell's wave wasn't a morning greeting; it was an order to meet the advancing rider. Farrell went inside without waiting to see if O'Brien did as desired.

Pleased to be singled out by the boss for this task, O'Brien lifted the loop from the pistol hammer in his holster, lifted the gun a few inches to make certain it wasn't stuck in the holster, and released it again. Satisfied with the gun's availability if needed, he hurried toward the advancing Lockhart. His spurs and batwing chaps were a symphony of jingling rowels and rustling leather.

"What be yur business at the Bar 5 this wee fine mornin', stranger?" he asked loudly, more for Farrell's sake than for Lockhart's.

Lockhart made no response and continued riding toward the house. O'Brien planted his feet in front of the horse, determined to perform his assigned task. With a nod, Lockhart acknowledged his presence but made no attempt to stop. O'Brien jumped sideways to avoid the black horse's continuing advance.

"By the bleemin' saints! You stop that hoss or yur mither will weep fur her son this fine mornin'. I asked what yur business with us be?"

"I want to talk to Mr. Farrell."

"By glory, 'tis a shame. The man has gone an' left me in charge. Hegan O'Brien hisself."

"Hegan O'Brien, go find him."

O'Brien was surprised at the hardness of the command. He thought only Vinegar Farrell had a voice like that. Behind him came two Bar 5 ranch hands easing themselves into the morning's work. Both wore belt guns; one carried a lariat, the other a shovel. They were upset about their morning routines being disturbed by this unexpected arrival. Both had ridden long enough with Farrell to expect trouble; those early outlaw days tended to lock a man into a careful way of thinking.

Flustered, the lanky cowboy with a pointed chin and high forehead, wearing faded cavalry breeches, stumbled over his shovel and fell. His companion's fiat belly shook in response to the misfortune. But the short-barreled man's laughter was more subdued than it would have been if they were alone. Smiling, the shorter cowboy held his lariat in one hand and picked up the shovel with the other. He handed the tool to his friend after the lanky man stood again, and they continued walking toward Lockhart.

Without slowing his horse, Lockhart said, "Relax, boys. If I wanted trouble, none of you would be standing now. I came to buy horses from Mr. Farrell."

O'Brien caught the confidence in the statement, casual yet ominous. He could see the same question in the faces of the other two Bar 5 men: Who was this man? Maybe it was a bluff. The stranger was obviously a townsman from the looks of his tailored clothes. But O'Brien hadn't missed the shoulder holster under his coat or the saddle weapons either. He hesitated, glanced at the others, and said, "I'll be a-goin' for himself, Mr. Farrell."

"Good, Hegan O'Brien."

By the time Lockhart reined his horse beside the front porch, O'Brien had disappeared inside the house. He could hear a booming voice obviously not happy at being disturbed. Finally O'Brien came to the door, paused, and said, "Himself, Mr. Farrell, will be a-comin'. You wait right thar, if'n ya please."

Lockhart nodded and watched the ranch hand half walk, half run toward the safety of the corrals, away from Mr. Farrell's temper and the uneasiness he felt around this stranger. The corrals were filled with young horses, milling, stamping, and staking territories. Brown, black, and sorrel shapes swirled in a distinctive blend of color and motion.

A silhouette moved from the shadows of the far yard toward the closest corral. Something about the way the man walked was familiar. Was that Touches-Horses? It had to be! Lockhart couldn't make out his features from here. Four other silhouettes appeared behind him. By their walk, he knew they were Indians, too.

"Are you from the government, son? We're always glad to have officials visit us. What can I do for you?" The thundering voice pulled Lockhart back to the porch. The smile on Farrell's face was pasted on and hard for him to hold.

Farrell stood with his arms folded, a cigarette stuck in the corner of his mouth. He had put on his coat hurriedly, and the collar was raised behind his neck. Before Lockhart could speak, the rancher moved to the railing closest to him and squeezed it with both hands. He stood, looking down, his eyes calculating every aspect of Lockhart's appearance.

"Mister Farrell, I'm no Indian agent, no government anything. I'm Vin Lockhart. I came to buy horses."

The relief in Farrell's face was a lightning flash, and then he frowned.

"Afraid you had a long ride for no thin', Lockhart. My hosses are already bought. U.S. Army's got 'em," Farrell said, releasing his fists from the railing.

"All of them? I was hoping to get maybe fifty head. You pick them."

"Fifty? What the hell for? You don't look like no cow-man," Farrell said. His eyes flashed and his last sentence was intended to be critical.

Lockhart chuckled and shook his head. "No, sir, I don't—and I'm not. But my partner and I just bought a cow-calf operation near Denver City. The previous owner had money problems. We've got ourselves a good foreman to run it, and he said the best horses were coming from you."

"He did, did he?" Farrell said, his lip curling upward in satisfaction. He sucked on the cigarette, pulling in a mouthful of smoke.

"What would be his name?"

"Crawford. But he goes by Crawfish," Lockhart said, using his partner's name as that of the nonexistent fore-man.

"I see. Never heard of him. How'd he hear about me?"

"Ran into some army boys on good-looking mounts. Asked 'em. The man's got a good eye for horseflesh. So do I."

"Yeah. Where did you say this ranch was?" Cigarette smoke was ushered out with Farrell's raspy words.

"I didn't," Lockhart said. The bite of his voice matched Farrell's churlish manner.

The big rancher laughed. "By God, you didn't at that. Reckon I was poking along a back trail that weren't none of my business."

"It's the Double B."

"Double B? Hmm, don't think I know that outfit."

"You would if you were from Denver City," Lockhart said. The ranch existed, but it wasn't for sale.

"Weren't there no hosses on this hyar Double B?"

"As I said, the previous owner got himself in trouble. He'd already sold off the best head in his string and was going to sell his herd when we heard about it. We're trying to build it up right, starting with good horses."

Farrell studied Lockhart without speaking. Lockhart's eyes met the rancher's, and the older man seemed satisfied with both his words and his manner. Farrell flipped the butt of his cigarette over the porch railing and reached for the makin's in his vest pocket. Methodically, he creased a cigarette paper, then sprinkled tobacco along the line from his small bag of Bull Durham. After shoving the muslin sack back into his vest pocket, he rolled the paper in a tight cigarette, licked the open end of the paper, and sealed it by sliding his gloved fingers along the wet edge. All the while, his eyes never left Lockhart's face.

The silence was intentional, Lockhart thought. He must not speak until Farrell does. The rancher snapped a match on his pistol butt and brought it to the cigarette in his mouth. Smoke encircling his face, he said, "You expectin' trouble, Lockhart? Ain't seen many men packin' a sawed-off shotgun as a saddle gun."

Lockhart grinned, shook his head, and said, "Didn't mean to alarm you. I just said I was a city fellow." He patted the stock of the gun. "Belongs to a friend of mine. He thought I should carry this thing. Said a 'belly gun,' I believe that's what he called it, would be good for road agents—or Indians. I'm no sharpshooter, that's for sure, but I didn't think it was too smart to ride out here without being armed either."

Farrell nodded his approval. "Lockhart, I like you. You

look like a man who can handle himself—city fella or no—and I respect that. But I can't sell you any hosses. The army has got a contract fer every piece of hossflesh I can deliver."

"I'll double their price."

"Reckon you would," Farrell said, grinning. "But what do I tell those army boys when they come for their hosses?"

"Tell them to be patient."

Farrell laughed. Deeply. His belly shook and tears came to the corners of his eyes, then he coughed. "You're a good one, Lockhart. I like you."

"Well, I had to try," Lockhart said with a returning smile. "I understand, dammit, wish I didn't. Says a lot about the way you're breeding them—and breaking them. My foreman must be right."

"I reckon you've heard about how I do the hoss-breakin'."

Lockhart paused. "Well, I heard a wild story about you using Indians. Figured it was whiskey talk. How do you do it?"

"Ain't no whiskey about it, Lockhart. I got the best damn hoss wranglers in the whole territory—an' they're redskins. Got one that's better'n any white hossman I ever seed."

"Oh, come on now, I'm not that green."

"I'm not funnin' you, Lockhart."

"My God, aren't you worried about those savages attacking you?"

Farrell laughed deep in his belly, his eyes flashing a secret joke, and said, "Not hardly. We keep 'em whipped, hungry, 'n' thirsty—an' tied up at night. Takes the starch out of the toughest o' them red bastirds. Makes the best part of their day workin' hosses. Hell, Lockhart, they don't know no better, anyway. Come on, I'll show you."

Farrell jumped down from the porch and walked briskly

toward the corrals, where activity was under full swing. He rolled another cigarette and lit it as he went. Farrell's dog shot out from the side of the house to run after him. Happy to be close to its master, the dog brushed against Farrell's leg, and he stumbled but caught himself.

"You stupid dog! Get away!" he yelled, and kicked in its direction. The dog's tail dropped and it trotted at a more discreet distance.

Biting the inside of his cheeks to cut off bristling disgust, Lockhart wheeled his black to follow. Farrell didn't turn to see if he was coming or not. Halfway down the hill, it was obvious to Lockhart that Touches-Horses was the earlier silhouette. The gentle Indian was concentrating on a long-legged sorrel and not looking toward the main house as Lockhart advanced. The high-strung animal stamped, snorted, and snapped at other horses, demonstrating a fiery leadership. But when Touches-Horses approached, the horse lowered its proud head and looked more like a docile farm animal. Lockhart chuckled to himself at the sight. No one would believe it if he didn't see it for himself.

He counted six Indians, including his friend: four Oglala Sioux and two Cheyenne. Three were in the farthest corral, two in the middle corral, and Touches-Horses was working alone in the closest enclosure. A cruel-eyed half-breed was apparently in charge of the Indians, yelling his orders first in Lakotan and then in Cheyenne.

As Lockhart approached the corral, anger splashed within him as he heard Bar 5 hands cursing and laughing at Touches-Horses and the others. A stocky cowboy with a black patch over his left eye was trying to rope a reluctant bay. He backed into Touches-Horses, who was putting a blanket on the sorrel and missed his throw at the bay. In response to the hoots from the men watching from the fence, the Bar 5 hand shoved Touches-Horses to the ground and kicked him in the ribs. Touches-Horses grunted in pain and gritted his teeth to keep any further sound from coming out.

Lockhart's fist grabbed for the pistol inside his coat. But a calmness washed over him the instant his hand moved. This was not the time. Reacting now would only get some of the Indians killed. Most likely Touches-Horses. He must wait and return in the darkness, just like he planned. His hand slowly left his shoulder holster and returned to his side. No one had noticed his movement, and he must not let them see him care.

Looking up, the half-breed saw Farrell and slipped through the corral poles to meet him but made no effort to shake his hand. A flat-brimmed hat shaded dark eyes assessing the strange rider coming behind Farrell. The half-breed's age could have been twenty or forty—Lockhart couldn't read that from his cruel face. But he could read gunmen, not horsemen.

The half-breed's two belted guns weren't for show. The left holster held a Colt with the butt forward; the right held its weapon with the handle the other way. Just behind it was a seven-pound bowie knife in a beaded sheath. Lockhart instinctively noticed that the walnut handles carried an engraved symbol. Cheyenne, Lockhart thought. But the sheath's beadwork was Lakotan. A quirt dangled from the half-breed's right wrist.

Farrell gestured to Lockhart, who reined his horse behind the rancher. "Lockhart, this here's Valentine. It's the 'breed's job to keep these damn wild savages in line. He's a good one for it. Half heathen himself."

Valentine's eyes relocked with Lockhart's.

"Nice to meet you, Mr. Valentine," Lockhart said in a smooth voice.

"Oh, it's just Valentine," Farrell corrected. A smile caught only the right side of his mouth. "Has to do with his reputation for killing. Always the heart, they say. A man in my position needs someone like Valentine, don't ya know."

Valentine grinned a face-wide, toothy line that Lockhart thought made him look like a rattlesnake. His gaze was torn from Valentine as his peripheral vision caught the cowboy kick Touches-Horses again as he tried to stand. The Indian flopped to the corral's torn ground, caught his breath, and gradually staggered to his feet. Lockhart bit the inside of his mouth again to keep from reacting. He looked back at Valentine, and he was watching the corral too.

Lockhart got a good look at his friend as he stood. The gentle Touches-Horses was filthy; his hair was matted with blood and horse manure. What had once been a buckskin warshirt was ripped open in the back; it was held in place by the leather band that held his mud-streaked breechclout. Most of the beadwork was gone; what remained hung like dead flowers, clinging to the shirt by threads. One of his moccasins was torn almost to his heel. When Touches-Horses turned to find the sorrel, Lockhart saw the marks of a whipping on his bare back. Valentine's quirt? He swallowed to keep from blurting out the accusation.

Something made Touches-Horses glance toward Farrell and the mounted stranger near him. Touches-Horses's soul jumped. Even with shortened hair and *wasicun* clothes, he recognized his old friend and blurted in Lakotan, "*Kola! Kola!* Panther-Strikes, it is Touches-Horses!" He ran toward the corral fence closest to them. A Bar 5 hand with a roped bay under control drew his pistol, aimed at the frantic Indian, and commanded him to stand still. Touches-Horses took two more steps, shuffled to a stop, and dropped his head against his chest. He stared straight at the ground, not daring to raise his eyes again. The half-dozen men at the corral turned to see what he was yelling at. Dish Holt, a large man with a blubbery face and turkey second chin, shoved Touches-Horses hard against the corral, jamming his cheek against the top pole. Blood popped from the opened cut.

O'Brien laughed and said, "Crazy redskin, yourself best be a-gittin' to your hoss work."

Stunned by the recognition and the heartfelt outburst, Lockhart's mind was whirring with the realization of the danger he was suddenly in. His mind tried to lock in on a rehearsed response in such a case. After a slight hesitation, he turned in his saddle and gazed toward the house, as if he, too, was trying to see what the Indian was yelling at. Without thinking about it, he reached inside his pocket and felt the pebble earring.

"Hell's bells, that Injun knows you," Farrell said, examining Lockhart as if he had just ridden in. He flipped his cigarette away to free his right hand.

Valentine grunted, "*Kola.* Mean 'best friend.' "

Lockhart forced a loud laugh. "Well, gentlemen, that's a good one. A city boy is *best friends* with a savage. Hell, maybe we're brothers. We look a lot alike."

Farrell grunted at the joke and nodded appreciatively.

"He must be saying something else, Valentine," Lockhart continued. "Or else he's talking to you. It's obvious I've never even met a red man like that before."

"No-o-o. He speak to you," Valentine said. His eyes didn't miss the bulge under Lockhart's coat. The sneer that followed indicated he hoped Lockhart would try to use the gun?

Withdrawing his hand casually from his pocket, Lockhart grinned and said, "Well, there you have it, Farrell. Your best redskin hoss wrangler likes me. He must think I'm here to buy him. That must mean you've got to sell him to me. How about three thousand—just for the noisy one?"

Farrell's skeptical frown vanished, and he smiled his pleasure at the remark. Pulling the tobacco sack from his vest pocket, he growled, “Valentine, get that silly red sonuvabitch working. We’ve got hosses to deliver—and you’re behind schedule.”

Valentine absorbed the order without showing any signs of emotion. He looked again at Lockhart and turned away. Then he stopped and said in Lakotan, “Afiye *nita kola kte. Miye niye kte.* I kill your friend. I kill you.”

Chapter Sixteen

Valentine watched Lockhart's face for a reaction to his evil promise. But Lockhart was ready for the trick and glanced to the left, then the right, as if to see whom Valentine was talking to.

"Oh, are you talking to me, Valentine? I'm sorry, I don't know any French."

"No speak that. Speak Lakotan. He speak Lakotan. You his friend. You speak Lakotan."

"Valentine, I think you'd better do what your boss says. You're starting to sound a little silly," Lockhart said.

"Go on, Valentine!" The command was Farrell's, and it spat hard.

Farrell ignored the half-breed after that, lighting a new cigarette as he looked up at Lockhart. "Sorry for the confusion, Lockhart. We've been pushing them Injuns hard the last week or so. I've got a hundred head due at the post by the end of the week."

"Don't apologize. I'm the one that evidently caused things to stop. I'm sorry."

"Oh hell, them Injuns are always yellin' about somethin'," Farrell said.

Lockhart tried to keep his attention completely on Farrell and not let his eyes wander the slightest toward Touches-Horses. From his peripheral vision, though, he saw two hands lead him back to the milling horses. The other Indians were slowly taking positions around the corral.

"You might try Axel Hoback for horses. Lazy H. It's about a mile east of here. You can't miss it. Big, long barn you can see from the trail. Not as good as mine, but he's selling, I hear tell."

"Yeah, they mentioned him in town. I'll head there, since I've got no choice," Lockhart said, and extended his hand to Farrell.

Farrell shook it vigorously and said, "I'll be in Laramie City come Saturday. If'n you're still in town, let's share a steak—-or a good bottle of whiskey—or a bad woman."

Lockhart laughed. "Or all three! I'm staying at the Bighorn Hotel."

"Good enough."

Lockhart swung his horse toward the ranch gate entrance and nudged the mustang forward with a squeeze of his legs. A tiny murmur reached his ears. *Was it coming from my pocket*? *What in the world*? How strange, he thought as he trotted away. The sound grew louder, and he couldn't ignore it any longer. He reached into his pocket to withdraw and grabbed the first thing he felt, the small pebble earring. As his fingers pulled it free, the humming stone slipped from his grasp. Startled, he leaned over to grab for the falling earring but missed. A bullet roared past his lowered shoulder.

He reined the black hard to the left and his spurs jolted

it forward in the same motion. More bullets punched where he had been; one knocked off his hat; another clipped his coattail. In one motion he drew his pistol and wheeled the responsive mustang toward Vinegar Farrell, who was cursing and shooting his gun at the same time. Lockhart charged directly at him, screaming "Hokay Hey!" and firing at the big man's face and chest.

Touches-Horses sprang from the corral fence at the first shot and yanked a pistol from the holster of the surprised Dish Holt. The enslaved Indian shot him in the stomach and lurched free as the big man grabbed first for Touches-Horses's shoulder and then for his own reddening stomach.

Valentine had also turned instinctively toward the gunfire, drawn one of his belt guns, and cocked it to bring down Lockhart. Silently, he cursed Farrell for not having him take care of this stranger, whoever he was. Touches-Horses's gun blast and the trailing cry from Holt broke his attention, and Valentine glanced to see what had happened. Touches-Horses immediately fired twice and caught Valentine in the thigh and lower shoulder. Off balance and reeling from the hits, Valentine saw his first returned shot clip the corral post; his second drove Touches-Horses backward into the swirling horses.

Inside the corral, frightened horses careened into the corral fence and each other, wild for freedom. O'Brien and the other three Bar 5 men were caught up in the sudden blur of color and hooves, trying to keep the animals under control and themselves from being trampled. The Indians were forgotten. The cowboy next to O'Brien got bumped sideways by a passing horse, lost his balance, and disappeared in the clouds of dust and desperate hooves. A tall, nearly naked Cheyenne grabbed O'Brien from behind and savagely snapped his neck. A throaty war cry followed the Cheyenne's grab of the dead Irishman's pistol.

Lockhart didn't feel the bullet that hit his shoulder as

three slugs from his pistol tore into Farrell. His fourth shot missed Valentine just after the evil half-breed fired at Touches-Horses; Lockhart's fifth shot slammed into Valentine's back.

With blood foaming from his mouth, Farrell took a jerky step forward and tried to aim his pistol at the black thunder coming straight for him. Lockhart's sixth shot spun Farrell halfway around and the big man sank awkwardly to the ground. Without hesitating, Lockhart switched the empty pistol to his left hand and drew the sawed-off shotgun from its saddle quiver in one smooth motion as he galloped past Farrell's body. He reined the wide-eyed horse toward the corral, but Valentine's bullet took him from the saddle.

Shaking off the effects of the ground's impact, Lockhart stood, regained his balance, and ran at the wounded Valentine, who fired and hit Lockhart in the left arm, forcing his pistol to fly away. Lockhart's sawed-off shotgun barked once and Valentine's face disappeared into a red rash. The half-breed killer screamed like an animal and fired twice again. One shot clipped Lockhart's coat sleeve above his right elbow and the other thumped into Farrell's unmoving body.

Valentine spat, "*Miye nita kola kte. Miye niye kte.*" He staggered sideways and tried to cock his pistol.

The second barrel of Lockhart's sawed-off shotgun exploded into the killer's chest and slammed him against a rail of the corral. Valentine's crimson face looked upward, unseeing, then he slid down the post into a crumpled heap. Lockhart dropped his empty gun and picked up Valentine's pistol lying a foot from his curled hand.

In the corral, the remaining two Bar 5 cowboys raised their hands too and yelled to Lockhart for protection from the Indians. "Help! We give up, please! Don't let these Injuns git us, mister! Please!"

"That's your problem," Lockhart snarled, his body not yet reacting to the shock of being hit. In Lakotan, he yelled, "Touches-Horses! *Kola!* Are you all right?"

"Many times Touches-Horses hurt worse, *kola*," Touches-Horses said, easing himself to his feet. "Valentine bullet not stop Oglala." He spotted the sorrel he had been training and calmed the animal, then asked the other Indians to calm the agitated horses and to leave the Bar 5 men alone.

"God, that's good news," Lockhart blurted in English.

"Are you wounded bad, *kola*?" Touches-Horses returned the concern after watching the Indian captives respond to his.

Lockhart paused for a moment, suddenly feeling lightheaded. "Well, yes, I guess I am." He looked at himself and the reddened spots on his clothes. His right shoulder spasmed and the fury jerked him. Through his mind marched a fury of pain. Throbbing, unforgiving pain. He paused a minute to let it pass. "Ah, shoulder...well, would you look at this!" Examining his body to determine where else he had been hit, he felt along his stomach. It was sore where Valentine's bullet had been stopped by the wad of currency in his money belt. The piece of lead plopped to the ground as he felt the compressed dollar bills.

"Touches-Horses, *wasicun* money saved my life," he muttered in English.

Touches-Horses didn't understand but smiled widely. When he eased his thin body between the poles, Lockhart could see that his friend had been hit in the upper thigh.

"I knew you come, *kola.* I tell others this," Touches-Horses began to jabber as he cleared the corral and limped toward Lockhart. "Yesterday, I find stone, like one you wore behind ear. I knew this was sign you were close. This morning, I hear panther cry. I knew you were coming this day. I tell them."

With an explosion of pent-up emotion, they grasped each other's forearm in the traditional warrior's salute, then hugged heartily. Tears laced Touches-Horses's face only to be matched by the same on Lockhart's. They stepped back, and Lockhart said, "We'll gather food and horses—and some clothes too. Whatever guns we find. It's the least these bastards owe you and the others. Tell them, please. We'll leave as soon as everyone is ready."

Before leaving to talk to the other captured Indians, Touches-Horses said, "My brother, they know who you are. They know you are *Wanagi Yanka.* That is why they not speak. Much gratitude, but fear you take them to the grandfathers."

Lockhart swallowed and said, "Thank you, my *kola.* I understand. Tell them they are safe, the spirits will help them get home. I came for you, but I am happy they are free now too."

Touches-Horses grinned again and limped away to tell the good news. Lockhart watched and waves of nausea rolled through him rhythmically. His eyes kept losing their focus no matter how hard he tried to keep them steady on Touches-Horses or the surrendering Bar 5 men. A low whinny cut through his fuzziness. It was his black horse returning to his side. Lockhart hugged the animal's neck, and it nuzzled him gently as if understanding the situation. Dried blood marked a bullet crease on the horse's right flank. The black's well-shaped head was down; his powerful body heaved for air that wouldn't enter fast enough- For an instant Lockhart thought he was going to pass out as the full shock of his shoulder wound brought teeth-gritting torment. After a minute of trying to breathe evenly and not gasp, he felt his head stabilize. Vomiting was held back only by gulping air.

Realizing he might pass out, Lockhart hurried to the corral for something to lean against. Turning his head swiftly was a mistake. The sudden movement made him very dizzy. He vomited. Nothing was in focus. The ground was moving. His head was roaring. His head was leaving the ranch. Spinning. He must grab something to keep from flying away. Lockhart was unconscious.

His white father put his hand on Lockhart's shoulder to show the boy something in their house. His mother smiled at him from the kitchen; she was making stew in a huge kettle. All of the windows were open, and sunlight made the small house bright. His father disappeared before Lockhart could turn to see what he wanted to show him. His mother held a hand to her mouth to hold back tears. Young Evening appeared to comfort her. Then Mattie appeared with both women. Crawfish was beside him now and helped him to his feet. Before Lockhart could say thanks, the prospector left to talk with Stone-Dreamer. They were standing by the tipi with his own warrior's markings decorating its sides. Crawfish had a huge gold rock in his hands. Lockhart's white father and mother joined them. Lockhart yelled at them to come and help him, but they didn't hear his plea.

"*Kola...kola*, wake."

Lockhart's breath came in short white bursts. He was feverish and trembling. His first thoughts were of Stone-Dreamer, then of Mattie Bacon...and Young Evening...and then of Touches-Horses. And Crawfish. Mattie...Mattie. She seemed so far away. His wonderful Silver Queen saloon seemed like a dreamworld. So did Denver City. So did the village of Oglalas.

"Kola, hold this *tunkan.* It make you well." Touches-Horses pointed to the small pebble earring lying on Lockhart's stomach. "We find in grass."

"W-w-what happened?"

"Wounds take you away to distant place. *Tunkan* bring you back."

"W-w-where?"

Touches-Horses helped him sit up as he explained, "*Wasicun* afraid you die and we kill them. They run on foot. We gather food, horses, guns, blankets, clothes.

See?" He stood so Lockhart could view his new shirt and pants. Behind him the other Indians sat silently on horses. They were clothed in white man's shirts, coats, and pants. Two wore hats. All wore pistol belts and carried rifles. An extra horse was packed with other treasures they had found in the ranch house.

"Good. We should ride now. Fast," Lockhart said, placing an arm on his friend's shoulder to help him stay balanced. His shoulder had stiffened into an agonizing burn.

"No think you can ride, *kola.* Hurt bad."

"Get me on my black and I'll be fine. You can tie my hands to the horn."

"Black fine horse."

"I know. My best friend gave it to me."

Touches-Horses smiled and said, "I clean wound on black horse. Not deep."

"Touches-Horses?"

"Yes, *kola*?"

"I can't wait to see Stone-Dreamer and tell him. I heard the stone sing."